The Last Hurrah
of the
Golden Horde

The
Last Hurrah
of the
Golden Horde

by NORMAN SPINRAD

NELSON DOUBLEDAY, Inc.

Garden City, New York

Acknowledgments

Thanks are due the following for permission to reprint:

"Carcinoma Angels" from DANGEROUS VISIONS.
  Copyright © 1967 by Harlan Ellison.

"The Age of Invention" and "Neutral Ground"
  from *The Magazine of Fantasy and Science Fiction.*
  Copyright © 1966 by Mercury Press, Inc.

"Outward Bound," "The Equalizer," "The Last of the
  Romany," "Technicality," and "Subjectivity" from
  Analog Science Fiction/Science Fact. Copyright ©
  1963, 1964, 1966 by *The Condé Nast Publications, Inc.*

"A Child of Mind" and "The Ersatz Ego" (under the title,
  "Your Name Shall Be . . . Darkness") from *Amazing
  Stories.* Copyright © 1964, 1965, by Ziff-Davis
  Publishing Company.

"The Rules of the Road" from *Galaxy Magazine.*
  Copyright © 1964 by Galaxy Publishing Corporation.

"Dead End" from *If.* Copyright © 1969
  by Universal Publishing and Distributing Corporation.

"A Night in Elf Hill" from THE FARTHEST REACHES.
  Copyright © 1968 by Joseph Elder.

"Deathwatch" from *Playboy.* Copyright © 1965
  by HMH Publishing Company.

"Once More, with Feeling" from *Knight.*
  Copyright © 1969 by Sirkay Publishing Co.

"It's a Bird! It's a Plane!" from *Gent.*
  Copyright © 1967 by Dugent Publishing Co.

"The Entropic Gang Bang Caper" and "The Last Hurrah of
  the Golden Horde" from *New Worlds.*
  Copyright © 1969 by *New Worlds.*

Dedicated to
The Grand Old Men
of Science Fiction

Contents

Carcinoma Angels

At the age of nine, Harrison Wintergreen first discovered that the world was his oyster when he looked at it sidewise. That was the year when baseball cards were *in*. The kid with the biggest collection of baseball cards was *it*. Harry Wintergreen decided to become *it*.

Harry saved up a dollar and bought one hundred random baseball cards. He was in luck—one of them was the very rare Yogi Berra. In three separate transactions, he traded his other ninety-nine cards for the only other three Yogi Berras in the neighborhood. Harry had reduced his holdings to four cards, but he had cornered the market in Yogi Berra. He forced the price of Yogi Berra up to an exorbitant eighty cards. With the slush fund thus accumulated, he successively cornered the market in Mickey Mantle, Willie Mays and Pee Wee Reese and became the J. P. Morgan of baseball cards.

Harry breezed through high school by the simple expedient of mastering only one subject—the art of taking tests. By his senior year, he could outthink any testwriter with his gypsheet tied behind his back and won seven scholarships with foolish ease.

In college, Harry discovered Girls. Being reasonably good-looking and reasonably facile, he no doubt would've garnered his fair share of conquests in the normal course of events. But this was not the way the mind of Harrison Wintergreen worked.

Harry carefully cultivated a stutter, which he could turn on or off at will. Few girls could resist the lure of a good-looking, well-adjusted guy with a slick line who nevertheless carried with him some secret inner hurt that made him stutter. Many were the girls that tried to delve Harry's secret, while Harry delved *them*.

In his sophomore year, Harry grew bored with college and reasoned that the thing to do was to become Filthy Rich. He assiduously studied sex novels for one month, wrote three of them in the next two which he immediately sold at a thousand a throw.

With the $3,000 thus garnered, he bought a shiny new convertible. He drove the new car to the Mexican border and across into a notorious bordertown. He immediately contacted a disreputable shoeshine boy and bought a pound of marijuana. The shoeshine boy of course tipped off the border guards, and when Harry attempted to walk across the bridge to the states, they stripped him naked. They found nothing and Harry crossed the border. He had smuggled nothing out of Mexico, and in fact had thrown the marijuana away as soon as he bought it.

However, he had taken advantage of the Mexican embargo on American cars and illegally sold the convertible in Mexico for $15,000.

Harry took his $15,000 to Las Vegas and spent the next six weeks buying people drinks, lending broke gamblers money, acting in general like a fuzzy-cheeked Santa Claus, gaining the confidence of the right drunks and blowing $5,000.

At the end of six weeks he had three hot market tips which turned his remaining $10,000 into $40,000 in the next two months.

Harry bought 400 crated government surplus jeeps in four one-hundred-jeep lots at $10,000 a lot and immediately sold them to a highly disreputable Central American Government for $100,000.

He took the $100,000 and bought a tiny island in the Pacific, so worthless that no government had ever bothered to claim it. He set himself up as an independent government with no taxes and sold twenty one-acre plots to twenty millionaires seeking a tax haven at $100,000 a plot. He unloaded the last plot three weeks before the United States, with U.N. backing, claimed the island and brought it under the sway of the Internal Revenue Department.

Harry invested a small part of his $2,000,000 and rented a large computer for twelve hours. The computer constructed a betting schema by which Harry parlayed his $2,000,000 into $20,000,000 by taking various British soccer pools to the tune of $18,000,000.

For five million dollars, he bought a monstrous chunk of useless desert from an impoverished Arabian sultanate. With another two million, he created a huge rumor campaign to the effect that this patch of desert was literally floating on oil. With another three million, he set up a dummy corporation which made like a big oil company and publicly offered to buy his desert for seventy-five million dollars. After some spirited bargaining, a large American oil company was allowed to outbid the dummy and bought a thousand square miles of sand for $100,000,000.

Harrison Wintergreen was, at the age of twenty-five, Filthy Rich by his own standards. He lost his interest in money.

He now decided that he wanted to Do Good. He Did Good. He toppled seven unpleasant Latin American governments and replaced them with six Social Democracies and a Benevolent Dictatorship. He converted a tribe of Borneo headhunters to Rosicrucianism. He set up twelve rest homes for over-age whores and organized a birth control program which sterilized twelve million fecund Indian women. He contrived to make another $100,000,-000 on the above enterprises.

At the age of thirty, Harrison Wintergreen had had it with Do-Gooding. He decided to Leave His Footprints in the Sands of Time. He Left His Footprints in the Sands of Time. He wrote an internationally acclaimed novel about King Farouk. He invented the Wintergreen Filter, a membrane through which fresh water passed freely, but which barred salts. Once set up, a Wintergreen Desalinization Plant could desalinate an unlimited supply of water at a per-gallon cost approaching absolute zero. He painted one painting and was instantly offered $200,000 for it. He donated it to the Museum of Modern Art, gratis. He developed a mutated virus which destroyed syphilis bacteria. Like syphilis, it spread by sexual contact. It was also a mild aphrodisiac. Syphilis was wiped out in eighteen months. He bought an island off the coast of California, a five-hundred-foot crag jutting out of the Pacific. He caused it to be carved into a five-hundred-foot statue of Harrison Wintergreen.

At the age of thirty-eight, Harrison Wintergreen had Left sufficient Footprints in the Sands of Time. He was bored. He looked around greedily for new worlds to conquer.

This then, was the man who, at the age of forty, was informed that he had an advanced, well-spread and incurable case of cancer and that he had one year to live.

Wintergreen spent the first month of his last year searching for an existing cure for terminal cancer. He visited laboratories, medical schools, hospitals, clinics, Great Doctors, quacks, people who had miraculously recovered from cancer, faithhealers and Little Old Ladies in Tennis Shoes. There was no known cure for terminal cancer, reputable or otherwise. It was as he suspected, as he more or less even hoped. He would have to do it himself.

He proceeded to spend the next month setting things up to do it himself. He caused to be erected in the middle of the Arizona desert an air-conditioned walled villa. The villa had a completely automatic kitchen and enough food for a year. It had a five-million-dollar biological and biochemical laboratory. It had a three-million-dollar microfilmed library which contained every word ever written on the subject of cancer. It had the pharmacy to end all pharmacies: a liberal supply of quite literally every drug that existed—poisons, pain-killers, hallucinogens, dandricides, antiseptics, antibiotics, viricides, headache remedies, heroin, quinine, curare, snake oil—everything. The pharmacy cost twenty million dollars.

The villa also contained a one-way radiotelephone, a large stock of basic chemicals, including radioactives, copies of the Koran, the Bible, the Torah, the Book of the Dead, *Science and Health with Key to the Scriptures,* the *I Ching* and the complete works of Wilhelm Reich and Aldous Huxley. It also contained a very large and ultra-expensive computer. By the time the villa was ready, Wintergreen's petty cash fund was nearly exhausted.

With ten months to do that which the medical world considered impossible, Harrison Wintergreen entered his citadel.

During the first two months, he devoured the library, sleeping three hours out of each twenty-four and dosing himself regularly with benzedrene. The library offered nothing but data. He digested the data and went on to the pharmacy.

During the next month, he tried Aureomycin, bacitracin, stannous fluoride, hexylresercinol, cortisone, penicillin, hexachlorophene, shark-liver extract and seven thousand three hundred and twelve assorted other miracles of modern medical science, all to no avail. He began to feel pain, which he immediately blotted out and continued to blot out with morphine. Morphine addiction was merely an annoyance.

He tried chemicals, radioactives, viricides, Christian Science, Yoga, prayer, enemas, patent medicines, herb tea, witchcraft and yogurt diets. This consumed another month, during which Wintergreen continued to waste away, sleeping less and less and taking more and more benzedrene and morphine. Nothing worked. He had six months left.

He was on the verge of becoming desperate. He tried a different tack. He sat in a comfortable chair and contemplated his navel for forty-eight consecutive hours.

His meditations produced a severe case of eyestrain and two significant words: "spontaneous remission."

In his two months of research, Wintergreen had come upon numbers of cases where a terminal cancer abruptly reversed itself and the patient, for whom all hope had been abandoned, had been cured. No one ever knew how or why. It could not be predicted, it could not be artificially produced, but it happened nevertheless. For want of an explanation, they called it spontaneous remission. "Remission," meaning cure. "Spontaneous," meaning no one knew what caused it.

Which was not to say that it did not have a cause.

Wintergreen was buoyed; he was even ebullient. He knew that some terminal cancer patients had been cured. Therefore terminal cancer could be cured. Therefore, the problem was removed from the realm of the impossible and was now merely the domain of the highly improbable.

And doing the highly improbable was Wintergreen's specialty.

With six months of estimated life left, Wintergreen set jubilantly to work. From his complete cancer library, he culled every known case of spontaneous remission. He coded every one of them into the computer—data on the medical histories of the patients, on the treatments employed, on their ages, sexes, religions, races, creeds, colors, national origins, temperaments, marital status, Dun and Bradstreet ratings, neuroses, psychoses and favorite beers. Complete profiles of every human being ever known to have survived terminal cancer were fed into Harrison Wintergreen's computer.

Wintergreen programmed the computer to run a complete series of correlations between 10,000 separate and distinct factors and spontaneous remission. If even one factor—age, credit rating, favorite food, *anything*—correlated with spontaneous remission, the spontaneity factor would be removed.

Wintergreen had shelled out $100,000,000 for the computer. It was the best damn computer in the world. In two minutes and 7.894 seconds it had performed its task. In one succinct word it gave Wintergreen his answer:

"Negative."

Spontaneous remission did not correlate with *any* external factor. It was still spontaneous; the cause was unknown.

A lesser man would've been crushed. A more conventional man would've been dumbfounded. Harrison Wintergreen was elated.

He had eliminated the entire external universe as a factor in spontaneous remission in one fell swoop. Therefore, in some mysterious way, the human body and/or psyche was capable of curing itself.

Wintergreen set out to explore and conquer his own internal universe. He repaired to the pharmacy and prepared a formidable potation. Into his largest syringe he decanted the following: Novocaine; morphine; curare; *vlut,* a rare Central Asian poison which induced temporary blindness; olfactorcaine, a top-secret smell-deadener used by skunk farmers; tympanoline, a drug which temporarily deadened the auditory nerves (used primarily by filibustering Senators); a large dose of benzedrene; lysergic acid; pscilicibin; mescaline; peyote extract; seven other highly experimental and most illegal hallucinogens; eye of newt and toe of dog.

Wintergreen laid himself out on his most comfortable couch. He swabbed the vein in the pit of his left elbow with alcohol and injected himself with the witches' brew.

His heart pumped. His blood surged, carrying the arcane chemicals to every part of his body. The Novocaine blanked out every sensory nerve in his body. The morphine eliminated all sensations of pain. The *vlut* blacked out his vision. The olfactorcaine cut off all sense of smell. The tympanoline made him deaf as a traffic court judge. The curare paralyzed him.

Wintergreen was alone in his own body. No external stimuli reached him. He was in a state of total sensory deprivation. The urge to lapse into blessed unconsciousness was irresistible. Wintergreen, strong-willed though he was, could not have remained conscious unaided. But the massive dose of benzedrene would not let him sleep.

He was awake, aware, alone in the universe of his own body with no external stimuli to occupy himself with.

Then, one and two, and then in combinations like the fists of a good fast lightweight, the hallucinogens hit.

Wintergreen's sensory organs were blanked out, but the brain centers which received sensory data were still active. It was on these cerebral centers that the tremendous charge of assorted hallucinogens acted. He began to see phantom colors, shapes, things without name or form. He heard eldritch symphonies, ghost echoes, mad howling noises. A million impossible smells roiled through his brain. A thousand false pains and pressures tore at him, as if his whole body had been amputated. The sensory centers of Wintergreen's brain were like a mighty radio receiver tuned to an empty band—filled with meaningless visual, auditory, olfactory and sensual static.

The drugs kept his senses blank. The benzedrene kept him conscious. Forty years of being Harrison Wintergreen kept him cold and sane.

For an indeterminate period of time, he rolled with the punches, groping for the feel of this strange new non-environment. Then gradually, hesitantly at first but with ever-growing confidence, Wintergreen reached for control. His mind constructed untrue but useful analogies for actions that were not actions, states of being that were not states of being, sensory data unlike any sensory data ever received by the human brain. The analogies, constructed in a kind of calculated madness by his subconscious for the brute task of making the incomprehensible palpable, also enabled him to deal with his non-environment as if it were an environment, translating mental changes into analogs of action.

He reached out an analogical hand and tuned a figurative radio, inward, away from the blank waveband of the outside side universe and towards the as-yet-unused waveband of his own body, the internal universe that was his mind's only possible escape from chaos.

He tuned, adjusted, forced, struggled, felt his mind pressing against an atom-thin interface. He battered against the interface, an analogical translucent membrane between his mind and his internal universe, a membrane that stretched, flexed, bulged in-

ward, thinned . . . and finally broke. Like Alice through the
Looking Glass, his analogical body stepped through and stood
on the other side.

Harrison Wintergreen was inside his own body.

It was a world of wonder and loathsomeness, of the majestic
and the ludicrous. Wintergreen's point of view, which his mind
analogized as a body within his true body, was inside a vast net-
work of pulsing arteries, like some monstrous freeway system. The
analogy crystalized. It *was* a freeway, and Wintergreen was driving
down it. Bloated sacs dumped things into the teeming traffic:
hormones, wastes, nutrients. White blood cells careened by him
like mad taxicabs. Red corpuscles drove steadily along like stolid
burghers. The traffic ebbed and congested like a crosstown rush-
hour. Wintergreen drove on, searching, searching.

He made a left, cut across three lanes and made a right down
toward a lymph node. And then he saw it—a pile of white cells
like a twelve-car collision, and speeding towards him a leering
motorcyclist.

Black, the cycle. Black, the riding leathers. Black, dull black,
the face of the rider save for two glowing blood-red eyes. And
emblazoned across the front and back of the black motorcycle
jacket in shining scarlet studs the legend: "Carcinoma Angels."

With a savage whoop, Wintergreen gunned his analogical car
down the hypothetical freeway straight for the imaginary cyclist,
the cancer cell.

Splat! Pop! Cuush! Wintergreen's car smashed the cycle and
the rider exploded in a cloud of fine black dust.

Up and down the freeways of his circulatory system Wintergreen ranged, barreling along arteries, careening down veins, inching through narrow capillaries, seeking the black-clad cyclists, the
Carcinoma Angels, grinding them to dust beneath his wheels. . . .

And he found himself in the dark moist wood of his lungs, riding
a snow-white analogical horse, an imaginary lance of pure light
in his hand. Savage black dragons with blood-red eyes and flickering red tongues slithered from behind the gnarled boles of great
airsac trees. St. Wintergreen spurred his horse, lowered his lance
and impaled monster after hissing monster till at last the holy
lung-wood was free of dragons. . . .

He was flying in some vast moist cavern, above him the vague bulks of gigantic organs, below a limitless expanse of shining slimy peritoneal plain.

From behind the cover of his huge beating heart, a formation of black fighter planes, bearing the insignia of a scarlet "C" on their wings and fuselages, roared down at him.

Wintergreen gunned his engine and rose to the fray, flying up and over the bandits, blasting them with his machine-guns, and one by one and then in bunches they crashed in flames to the peritoneum below. . . .

In a thousand shapes and guises, the black and red things attacked. Black, the color of oblivion, red, the color of blood. Dragons, cyclists, planes, sea-things, soldiers, tanks and tigers in blood vessels and lungs and spleen and thorax and bladder— Carcinoma Angels, all.

And Wintergreen fought his analogical battles in an equal number of incarnations, as driver, knight, pilot, diver, soldier, mahout, with a grim and savage glee, littering the battlefields of his body with the black dust of the fallen Carcinoma Angels.

Fought and fought and killed and killed and finally. . . .

Finally found himself knee-deep in the sea of his digestive juices lapping against the walls of the dank, moist cave that was his stomach. And scuttling towards him on chitinous legs, a monstrous black crab with blood-red eyes, gross, squat, primeval.

Clicking, chittering, the crab scurried across his stomach towards him. Wintergreen paused, grinned wolfishly, and lept high in the air, landing with both feet squarely on the hard black carapace.

Like a sun-dried gourd, brittle, dry, hollow, the crab crunched beneath his weight and splintered into a million dusty fragments.

And Wintergreen was alone, at last alone and victorious, the first and last of the Carcinoma Angels now banished and gone and finally defeated.

Harrison Wintergreen, alone in his own body, victorious and once again looking for new worlds to conquer, waiting for the drugs to wear off, waiting to return to the world that always was his oyster.

Waiting and waiting and waiting. . . .

Go to the finest sanitarium in the world, and there you will find Harrison Wintergreen, who made himself Filthy Rich, Harrison Wintergreen, who Did Good, Harrison Wintergreen, who Left his

Footprints in the Sands of Time, Harrison Wintergreen, catatonic vegetable.

Harrison Wintergreen, who stepped inside his own body to do battle with Carcinoma's Angels, and won.

And can't get out.

The Age of Invention

One morning, having nothing better to do, I went to visit my cousin Roach. Roach lived in one of those lizard-infested caves on the East Side of the mountain. Roach did not hunt bears. Roach did not grow grain. Roach spent his daylight hours throwing globs of bearfat, bison-chips and old rotten plants against the walls of his cave.

Roach said that he was an Artist. He said it with a capital "A." (Even though writing has not yet been invented.)

Unlikely as it may seem, Roach had a woman. She was, however, the ugliest female on the mountain. She spent her daylight hours lying on the dirty floor of Roach's cave and staring at the smears of old bearfat, moldy bison-chips and rotten plants on the wall.

She used to say that this was Roach's Soul. She would also say that Roach had a very big soul.

Very big and *very* smelly.

As I approached the mouth of Roach's cave, I smelt pungent smoke. In fact, the cave was filled with this smoke. In the middle of the cave sat Roach and his woman. They were burning a big pile of weeds and inhaling the smoke.

"What are you doing?" I asked.

"Turning on, baby," said Roach. "I've just invented it."

"What does 'turning on' mean?"

"Well, you get this weed, dig? You burn it, and then you honk the smoke."

I scratched my head, inadvertently killing several of my favorite fleas.

"Why do that?" I asked.

"It like gets you high."

"You don't seem any further off the ground than I am," I observed. "And you're still kinda runty."

Roach snorted in disgust. "Forget it, man," he said. "It's only for Artists, Philosophers and Metaphysicians, anyway. (Even though Philosophy and Metaphysics have not yet been invented.) Dig my latest!"

On the nearest wall of the cave, there was this big blob of bearfat. In the middle of it was this small piece of bison-chip. Red and green and brown plant stains surrounded this. It smelt as good as it looked.

"Uh . . . interesting. . . ." I said.

"Like a masterpiece, baby," Roach said proudly. "I call it 'The Soul of Man'."

"Uh . . . 'The Sole of Man'? Er . . . it *does* sort of look like a foot."

"No, no, man! *Soul,* not *sole!*"

"But Roach, spelling hasn't been invented yet."

"Sorry. I forgot."

"Anyway," I said, trying to make him feel a little better, "it's very Artistic." (Whatever that meant.)

"Thanks, baby," Roach said sulkily.

"What's the matter, Roach?" I asked. He really looked awful.

"We haven't eaten in a week."

"Why don't you go out and kill a bear or something?" I suggested.

"I don't have the time to waste on hunting," Roach said indignantly. "I must live for Art!"

"It appears that you are dying for Art," I replied. "You can't do very much painting when you are dead."

"Well anyway," said Roach, in a very tiny voice, "I'm a pretty lousy hunter in the first place. I would probably starve even if I spent the whole day hunting. Or maybe a bear would kill *me*. This way, I'm at least like starving for a Reason."

I must admit it made a kind of sense. Roach is terribly nearsighted. Also amazingly scrawny. The original 90 pound weakling.

"Mmmmmmmm. . . ." I observed.

"Mmmmmmmm. . . . *what?*" asked Roach.

"Well, you know old Aardvark? He can't hunt either. So what

he does is he makes spearheads and trades them for bears. Maybe you could . . . ?"

"Go into *business?*" Roach cried. "Become bourgeois? *Please! I* am an Artist. Besides," he added lamely, "I don't know how to make spearheads."

"Mmmmm. . . ."

"Mmmmm. . . ."

"I know!" I cried. "You could trade your paintings!"

"Cool, baby!" exclaimed Roach. "Er . . . only why would anyone want to trade food for a painting?"

"Why because . . . er . . . ah. . . ."

"I guess I'll just have to starve."

"Wait a minute," I said. "Er . . . if I can get someone to trade food for your paintings, will you give me some of the food, say . . . oh, one bear out of every ten?"

"Sure," said Roach. "What've I got to lose?"

"It's a deal then?"

"Deal, baby!"

I had just invented the Ten-Percenter.

So I went to see Peacock. Peacock lived in the weirdest cave on the mountain—all filled up with stuff like mooseskins dyed pink, stuffed armadillos, and walls covered with withered morning-glories. For some reason which I have not yet been able to fathom, the women of the more henpecked men on the mountain give Peacock bears to make the same kind of messes in their caves.

Peacock is pretty weird himself. He was dressed in a skin-tight sabertooth skin dyed bright violet.

"Hello sweets," Peacock said, as I entered his perfumed cave.

"Hello, Peacock," I said uneasily. "Heard about Roach?"

"Roach?" shrilled Peacock. "That dirty, dirty man? That beatnik with the positively *unspeakable* cave?"

"That's him," I said. "Roach the Artist. Very good Artist, you know. After all, he invented it."

"Well what about that dreadful, dreadful creature?"

"Well you know your friend Cockatoo—?"

"Please, sweets!" shrieked Peacock. "Do not mention that *thing* Cockatoo in my presence again! Cockatoo and I are on the outs. I don't know what I ever saw in him. He's gotten so unspeakably *butch*."

Cockatoo was this . . . uh . . . *friend* of Peacock's . . . or *was*. They . . . uh . . . invented something together. Nobody is quite sure what it was, but we've organized a Vice Squad, just in case.

"Yeah," I muttered. "Well anyway, Cockatoo is paying Roach twenty bears to do a painting in his cave. He says that having an Original Roach in his cave will make your cave look like . . . er . . . 'A *positive* sloth's den, bubby,' I think his words were."

"Oooooh!" shrieked Peacock. "Oooooh!" He began to jump around the cave, pounding his little fists against the walls. "That monster! That veritable *beast!* Oooh, it's *horrid,* that's what it is! What am I going to do, sweets, whatever am I going to do?"

"Well," I suggested, "Roach is my cousin, you know, and I do have some pull with him. I suppose I could convince him to do a painting in *your* cave instead of Cockatoo's. Especially if you paid *thirty* bears instead of twenty. . . ."

"Oh, *would you* sweets? Would you really?"

"Well I don't know. I do kind of like you, Peacock, but on the other hand. . . ."

"Pretty, pretty, *pretty* please?"

I sighed heavily. "Okay, Peacock," I said. "You've talked me into it."

So Peacock got his Original Roach for thirty bears. Next week, I went to see Cockatoo, and I told him the story.

I got *him* to pay *forty* bears. Forty and thirty is seventy. Which gave me seven. Not bad for a couple hours' work. I better watch out, or someone'll invent income tax.

I saw Roach last week, the ingrate. He has moved to a bigger cave on the *West Side* of the mountain. He has a fine new leopard skin and *three* new women. He has even invented the Havana cigar, so he can have something expensive to smoke.

Unfortunately, he has discovered that he no longer needs me to make deals for him. His going price is eighty bears a painting. I, like a dope, neglected to invent the renewable exclusive agency contract. Can't invent 'em all, I suppose.

Roach has become truly insufferable, though. He now talks of "art" with a small "a" and "Bears" with a capital "B". He is the first Philistine.

He is going to get his.

How do you like my fine new leopard skin? Would you like one of my Havana cigars? Have you met this new woman yet? Have you seen my new cave?

I can buy and sell Roach now. I am the first tycoon. How did I do it? Well. . . .

Hog was the mountain bum. He never trimmed his beard. He didn't have a woman, not even an *ugly* one. He laid around his filthy cave all day, doing nothing but belching occasionally. A real slob.

But even a jerk like Hog can throw bearfat and bison-chips against a cave wall.

I made an Artist out of Hog. I did this by telling him he could make fifty bears a day just by throwing bearfat and bison-chips against the walls of other people's caves.

This appealed to Hog.

This time I did *not* neglect to invent the renewable exclusive agency contract. It was another ten percent deal.

Hog gets ten percent.

Then I went to Peacock's cave. I stared in dismay at Roach's painting. "What is *that?*" I sneered.

"That, sweets, is an Original Roach," Peacock crooned complacently. "Isn't it divine? Such sensitivity, such style, such grace, such—"

"*Roach?*" I snorted. "You *can't* be serious. Why that Neopseudoclassicalmodern stuff went out with the Brontosaurs. You're *miles* behind the times, Peacock," I said, thereby inventing the Art Critic. "*The* Artist today is of course the Great Hog."

"Hog?" whined Peacock. "Hog is beastly, beastly. A rude, stupid, smelly thing, a *positive* slob. Why his whole cave is a wretched mass of slop!"

"Exactly," I answered. "That's the source of his greatness. Hog is the mountain's foremost Slop Artist."

"Oooooh. . . . How much do the Great Hog's paintings cost?"

"One hundred bears apiece," I said smugly. "Cockatoo is already contracting to—"

"I told you never to mention that *creature* to me again!" Peacock shrieked. "He must not steal an Original Hog from me, do you hear? I simply couldn't *bear* it! But all this is getting so *expensive.* . . ."

I gave Peacock my best understanding smile. "Peacock, old man," I said, "I have a little business proposition for you. . . ."

Well, that's all there was to it. You guessed it, now when Peacock makes one of his messes in some henpecked caveman's cave, it always includes at least one Original Hog, or maybe a couple Original Treesloths—Treesloth being another jerk Artist I have under contract. I sell the painting to Peacock for a hundred bears, and he charges his suck—er, *client, two* hundred bears for the same mess of bearfat and bison-chips. Peacock calls this Interior Decorating.

I call it "Civilization." Maybe it'll last for a couple of months, if I'm lucky.

Outward Bound

Captain Peter Reed floated closer to the big central viewport of the conning globe.

Before him, filling half his field of vision, was the planet Maxwell, green continents and blue seas reminding him of Earth.

He shook his white-haired head. Earth was fifty light-years off, or to put it another way, seventy years ago, or in another way, only four months.

Reed shrugged, not an easy task for a seventy-year-old man in free fall. Or to put it another way, an eight-hundred-year-old man.

Reed could not help laughing aloud. Fifty subjective years in space, he thought, eight hundred years in objective time, and still it has its wonder for me.

As he watched, a mote of light detached itself from the disk of Maxwell, and arced upward.

That would be Director Horvath's ship, thought Reed. Last time the *Outward Bound* was at Maxwell, it had been ruled by a hereditary king. But that was three hundred years ago. King La Farge, thought Reed sadly, dead and gone three hundred years.

This Lazlo Horvath, now. He seems to be a different proposition. Ambitious, dangerous.

Reed smiled wryly. If he keeps up this way, he may soon be honored by a visit from Jacob ben Ezra.

The captain spoke into the communicator. "Rog, get the reception room ready. Our customer's on the way."

He paddled awkwardly to the rear of the conning globe, grabbed a guard rail, and pulled himself through the rotating doorway, into the main cylinder of the *Outward Bound*.

Immediately, he felt the tug of gravity. The *Outward Bound* was an untidy collection of cylinders and globes, held together by spars. While in orbit, the whole conglomeration spun about a central axis, creating an artificial gravity. But, of course, it was necessary that the conning globe be stationary, so it hung in front of the main cylinder, mounted on frictionless bearings, so that it alone did not share the ship's rotation.

Captain Reed made his way to the reception room. Lazlo Horvath should be an eager customer. The last tradeship to hit Maxwell had been the *Stargod,* one hundred years ago, and that was still in the days of the Kingdom.

Director Horvath was new and ambitious, and like all planetary leaders, he chafed under the yoke of Earth. An ideal customer.

Roger Reed was already in the reception room when his father arrived. There was some family resemblance. He had his father's large frame, but on him it was well-muscled, not hung with loose flesh. His hair was a flamboyant red, and he was going through one of his periods of experimentation with mustaches. This one was only a week old, and its ultimate nature could not yet be discerned.

"Horvath's on board, Dad," he said.

"Please, Roger," said the old man, with a weariness born of endless repetition, "at least when there is a customer aboard, *don't* call me 'Dad'."

"Sorry, sir."

Captain Reed looked about the reception room. It was the one area of calculated ostentation on the ship. It was paneled in real knotty pine. A genuine wool carpet lined it from wall to wall. The captain sat behind a huge mahogany desk, on a genuine red leather covered chair. Three other such chairs were scattered about the room. A viewer was built into one wall.

The room always made Peter Reed feel uncomfortable.

"Well, Roger," said the captain, "do you think this'll be a good haul?"

"Don't see why not, da . . . *sir.* The Directory of Maxwell seems to be at that stage when they think that with a *little* help, they can break the Terran hegemony. They ought to go quite high for the force field, for instance."

The old man sighed. "They never learn, do they?" he said. "No doubt Horvath will think that the force field is an ultimate weapon.

He'll never stop to realize that on Earth, it's already seventy years old."

"Why so glum, *captain?*" said the younger Reed. "After all, it's our stock in trade."

"So it is, so it is."

An orderly appeared at the door. "Captain Peter Reed," he said formally, "it is my honor to present Lazlo Horvath, Director of Maxwell."

A short, squat man, of about fifty, stalked into the room. He was dressed in a black uniform, with gold trim, encircled by a wide Sam Browne belt. He wore heavy black boots.

Oh, no, thought Peter Reed, not one of *them!*

Nevertheless, he rose politely, wryly aware of the plainness of his simple light-green coveralls. "Director Horvath."

"Captain Reed."

"My second, Roger Reed."

"Mr. Reed."

"Sit down, Director," said the captain.

Horvath perched himself on the edge of one of the chairs.

"It has been a while since a starship visited Maxwell," he said. His voice was deep and crisp.

"Yes, I know. The trader *Stargod,* one hundred years ago."

For a moment, there was a flicker of puzzlement on Horvath's tough face. "Ah, yes, the *Stargod,*" he said smoothly. "Well, Captain Reed, what have you to offer?"

"Several new concepts," said Peter Reed, studying the Director. It was obvious that the man had let something slip. But what?

"Such as?"

"For one thing, an amusing new concept in drinks. Roger, the refreshments."

Roger Reed waved his hand, and a panel slid aside, revealing a pitcher of red liquid, and three glasses on a tray. He poured the drinks.

Captain Reed smiled as he saw the perplexed look on Horvath's face. The drink was made up of two different wines, one hot, one cold, kept separate by a new chemical technique so that one tasted alternately hot and cold liquid. It was a strange feeling.

"Very amusing, Captain Reed," said Horvath. "But surely you

don't expect Maxwell to pay good radioactives for such a parlor trick."

Reed grinned. The hot-and-cold liquid technique was just a come-on, of course. The really big commodity he had to sell was the force field.

"Director," he said, "as you know, traders don't sell *products*, except radioactives, at times. What we sell is science, knowledge, techniques. Now the drink may be a parlor trick, but there can be practical applications of the technique."

"Perhaps, perhaps," said Horvath shortly, "but what *else* do you have? Perhaps . . . perhaps you at last have the secret of Overdrive?"

Peter Reed laughed. "Maybe I have the Philosopher's Stone, as well?" He saw that Horvath was not amused. "I'm sorry, Director," he said. "It's just that we've never made port on any planet, in the eight hundred years that the *Outward Bound* has been in space, where they didn't ask that question. No, we don't have the secret of Overdrive. It is my opinion that there never will be an Overdrive. Man will never travel faster than light. It's a chimera, a schizophrenic compulsion to leave the limiting realm of the real universe, to find a never-never land called Hyperspace, or what have you, where reality is suspended, and the Galaxy belongs to Man."

Horvath frowned. "A very pretty little speech," he said. "So easy for *you* to say. But then, you are not under the heel of Earth. You starmen are by nature free agents. But we, we *colonials,* we know what it is to suffer the tyranny of time. Maxwell is fifty light-years from Earth. Therefore, since we were settled from Earth, from an Earth that was already sixty years ahead of us when we emerged from Deep Sleep, we will *always* be sixty years behind Earth, just as the outer ring will always be two hundred years behind. To you, an Overdrive would be just one more thing to peddle, although it would bring the best price in history. To us, an Overdrive would mean freedom."

"Of course, you are right, Director," said Captain Reed. "Nevertheless, that doesn't make Overdrive any more possible. However" —he noticed Horvath's anticipation with satisfaction—"we do have something new, something big. I suppose they've been looking for this as long as they've been looking for an Overdrive—*a force field.*"

Horvath's eyes widened. *"A force field?"*

"Ah, you are interested."

"Of course. It would be idiotic to try and hide it. *This,* Maxwell wants."

"And what have *you* to offer?" asked Peter Reed softly.

"One ton of thorium."

"Oh really, Director!" said Reed. "That's all right for the hot-cold technique, but—"

"Two tons!"

"Come, come Mr. Horvath. A force field is the ultimate defensive weapon, after all. Two measly tons—"

"Ten tons!"

"Now, what are we going to do with all that thorium? Can't you do better? We deal in knowledge, you know. Perhaps you have something in that area—"

"Well," said Horvath, his hard eyes narrowing, "there was another ship here, only three years ago."

"Oh?"

"Colonizer, heading for the outer ring. Direct from Earth."

"So what?"

"Well, captain, there was a *passenger* aboard."

"A passenger?"

"Yes, a Dr. Ching pen Yee. Had to leave Earth quickly, so it seems, some kind of mathematical physicist. We're holding him."

"I don't see what this has to do with *us,*" said Peter Reed.

Horvath smiled crookedly. "Grand Admiral Jacob ben Ezra is on his way to Maxwell. In fact, he's decelerating already. Should be here in about a month."

Captain Reed stroked his nose. If Earth was sending ben Ezra himself after Dr. Ching, the man must be someone really important. Earth virtually *never* pursued a fugitive beyond the twenty-five light-year radius of the Integral Control Zone. And Horvath knew it.

"So what are you offering?" he said slowly.

"Ben Ezra can't know that he was put off here," said Horvath.

"He'll be eager to get away. I propose that I trade you Ching for the force-field theory."

"But neither of us knows whether Ching has anything of value," said Reed, knowing that anyone who was being pursued by Jacob ben Ezra over fifty light-years must know something *very* valuable indeed.

But Horvath knew it, too. "Come, captain. We both know that Earth would not send ben Ezra, unless Ching was very important indeed. Ching and one ton of thorium for the force field."

"Ching and three tons," said Reed, with a little smile.

"Ching and two tons."

Peter Reed laughed. "Ching and three tons for the force field *and* the hot-cold technique."

"Very well, captain," said Horvath, rising and sticking out his hand, "you've got a deal."

The two men shook hands.

"Have your men begin bringing up the thorium immediately," said Reed, "and get your scientists up here quick, to learn the techniques. I certainly don't want to be in this system when ben Ezra gets here."

"Of course not," said Horvath, with a grin. "Rest assured, captain, I'm a very good liar. And believe me when I say it has been a pleasure doing business with you."

"The same, Director. Mr. Reed will show you to the air lock."

As Roger Reed opened the door, Horvath stopped and turned.

"Captain," he said, "one thing. If you ever do get hold of an Overdrive, Maxwell will match anyone's price for it. You can write your own bill of sale."

Captain Reed frowned. "You know as well as I do, that we traders sell the same knowledge to every planet we touch."

Horvath eyed him thinly. "I am aware of the practice," he said. "However, in the case of an Overdrive, Maxwell would make it well worth your while to make it an *exclusive* sale."

Reed shook his head, and grinned. "I'll keep it in mind, Director," he said.

Grand Admiral Jacob ben Ezra finished his fourth cigarette of the morning. On a starship, with its own self-contained atmosphere to maintain, smoking was a hideous luxury. But Admiral ben Ezra was a man with privileges. A small, frail old man of eighty subjective years, he had been in space for over seven hundred objective years, and was something of a living legend.

Right now, he was nervous. He turned to his aide. "David," he said, "can't we cut a week or two off the time?"

"No, sir," replied the young commander. "We're using maximum deceleration as it is. Photon sails, plus ion drive."

"What about using the atomic reaction rockets as well?" asked the admiral, knowing full well what the answer would be.

"We just don't have the reaction mass to spare," said the commander. "Photon sails, of course, cost no fuel, and the ion rockets use very little, but with the ion drive going, and three weeks left till planetfall, we can't use the rockets for even an hour. Besides—"

"Besides, our course is already plotted, and we'd undershoot," said ben Ezra. "David, David, don't you know when an old man is talking just to let off steam?"

The young commander fidgeted with embarrassment.

"Nevertheless," said the Grand Admiral, rubbing the end of his long nose, "I wish we could. It's going to be a close thing."

"Why, sir?"

Jacob ben Ezra lit a fifth cigarette. "The *Outward Bound* left Earth just about when we did. They're scheduled to stop at Maxwell. No doubt, the *SS-185* will put Ching off somewhere before they get to Toehold. My guess is that it'll be Maxwell."

"So, sir?"

Ben Ezra exhaled a great cloud of smoke.

"Sorry, David," he said. "Somehow, I'm beginning to find it difficult to remember that not everyone is as old as I am. The *Outward Bound* is one of the oldest tradeships around, in fact, if my memory serves me correctly, it was the *first* one built specifically for the purpose. Her captain is Peter Reed. He's been in space longer than *I* have."

"Longer than *you*, sir?"

Ben Ezra laughed. It was not the laugh of an old man. It felt good to laugh, especially under the circumstances.

"Yes, my incredulous young friend," he said, "longer than I have. Reed is one of the cleverest captains in space. Also, don't forget, he has the force field to sell, this trip."

"You mean you think Maxwell will trade *Ching* for the force field? But, sir, once they find out why Ching's out here, *no one* would trade him for *anything*."

Jacob ben Ezra puckered his leathery lips. "You are assuming that Dr. Ching will talk. I doubt that very much. He knows that we'd follow him to Andromeda, if we had to. My guess is that he'll figure his only hope is to change ships as often as possible, and not tell *anyone* why he's on the run."

"Then why would Captain Reed accept him in trade?"

"Because," said the Grand Admiral, raising his bushy white eyebrows, "Reed is clever *and* experienced. He will *know* that anyone who is being pursued by us, all the way from Earth, is someone who has something of vital importance."

Jacob ben Ezra crushed his cigarette against the bulkhead. He shook his head violently.

"If only he knew," he said, "if only he *knew*."

The *Outward Bound* orbited low over Maxwell. She was an untidy spectacle—one great central cylinder, around whose girth the space gigs were clustered; three lesser cylinders, connected to the main body only by spars; the conning globe; and, far astern, the propulsion reactor, a dull black globe, behind which sprouted two sets of rockets—the small, almost inconspicuous ion drive, and the great reaction rockets, which fed off whatever reaction mass happened to be in the huge fuel tanks, located just forward of the reactor.

To make the whole thing even more messy looking, the main cylinder and its auxiliaries were pocked with globes, tubes and blisters, looking for all the world like budding yeast under a microscope. Like Topsy, the successful tradeship just *grew,* adding a cylinder here, a globe there, a blister in another place, as the ship's fortune waxed. In deep space, where friction was no factor, this wild messiness was a status symbol, a sign of prosperity.

Now, Maxwellian ships were coming and going constantly, bringing thorium, food, water, scientists. They had one great navigational hazard to overcome. Four mile-long spars sprouted from amidships on the main cylinder. During acceleration away from a sun, or deceleration towards a sun, four immense triangles of ten-molecule-thick plastic would stretch from the spars, catching the energy of photon packets outward bound from light sources. By grams-per-square-yard, the solar sails provided negligible thrust, but cumulatively, over two square miles of surface area, they were good for a steady, if mild acceleration. Besides, the energy they provided was free.

But now, since the spars were empty, and the ship was spinning about its central axis, the spars were the arms of a monstrous windmill, which the Maxwellian ships had to avoid.

Captain Reed smiled as he watched the ships thread their way gingerly toward the *Outward Bound*. No doubt, there were simple ways of making the spars stationary while the ship spun, perhaps using the same circle-in-circle bearings that served to immobilize the conning globe. But no starship *he* had ever heard of had bothered to try. It was just too amusing watching the planethogs dodge the whirling spars.

Well, this would be the last day they'd have to brave the whirl-wind. The last of the thorium was aboard, the Maxwellians had their force field and hot-cold technique, and Ching would be com-ing aboard on the last ship.

None too soon, either, thought Peter Reed. Ben Ezra will be here in another ten days. Ten days to get here, perhaps a week or two to break Horvath. Captain Reed had few illusions about *that* individual. Within three weeks, at the outside, Jacob ben Ezra would know that Ching pen Yee was aboard the *Outward Bound*.

Ben Ezra would be able to close the gap to a week or less, at the next planetfall, Nuova Italia, only ten light-years away.

But by that time, thought Reed, I'll know whether Ching's worth keeping. If he isn't, ben Ezra can have him at Nuova Italia. But if he is . . . well, ben Ezra will probably have to take on supplies at Nuova Italia. We can get away from him once more, if we have to. But . . . he can catch us easily, and wherever we head, he can be there before us, with us only having a couple of days lead.

We'll jump off that bridge when we come to it, thought Captain Reed.

"Dr. Ching is aboard," came a voice from the communicator.

"Good," said Reed. "How soon can we break orbit?"

"Everything'll be secured in another three hours, Dad."

"Roger!"

"Sorry, sir."

"All right, Roger," said the old man. "Make ready to break orbit as soon as possible. And send Ching to the reception room.

Have Olivera there, too. In fact, stall Ching a bit, and have Manny get there a few minutes earlier. Tell him I'll be right down."

"Yes, *sir*."

"But, Peter," said Manuel Olivera, his dark eyes raised to the ceiling in supplication, "I am *not* a theoretical physicist. I am *not* a mathematician. I am a tinkerer, a librarian, a maker of stinks, a—"

"Manny! Manny! Please!" said the captain. "I know the whole song and dance by now. Nevertheless, you *are* the *Outward Bound*'s chief scientist."

"Yes, yes," said the small dark-skinned man excitedly, "but you know as well as I do that all that means is that I'm a glorified librarian. We—"

"All right, all right. All I want you to do is *be* here, and pay attention. This Dr. Ching has something of value, I'm *sure* of it. And we may not have him very long. We've got to be quick, and—"

"Dr. Ching pen Yee to see you, captain," said an orderly.

"Send him in."

Dr. Ching was a small, though well-built man of about sixty. His straight black hair was parted neatly in the middle. Only his shifting eyes betrayed his nervousness.

"Thank you for accepting my passage, Captain Reed," he said.

"Not at all, Dr. Ching. Frankly, we hope you may be of value to us. As you know, the lifeblood of a tradeship is knowledge. We sell it, and we buy it. To be blunt, we have *bought* you from Maxwell. You get passage with us, for as long as you want, and in return, we expect you to share your knowledge."

"But, captain," said Ching nervously, "I am a mathematical physicist. You are engaged in the business of selling practical technological knowledge. We mathematical physicists are not noted for producing marketable knowledge."

Reed frowned. This Ching was cool, and he was scared. A tough combination to crack.

"Please let Mr. Olivera and myself be the judge of that. By the way, I believe I've forgotten to introduce you. This is Manuel Olivera, our chief scientist."

"How do you do, Mr. Olivera," said Ching smoothly. "Captain Reed, really you are wasting your time. I am purely a theorist."

Reed wondered if he should spring his knowledge of Admiral ben Ezra's pursuit. He decided it could wait.

"Suppose you just tell us what you're working on?" he said.

Ching fidgeted. "Mathematical theory," he said.

"Come now, Dr. Ching," snapped Olivera, "we are not complete scientific ignoramuses, you know. What sort of theory?"

"A development of a small corollary to the Special Theory of Relativity."

"Oh?" said Olivera. "Involving what?"

Ching's eyes flickered from focus to focus like a bird's. "Involving . . . some work with transfinite substitutions," he said vaguely.

Olivera continued his pursuit. "Transfinite substitutions? Where? For what?"

Ching laughed falsely. "Really, Mr. Olivera," he said. "It's all a complicated mathematical exercise. It amuses me to substitute infinite and transfinite numbers for some of the variables. As I said, nothing practical."

"Just why are you doing this?" snapped Olivera.

"Really," said Ching blandly, "that's an unanswerable question. Indeed. Why do men climb mountains? Because they are there. Really, gentlemen, I'm quite tired. May I be excused?"

Olivera was about to continue his sortie, but the captain waved him off.

"Of course," he said. "We will soon be leaving for Nuova Italia. In about two hours. We will have time to talk again, before we all go into Deep Sleep. By all means, rest up."

"Thank you, captain," said Ching. An orderly was called, and he led Ching off.

"Well, Manny?" asked the captain.

"Well, *what?* Am I a mind reader? Gibberish. Vagueness. Perhaps outright lies. I ask you, Peter, would Jacob ben Ezra travel fifty light-years after someone engaged in 'a complicated mathematical exercise?' Would Earth give a damn?"

"Of course not," said the captain.

"Then why in space didn't you tell him that you knew ben Ezra was after him?" snapped Olivera.

Peter Reed smiled thinly. "Time enough for that between now and Deep Sleep. That's a whole week. I think the strategic time to

spring it is just before he goes into Deep Sleep. Impending Deep
Sleep makes a man realize just how dependent he can be."

"You'd *better* loosen him up by then," said Olivera, "because
it's just possible that when we wake up, we'll find ben Ezra right on
our tails."

A three minute burst on the huge reaction rockets kicked the
Outward Bound out of orbit.

As she drifted slowly outward, the huge triangular photon sails
were reeled out onto the mile-long spars, blotting out whole sectors
of stars.

The pale, almost invisible, blue stream of the ion drive shot
noiselessly, vibrationlessly out of the nozzles.

The *Outward Bound* was on her way to Nuova Italia.

During the next week, the ship would be secured, the automatic
systems checked, re-checked, and finally given command of the
ship. There would be a final course correction, and then the thousand men, women and children who made up the crew of the
Outward Bound would go into Deep Sleep.

Deep Sleep was the technique that had given Man that insignificant portion of the Galaxy which he possessed. A starship could
accelerate to nearly three-quarters the speed of light, but this took
over a year, and, although it had been proven true that subjective
time on a fast-moving starship *did* contract, as Einstein had predicted, the factor was still far too short. The spaces between the
suns would still eat up lifespans.

Deep Sleep had been developed to deal with this dilemma.
Partly it was a technique developed from yoga, partly it was simply a careful, controlled lowering of the body temperature, till life
slowed down to the barest crawl. The elements of the technique
had been known even before rudimentary spaceflight. But it took
the technical integration of all the factors to make Deep Sleep an
effective and relatively safe form of suspended animation, and to
give Man the stars.

Peter Reed was getting disgusted. It was now time to go into
Deep Sleep, and still no one had been able to get anything out of
Ching. Clearly, the man was scared silly.

Well, thought Reed, maybe I can shock him out of it now.

He was standing in one of the Deep Sleep chambers. The walls

were lined with transparent plastic cubicles, coffin-sized, honey-
combed with passages, through which liquid oxygen was passed.

Another of the ship's economies, thought the captain. The same
oxygen that served as the ship's air supply was cooled by the cold
of space, and used to freeze the Deep Sleep chambers. It took a
lot of liquid oxygen, in fact, the entire ship's supply, but since no
one would be needing it while the crew was in Deep Sleep, and
since it was re-usable, it made a neat saving.

Most of the crew were already in Deep Sleep. The cubicles were
filled with frozen crewmembers, the Environment Masks snugly
fitted over their faces. Only the skeleton Deep Sleep detail, the captain and Dr. Ching remained unfrozen. Now, the captain and the
passenger would take their places, and then the automatics would
handle the Deep Sleep detail.

A crewman was escorting Ching to his cubicle. The mathematician's face was pasty and pale. His eyes flickered furiously over
the frozen figures in the plastic coffins.

Reed smiled, half in sympathy, half in satisfaction. He had spent
a total time of nearly seven hundred years in those cubicles. Still,
it always made him shudder a bit. But Ching had only experienced
Deep Sleep once, and somehow, the second time was always the
hardest.

"Well, Dr. Ching," he called out, "how do you feel?"

"A bit foolish, captain. I must admit that I am afraid, and yet
there is really nothing to be afraid of."

For a moment, Reed's distaste for Ching was washed away. The
Grand Admiral of Earth's fleet had hounded him across fifty light-
years, and now he was facing what must to him be a great irrational
fear. And yet, he's so calm.

"I don't see why a man like *you* should be afraid," said the
captain deliberately, hating what he was doing.

"Captain?"

"Well, it seems to me that a man who's being chased across the
Galaxy by Jacob ben Ezra, and still refuses to tell me *why*, must
have a surplus of guts."

For a moment, Ching trembled. Then he smiled slowly. "I
thought you knew," he said. "Why else would you be so interested
in me?"

"Why don't you tell me what this is all about Ching? What are
you on to? Why is Earth so concerned? I don't expect you to be-

lieve that we're your *friends* but surely you must realize that it's in our interest as traders to protect you if you're working on something important."

Ching sighed heavily. "Captain Reed," he said, "Earth is not after me because they *want* what I'm working on. I'm really not working on anything practical at all. Just a mathematical and physical concept."

"And yet, they're chasing farther than they've ever chased a fugitive before."

"Yes," said Ching. "Captain, some day you may know why I must keep my secret. If Jacob ben Ezra catches up to us, you will be *glad* that I've remained silent."

"Why, man, why?"

"Because," said Ching, "I'm fairly certain that ben Ezra has orders to kill anyone who knows what I know."

The captain frowned. "Perhaps you will change your mind when we come out of Deep Sleep at Nuova Italia."

"Perhaps, captain, *you* will change *yours*."

Peter Reed shrugged irritably. "Let's get on with it," he said to the attendant.

He climbed into his cubicle, and settled himself on the foam-rubber mattress. The attendant secured him with clamps. The ship's spin would stop when the crew was in Deep Sleep. There would be no gravity.

The soft, lined mask was fitted over his face. He inhaled the soothing tranquilizer vapor. He was comfortable, content. He vaguely felt the prick of a needle, then his senses began to dull, first sight, then sound, then feel, then smell. The last sensation was a dry taste in his mouth, and then that was gone, and he was an entity within himself, in his own private universe . . . a mote swimming in the sea of himself . . . and then, even the sense of mind began to dull . . . to fade . . . to softly melt away, like a mouthful of cotton candy.

A blinding redness which pervaded the universe . . . a pins-and-needles feeling . . . then warmth, overwhelming, welcome warmth, motion, smell, sound.

Jacob ben Ezra sat up in his Deep Sleep cubicle, slowly, patiently teaching his old eyes to focus.

You never get really used to it, he thought. What year is this?

Let's see . . . Maxwell to Nuova Italia means fourteen years in
Deep Sleep, and when we left Maxwell, it was 3297 A.D., or '98?
On Earth . . .

Ben Ezra gave a dry little laugh. Time! What is time? Does it
matter? I am eighty years old, I am eight hundred years old, or
maybe a thousand.

This life means giving up many things. A firm sense of time is
one of them. The people who've sent me after Ching, back on
Earth, are all dead. I'm a ghost, a shade, the expression of the
will of a group of men, all of whom are dead—in a sense.

Man was not meant for this kind of life, thought Jacob ben Ezra
sourly. This is a poor way to command the stars, a poor and pitiful
way.

He laughed bitterly. This is a life fit only for Gypsies and Jews.
Come to think of it, Gypsies don't have a sufficient sense of
history, in the long run.

Maybe that's why so many in the Fleet are Jews. To a Jew, a
thousand years is supposed to be a reasonable length of time. Or
so the legends say. So they say.

But what is a Jew? There is no such thing as Judaism, anymore.
There is hardly such a thing as race.

A Jew, thought Jacob ben Ezra, nowadays is anyone who thinks
of himself as one. *Homo interstellarus.*

Ben Ezra leaned on the shoulders of a waiting attendant, and
climbed down from the cubicle. His legs were a bit rubbery, but
he was used to it.

Homo interstellarus, he thought, as he made his way slowly to
the conning globe, lousy Latin, but very good sense.

It was as if Jews had been training to man the Great Fleet for
five thousand years. How long had they been a self-contained
culture, independent of geography, living, even, in their own time
stream? In the pre-stellar past, they had been feared for it,
damned for it, but now, it had a purpose. Who else could isolate
themselves on the twenty ships of the Great Fleet, but Jews? Knowing no planet, no time to call home?

"They, they," mumbled the admiral. Why not *we,* he thought.
Heh! Peter Reed is as much a Jew as I am. What does it mean
now? It means the exiles, the planetless ones, the timeless ones,
defying the Universe, spitting in the face of Einstein himself.

The steps of Jacob ben Ezra became firm and sprightly. He lit a cigarette.

"Feels good!" he said to no one in particular.

Several men were already in the conning globe—Chief Navigator Richard Jacoby, several minor crewmen, and his aide, David Steen.

"They're there, sir," said Steen. "We've got a fix on 'em."

The admiral frowned. This job was getting more odious to him every minute.

"How far behind are we?" he asked.

"About six days."

"Then they haven't made orbit yet?"

"No, sir."

"Good. That means we can keep an eye on them. Jacoby, is it possible for them to get away?"

The tall, thin navigator frowned. "Depends on what you mean, admiral. Wherever they go, of course, we can track them. Do you mean will we catch up to them before they leave orbit? Then, I'd have to say no, not if they're trying to get away."

"Can we *stop* them?" said the admiral.

"You mean *destroy* them, sir?"

"I don't mean make love to 'em, Jacoby! I know we can destroy them, but can we get close enough to disable 'em, carefully, without killing?"

"Hard to say, at six days' distance."

"That's what I was afraid of. Well, tomorrow, we'll radio 'em to heave-to and wait for us."

"Do you think they will, sir?" asked Steen.

"That depends, David, that depends. If they know why we're after Ching, they'll do *anything* to keep him. But, then, they may not know. In which case, they won't take any silly chances."

"And if they try to get away?"

Grand Admiral ben Ezra frowned. "If they try to get away, we have two choices. We can blast 'em, or we can plot their next course, and be waiting for 'em. Six days, we can easily make up on the next hop. The thing is, if we *do* blast 'em, and can't confirm that Ching was aboard, then we'll have to backtrack to Maxwell, maybe even back to Earth, and we'll never really *know*."

"But, sir," said Steen, "do you really think Reed would risk his ship for Ching, *even if* he found out?"

Jacob ben Ezra laughed, and shook his head. "I'm not sure," he said, "but I am sure that Captain Reed is as clever as I am. Which means, if he *does* find out, he'll know that we can't blast him without *knowing* that Ching is aboard. If he finds out, he'll run all right. And you know something, David?"

"What, sir?"

The admiral lit another cigarette. "I'd do the same thing myself," he said.

Captain Peter Reed cursed loudly. "Just great, just wonderful! Six days away! Six days away, and that bloody sphinx of a Ching hasn't—I've a good mind to call it a business loss and turn him over to ben Ezra."

"Sir," said the radioman fearfully, "Admiral ben Ezra is still calling—"

"Put it through to this 'visor, but *don't* answer. And stop all communications with Nuova Italia. I want it to look like our radio's dead."

"Yes, sir."

"Roger!" said Reed into the communicator. "Prepare to break orbit immediately, and stand by. And get Ching up to the conning globe on the double!"

"But, sir, Ching has never been in zero gravity before, he—"

"Drag him up here by the hair, if you have to!"

It was only three minutes later when Roger Reed hauled a green-looking Ching into the conning globe.

"Captain," said Ching, "is this *really* necessary? I—"

"I want you to hear something, my tight-lipped friend," said the scowling Peter Reed. "I want you to hear it directly."

He turned on the televisor. The tired, wizened face of Jacob ben Ezra filled the screen. Ching paled, even through his nausea.

". . . Calling the *Outward Bound* . . . Calling the *Outward Bound*. Calling Captain Peter Reed . . ."

The pale visage on the televisor paused to light a cigarette.

"Really, Peter," said Jacob ben Ezra, "this is ridiculous. I know you're reading me."

Peter Reed could not help smiling.

"Very well, Peter," said the voice of ben Ezra, "we'll play it your way. So *don't* answer me. *I'll* do the talking. You probably have a Dr. Ching pen Yee aboard. I want him. I've come all the way from Earth for him, and, by space, I'll have him, or I'll blow you to bits. You have five minutes, plus the time lag, to answer. If you don't answer *then,* I will take appropriate action."

Captain Reed turned the televisor off.

"Well, Dr. Ching," he said, "do I turn you over to ben Ezra, or do you talk?"

A new emotion crossed Ching's face. It did not seem to be fear, it was more of a manic defiance.

"You don't understand. I do not care about death, captain," he said. "I have not fled to save my life. Had I remained on Earth, my life would not have been endangered. But—"

"But *what?* You heard the admiral. You have five minutes to make up your mind."

Ching sighed. "It is my work that must go on. *That's* what they want to stop. Very well, captain, I must take the chance."

"So?"

"There is no simple way of explaining it. I have told you that I am working on a corollary to the Special Theory of Relativity. It is the Special Theory of Relativity, as you must know, which limits all speed to the speed of light. Essentially, it means that at the speed of light, mass is infinite, therefore it would take an infinite thrust to accelerate to that limit, and exceeding it would be impossible. But, as I have said, I am working on transfinite substitutions. I hope to evolve an equation—"

"Come to the point, man, come to the point!"

"There is no simple point, captain. I am engaged in the preliminaries of a work that some day may lead to a theoretical means of exceeding the speed of light within the Einsteinian Universe—"

"An Overdrive!" shouted Captain Reed.

"Not for a long time," said Ching pedantically. "It—"

But the captain was no longer listening. *An Overdrive!* Countless others had tried before, but Earth thought that *this* man was close enough to send ben Ezra sixty light-years to . . .

Reed's trader's brain analyzed the situation with the speed born of commercial instinct. An Overdrive would be the most valuable commodity any trader ever had to sell. The *Outward Bound* could sell it again and again, on each of the sixty-seven planets inhabited by Man, each time commanding a price undreamed of in all history!

And ben Ezra would not take the chance that Ching *wasn't* on
the *Outward Bound*. He would have to *know*. He couldn't . . .

"Hang on to something," shouted Peter Reed.

He yelled into the communicator: "Break orbit! *Do it now!*"

"What course, sir?" came the tinny voice.

"Who cares?" roared Reed. "Just get us away from here. Raise
the sails, activate the ion drive. Maximum thrust on the reaction
rockets! Do it now! Now! *Now!* NOW!"

Jacob ben Ezra shook his head, with a Gallic shrug. Reed was
running. What else could he do? But that means he *knows*. It must!

Ben Ezra lit a cigarette. "Change course," he said to his
navigator. "Accelerate. Follow them."

"Are we going to attack?" asked Commander Dayan, floating
alongside the admiral in the conning globe. His dark, mustachioed
face was alight with an eagerness that ben Ezra found distasteful.
But then, one could not really blame Dayan. Gunnery officers usually have nothing to do but sit around.

"Not now, at any rate," said the admiral. "Better strap in. Acceleration coming up."

Ben Ezra stared out the viewpoint at the stars.

My stars, he thought. *Our* stars. Mine and Peter Reed's. No
wonder my stomach isn't in this. Reed and I have been in space
longer than anyone else. In eight hundred years, we've met just
five times, and yet . . .

And yet, I feel closer to him than to all the politicians on Earth.
What do *they* know about the stars? All they're interested in is
preserving their petty little planet's rule over Man. They wouldn't
know what an Overdrive would mean. It would mean that Man
would have the Galaxy, it would mean that one wouldn't have to
be a pariah, a man without a planet or a time, to be a starman.

But is that what they think of? Huh! All they see is the end of
Earth's control. Of course, they're right. The only thing that makes
Earth undisputed master is *time*. Earth is always generations ahead
of the planets. Its head start in technology will hold up forever—

But not if there should be an Overdrive—not if Man could go
from Earth to the outer ring in months, not centuries.

He glanced at David Steen, strapped in beside him. Young but
intelligent. Some day—

"It's a dirty business, David," he said, almost involuntarily.

"Sir?"

"I said it's a dirty business. I never thought I'd be a hired murderer."

"But, sir, we have orders. It's a military mission. You have no reason to blame—"

"Orders! The orders of men who are all dead by now. The orders of an Earth that doesn't even give a damn about the possibility of Man *really* having the stars. Orders to destroy, orders of a willful, selfish . . . ah!"

"Admiral ben Ezra, our orders are simply to make sure Dr. Ching doesn't escape. Not necessarily to kill anyone. Besides, we're—"

"Yes," said ben Ezra bitterly, "yes, I know. We're soldiers." A new and narrow look came into his large gray eyes.

"But you have a point, David," he said. "Our orders are simply to bring back Ching, and eliminate all knowledge of his work. They don't say anything about blowing up traders, do they? I've not been ordered to kill Peter Reed."

"No, sir."

"No, indeed," said the admiral slowly.

"By all space," he roared, "we're going to carry out our orders! But we're going to do it without killing Captain Reed!"

"Well," said Manuel Olivera, "where do we go from here?"

"Out to the outer ring, I suppose," said Peter Reed. "We are in a very peculiar position. I'm *sure* that ben Ezra won't blast us without boarding. He's got to make sure he gets Ching. But wherever we go, he can plot our course, and be there first. Whatever we do, we've got to do it between now and the next planetfall."

He leaned his face in both hands, propped upon his elbows on the mahogany desk top.

Ching sat nervously in front of him, and Olivera paced the room.

"I still don't see *why* Earth wants to stop you, Dr. Ching," said Olivera.

"In a way, I do," replied Ching. "Positively speaking, the Overdrive would mean the inevitable end of Earth's domination. Without the time differential, Earth would be just another planet."

He managed a small grin. "But on the other hand," he said, "scientifically speaking, they're being most foolish. I am perhaps twenty years from an equation from which an Overdrive could be developed. All I have, right now, is a new point of view. For a thousand years, men have been searching for an Overdrive, always trying to escape from the Einsteinian Universe. Sometimes they look for a mythical thing called hyperspace, or subspace, or the fourth dimension. What I have done, is simply to begin an inquiry, *within* Relativity Theory, modifying not the equation, but the substitutions."

"What is all that about?" snapped Olivera.

"I'm not sure yet," said Ching abstractedly. "But basically, if you accept the Special Theory of Relativity, the reason that the speed of light cannot be exceeded is that mass is infinite at the speed of light, hence it would take an infinite force to accelerate it to that speed.

"*But,* if there were a drive whose thrust was a function of the mass it was accelerating, then, as mass increased, thrust would increase, and at the speed of light, theoretically, where mass was infinite, *thrust* would also be infinite. And if the thrust-mass equation involved a suitable exponential function—in theory, anyway —thrust could become *transfinite.*"

"Making it possible to go faster than light!" said Olivera excitedly. "Yes, yes, Dr. Ching. If there ever is an Overdrive, it will have to be developed along those lines! Tell me, how close are you?"

Ching laughed bitterly. "As I said, perhaps as much as twenty years away. Who can tell? Right now, all I have is a point of view, a direction in which to proceed. I must experiment with substitutions, then I must develop the proper thrust-mass equation. And at that point, the real work only begins. I must then develop a theoretical basis for a drive that can utilize the thrust-mass equation, a drive, where, not only does thrust depend on mass, but in the precise proper function as well. It's a very long way off."

"But man, it would be an Overdrive!"

"Not even then," said Ching. "That would be the end of *my* work, and the beginning of someone else's. I am not a practical scientist. Someone else would have to take my equations and develop the actual Overdrive."

He sighed and shrugged. "That's why I can't understand why Earth won't let me be. All I want is to be free to develop my equations. It's my whole life! I could build no drive, I—"

"When you rule an empire of more than sixty planets, over a

time differential of over two hundred years," said Captain Peter Reed, "you must plan and plot far ahead. You must take a very long view."

"Well, now that we know what we've got," said Olivera, "what are we going to do about it?"

Captain Reed drummed his fingers nervously on the desk top. "I'll be damned if I know," he said. "Fact: an Overdrive would be the greatest commercial coup in history. Fact: it would take about twenty years to develop one, from the start we have. And finally, fact: we will *have* to let ben Ezra aboard on our next planetfall. He'll be waiting for us, and there'll be no escaping. That's why he's let us get this far. This, gentlemen, is what is known as a bind."

"Time," said Ching absently, "why does it always come down to time? The Overdrive wouldn't even be necessary, if it weren't for the time factor. Then Earth would've let me continue my work unmolested. And now, it's a matter of time before ben Ezra gets me, too little time—"

"You're a mathematician," said Peter Reed. "You should know that time underlies the Universe, space . . . history—"

"Time," said Olivera. "Peter, we've just *got* to save the Overdrive! It's bigger than us; it's bigger even than the *Outward Bound.* It's bigger than Earth! We've just got to buy the time, *somehow.*"

"Twenty years," said Peter Reed. "In twenty *days,* we'll have to go into Deep Sleep, or we'll run the risk of depleting our oxygen, our food, our water. And when we come out, Jacob ben Ezra will be waiting for us."

A slow, grim smile parted Ching's tight lips. "Twenty years—" he said slowly. "Captain, where are we heading?"

"Out to the outer ring, maybe to Toehold."

"And how long will such a trip take?"

"About a hundred and twenty years."

"Captain," said Ching, "we don't *all* have to go into Deep Sleep, do we? There would be enough food and air for, say, one man to stay awake, for say, *twenty years?*"

Peter Reed suddenly became aware of the feverish glow of the abstract fanatic in Ching's eyes.

"You mean you would stay out of Deep Sleep? You would die in space, in the nothing between the stars? You would be alone, *utterly alone,* for twenty years."

"I am well aware of the consequences, captain. Nevertheless, it would enable me to complete my work. *That* is all that matters. Could it be done?"

Reed stared wonderingly at the small man. "Sure. There'd be plenty of food and air for one man to do it. By a factor of ten, at least."

"Well then, captain?"

"Are you sure, Dr. Ching? It's one thing to talk about it now, but when you've been alone for one, five, ten years—"

"I am willing to take that chance."

"Well . . . we could rig up a cubicle so that you could go into Deep Sleep any time it got to be too much for you—"

"Why, he might complete his work, and still make it to Toehold!" cried Olivera.

"He might," said Reed. "Of course, even then, we would still have the problem of dealing with ben Ezra—"

"Oh, space, Peter!" yelled Olivera. "One thing at a time. This is it! This is the *only* way!"

"I suppose you're right, Manny. Have your boys set up the necessary automatics. Let Dr. Ching get acquainted with our computer."

"Thank you, captain," said Ching. "We will beat them, after all."

"Perhaps," said Reed. Is your *we* the same as my *we,* he thought; is your *them* the same as my *them?*

Olivera had ceased his pacing. He appeared lost in thought.

"Manny," said the captain, reading his old friend's mood. "Manny, what is it?"

"Dr. Ching," said Olivera, "what will we have when your work is finished, I mean, what end result?"

"Why, I hope, an equation giving a principle upon which an Overdrive could be built," said Ching gravely.

"A *principle,*" said Olivera slowly, "an *equation.* But not *plans,* not *blueprints,* not even a schematic diagram."

"What do you expect of me?" said Ching plaintively. "I'm a mathematician, not an engineer. Such a thing would take a pragmatic scientist, working hand in hand with—"

"Yes," said Manuel Olivera, "so it would."

"*Manny!*" shouted the captain. "You wouldn't—"

"I must, Peter, I must! Someone must. We've got to have more than an equation, when we run into ben Ezra. If we've got pragmatic plans, we can send out all six of our gigs to Toehold. It's an undeveloped planet, they'd never be able to do anything with an equation. But plans— And ben Ezra would have to destroy seven targets, instead of one. Someone would get through."

"It would not be as bad for him, captain, as it will be for me," said Ching. "He could stay in Deep Sleep until I was ready for him. It would only be a few years for him."

"All right, Manny," said Reed, "you win."

But even as he gave the orders for setting up the automatics, something was nagging at the back of his mind.

Disperse the plans indeed! Sacrifice the *Outward Bound!* There must be a better way. Perhaps, ben Ezra could be fooled—just this once. What if he *got* Ching? Might it not be possible to convince him that Ching had never talked? Perhaps, perhaps—

Even as the nothingness of Deep Sleep overtook him, Peter Reed was still dreaming of the greatest commercial coup in history.

Jacob ben Ezra was dissatisfied, and he didn't know why. His ship was already orbiting Toehold, the *Outward Bound* had been spotted, a week away, all was set, and within eight days, he would have Ching.

But somehow, he felt dissatisfied.

"David," he said, "I feel *dirty*."

"But, sir, why?"

Ben Ezra lit a cigarette, the thirtieth of the twenty-four hour period. As far as he could remember, it was a record for him.

"We're men of space, David," he said. "We're no more emotionally bound to Earth than Reed is. *Homo Interstellarus,* I think of us as. An Overdrive is something we should welcome, not suppress."

The young commander was silent. To him, ben Ezra knew, orders were orders. He had been born aboard ship, the Fleet was all he knew or cared about. And the Fleet was an agent of Earth.

"Don't you see, David? Of course you don't! Our duty as officers is clear—to obey orders. But we have a duty as men, as well. And, by space, that duty is to preserve the Overdrive!"

"You would disobey direct orders, sir?"

"No, dammit! I've been in this service all my adult life. Orders must be obeyed. If the Fleet decided to take the law into its own hands, we'd be no better than pirates. No, David, orders must be obeyed. But that doesn't mean I have to like it. It won't help me sleep any better, or enable me to smoke less of these infernal cigarettes."

"No, sir."

"I almost hope . . . I almost hope—"

"What, sir?"

Ben Ezra grinned humorlessly. "I almost hope Peter Reed can figure out a good way to trick me. I'd almost like to see him get out of it."

Manuel Olivera held the sheaf of papers in front of him. "Seven years!" he said. "Seven awful, lonely years, the two of us working together. But here it is, here it is!"

Peter Reed looked in wonderment at Olivera. His hair was now flecked with gray. He had lost fifteen pounds. But the greatest change was in his eyes. There was a haunted fire, an emptiness. What those seven years must've been like, thought Reed.

"And now he's dead," said Olivera. "Dead of old age."

"But did he get into the cubicle?" asked Reed. It was essential to have Ching's body.

"Yes, he got in. But he was a broken old man. Even as I watched him go under, I knew he would never survive the thaw." Olivera sighed heavily. "It was hard for me, but what was it for him! Twelve years! Twelve years *alone!* It was a full twelve years before he thawed me out."

"But he did it," said Reed.

"Yes, he did it."

"And now we have ben Ezra to deal with. He's already orbiting Toehold. Six days—Manny?"

"What, Peter?"

"I don't suppose we could rig up an Overdrive? We have plans, blueprints—"

"Not a chance. There's a good three or four years' work, technical experimentation needed, and even if we had the time, we need things we couldn't possibly make ourselves."

Reed shrugged. "Just thought I'd ask. We're sitting on top of a mint—"

"A mint!" roared Olivera. "A mint! Is that all it means to you, a *commodity* to sell? Peter, I didn't think you were such a fool. Is that what Ching died for? To line our pockets?"

"Ching died for that mysterious thing called abstract knowledge, and you know it, Manny," said the captain. "He didn't care any more about giving the Overdrive to Man than he did about the profit!"

"Profit! You think you can make a profit out of this? Think, Peter, think. What will happen to the *Outward Bound* when Man has the Overdrive? We'll be finished. All tradeships will be finished. We owe our existence to the time lag, as much as Earth's rule does. I thought you realized that from the beginning. I thought you were willing to sacrifice it for Man. I . . . I was a bigger fool than you are!"

It hit Reed like a piledriver. Manny was right. The Overdrive meant the end of the tradeships. Selling the Overdrive would ultimately be the end of the *Outward Bound,* of the way of life he had followed for close to a thousand objective years.

Peter Reed knew that if the Overdrive became known, he would be the last captain of the *Outward Bound.*

"You're right, Manny," he said. "I suppose that solves our problem. We'll just give it all to ben Ezra."

"*Will we now,* captain?" sneered Olivera. "Even if you don't care what this means to Man, think of your own hide. What do you think ben Ezra will do if he knows *we* know?"

"Why, he'll—"

"Exactly. He'll kill every one of us. Or at least haul us back to Earth, where the best we can expect is to be imprisoned for the rest of our lives. *Without trial.*"

Reed cursed. It was true. The only thing to do, is to play it through. At least, if we can fool ben Ezra, I can make my own decision.

"Well, captain?"

"Destroy those plans. But first, microengrave them on some part of the ship, a wall, a toilet, anywhere. Don't even tell me where. I don't want anyone but you to know, till this is over. Then destroy our transmitters. Make it look like they've been out ever since Maxwell, but make it look like an accident."

"What about Ching? Should we destroy the body? Maybe we can convince ben Ezra that he was never aboard."

"Not a chance. I've got it! Rig his cubicle so that it looks like the machinery failed, and he died of old age, *inside* the cubicle. Can you do it?"

Olivera puckered his brows. "Won't be easy," he said, "but I think so."

"Well, that's all we can do until ben Ezra boards."

"You're going to try and convince ben Ezra that Ching never talked? You expect him to be so stupid as to swallow *that?*"

Peter Reed licked his lips.

"No," he said, "but I know Jacob ben Ezra. What I'm banking on, is that he'll try and convince himself."

"To what do I owe this pleasure, Jacob?" said Peter Reed, sitting behind the big mahogany desk.

"To what— Peter, you *know* I've followed you all the way from Maxwell," said Admiral Jacob ben Ezra.

"All the way from Maxwell!" exclaimed Peter Reed. "Why in blazes didn't you give me a call on the . . . oh, oh! I keep forgetting that the radio's out of commission. Then you *did* call me?"

Ben Ezra looked at his aide, and then at the ceiling. "Yes, I did call you. Is your radio *really* out of order?"

"Freak accident," said Reed. "Meteor hit the radio shack. Small one, but enough to smash things up. Say, you wouldn't have a spare F-46E transmitter housing?"

"I'll see what I can do," said ben Ezra coolly.

"Roger, get us some drinks, will you?"

Roger Reed produced four of the hot-cold cocktails.

"These are most amusing, Jacob," said Captain Reed.

"I left Earth about the same time you did, this time, Peter," said ben Ezra. He lit a cigarette.

"Still smoking those filthy things, eh?" said Peter Reed conversationally.

"*Captain* Reed," said ben Ezra, "aren't you even *interested* in why I've followed you for a hundred light-years?"

Reed laughed. "Something sinister, Jacob? I assumed that when you hailed us at Maxwell, and we didn't answer, you thought we were in trouble, and—"

"Really, Peter!" said ben Ezra. "*I'll* come to the point, even if you won't. Do you have a passenger?"

Peter Reed frowned. "So that's it," he said. "Look, Jacob, we're fully insured for this kind of thing. Million credit liability policy. It's a hefty premium, and the chances of it ever happening are so slight, but—"

"What in blazes are you talking about?"

"Why our passenger, of course," said Reed blandly. "Isn't that what *you're* talking about? I sure as hell don't know how you found out, but I assure you it was a legitimate accident, and we're fully covered."

"Covered? Accident?"

"Oh, come on, Jacob, stop playing cat and mouse with me!" snapped Reed. "All right, all right, if that's the way you want it, I'll tell you the whole thing as if you didn't know what happened."

"I certainly wish you would," said ben Ezra.

"Well, we *did* have a passenger. Picked him up on Maxwell. Strange little fellow called Ching pen Yee. That Director, what was his name?"

"Lazlo Horvath," said David Steen.

"Yes, yes, Horvath. The dirty crook. Told me some kind of fish story about how this Ching was some kind of important scientist. Well, ordinarily, you couldn't fool me with a thing like that, but as you know, we have the force field to sell this trip, and Horvath simply didn't have anything better to pay for it, so I took a chance on this Ching. What a joke!"

"Joke?"

"Yes," said Reed. "Scientist? Why the man was a raving lunatic! Classic case. Paranoid delusions. Thought the entire Terran hegemony was out to get him. Literally. Not only that, but delusions of grandeur as well. Why, he thought he was the greatest thing since Einstein! Secret of immortality, conversion bomb, all the usual mythical nonsense."

"A madman?" said ben Ezra, his eyes narrowing to slits.

"What a madman!" exclaimed the captain. "To top it all off . . . why do you know what, Jacob? He thought he had the secret of Overdrive as well!"

"*Really,*" said ben Ezra, perhaps a shade too dryly.

"I swear, I expected him to pull the Philosopher's Stone itself out of his pocket!" laughed Peter Reed.

"Indeed."

"Where is this Dr. Ching?" said David Steen.

Ben Ezra flashed him a dirty look.

"Ah, you know as well as I do, Jacob, don't you? A one in a

million accident, but it *did* happen. The automatics in his Deep Sleep cubicle malfunctioned. He died of old age on the last hop."

"Died?" said ben Ezra slowly.

"I assure you Jacob, there was no lapse in safety procedures, and we are fully covered."

"To be sure," said ben Ezra. "To be sure." His eyes were even more unreadable than usual.

"Do you by any chance have the body?" he said.

"Yes," replied Reed. "It's still in the cubicle."

"Good. Mr. Ching had relations on Galdwin, which . . . er . . . is our next stop. We will take the body to them. David, get a detail."

"But, sir—"

"David!"

"Yes, sir."

"A most unfortunate accident, Peter," said ben Ezra.

"Yes."

"But you say the man was mad anyway," said ben Ezra, bringing his face close to Reed's.

Reed stared back. "Very mad," he said evenly.

"You are *quite* sure?" said ben Ezra.

Reed drummed his fingers nervously on the desk. Ben Ezra's glance fell to Reed's hand, for a short moment. Reed's gaze followed. Then they were staring in each other's eyes again.

"Quite sure," said Peter Reed.

"I see," said Jacob ben Ezra. The corners of his mouth curled upward in the slightest suggestion of a grin.

Reed's mouth went dry.

"Well, Peter," said ben Ezra, suddenly and unexpectedly convivial, "it's been nice meeting you again. Very nice. But I really must be going."

"Sorry to see you leave so soon," said Reed.

"I'll bet you are!" said ben Ezra with a little laugh.

He walked to the door and opened it.

"Good-by, Peter," he said.

"Good-by, Jacob."

As he stepped through the doorway, the admiral swiveled his neck to face Reed.

"Perhaps," he said dryly, *"I'll be seeing you a lot sooner than you think I think."* Then he was gone.

"What in space did he mean by that, Dad . . . *sir?*" asked Roger Reed.

The captain stared at the empty doorway.

"I think I know," he said, "but I'm not sure I *want* to know."

Peter Reed floated by the viewport, watching ben Ezra's ship break orbit.

He's really going, Reed thought. But he did not feel like congratulating himself.

He *knew*. He *had* to know. Jacob would never have swallowed a cock-and-bull story like that unless he wanted to. Well, he's got Ching's body, and he'll take it back to Earth, and that'll be the end of it. The Overdrive is mine.

But what, he thought, am I going to do with it? The safe thing would be to destroy the plans . . . or—

It'd take time and money to build it. The *Outward Bound* could never do it alone, but there are planets out here on the outer ring who'd do the work, and not ask too many questions.

Or there's Maxwell. Horvath is dead, but there's never a dearth of his kind. The Overdrive would bring a fantastic price from someone like that. But what would he do with it? Rule the Galaxy?

The Galaxy . . . who can say anything about the Galaxy? Man has seen such a small piece of it. Naturally, the chance of running into another intelligent race has been nil, as long as we were confined to such a small volume of space. But now— What exists in the center?

Without realizing it, Peter Reed had made his decision.

Ching had died for the Overdrive, thought Reed. Manny's given seven years of his life for it, seven lonely years.

And Jacob—Jacob took the biggest chance of his career to give Man the Galaxy.

Captain Reed sighed resignedly. One doesn't go in for this kind of life unless one is something of a romantic, he thought, no matter what I may say about profits.

What have all the profits been for? Just to keep the *Outward Bound* in space. Why stay in space? What logical answer is there?

Reed remembered a quotation from a man thousands of years dead, so long his name had been forgotten.

"Why climb mountains?" they had asked the mountaineer.

"Because they are there," he had said.

Why go to the stars? *Because they are there*. It was enough.

Manny understood that. In a way, perhaps Ching understood it, too.

And Jacob had risked a thousand-year career so that Man could have the Galaxy. *Because it was there*.

And can I do less, thought Peter Reed. A few hundred light-years of space is no substitute for the Universe.

Roger may never be captain of the *Outward Bound*. The twilight of the tradeships has already begun—

Reed looked sadly out the 'port at ben Ezra's receding ship. Good-by, Jacob, he thought, good-by to a way of life a thousand years old.

But Man must have the Overdrive.

Jacob ben Ezra watched the green disk of Toehold slowly recede. Hidden on the other side of the planet now, was the *Outward Bound*.

By now, he thought, Peter will have decided to build an Overdrive.

He laughed softly to himself. We old foxes understand each other. We both have our excuses—Peter his profits, me my duty.

But when it comes down to it, we're both in space for the same reason, and neither of us can put it into words.

So Earth will be satisfied. They'll have the body of poor Ching. Little will they know, little will they know, until it's too late.

There are planets out here that will ask few questions. Peter has the force field to sell, and for that, he can get his Overdrive built. And after that—

After that, in the short run, who knows? Ben Ezra shifted his gaze to the vast, multi-colored cloud of stars that is the center of the Galaxy.

In the short run, who knows, he thought. Who cares? But in the long run—

In the long run, Man will have the Galaxy, perhaps not to himself, *certainly* not to himself, but have it he will.

The admiral put out his half-finished cigarette. I've been in this business so long, that I'm a legend, he thought. How ironic that the thing I can be most proud of is something that, once the Overdrive is a reality, will be called a failure.

He looked at the cloud of stars. They seemed to be looking right back. Come on, they seemed to say, we've been waiting.

A failure— Maybe you could call it that—

He grinned at the far glow of the Center.

"Coming!" he said.

A Child of Mind

Doug Kelton awoke in the middle of the night with the leaf-branches creaking in the forest like the rigging of a great sailing ship; with the sweet modulated whistles of the piperlizards saluting the twin moons; with a landcroc cooing somewhere deeper within the forest.

He stretched the muscles of his naked body minutely, one by one, careful not to awaken the sleeping woman whose limbs were intertwined with his in the hammock. It was a time for aloneness.

He felt perfect breasts press and relax, press and relax against his chest with the slow rhythm of her untroubled breathing. He brushed long silky strands of her hair from his face and inhaled the fragrance of her.

It was a light and perfumy smell, too perfect, too clean, too . . . antiseptic. A woman should not smell like that, a woman did not really smell like that, not after a night of lovemaking, not under less alien skies. . . .

He wondered how Blair's woman smelled, and Dexter's. He smirked wryly to himself. If he was any judge of men, Blair's woman would reek of fear and sweat mixed with crude perfume.

Dexter's woman would not smell at all.

Kelton found those dark, confused thoughts creeping up on him again, as he had every night for the past week or so. But there was something different about this night—he felt a decision forcing its way to the surface of his troubled mind. It was a decision he had tried so hard to avoid. . . .

Don't be a fool! he told himself. You've got everything here a man could ever want. A garden of a planet, warm, lush, full of food, without any really dangerous lifeforms. . . .

Nevertheless, he found his mind forming the cold steel image of the ship.

Idiot! The woman of your dreams, the perfect mate, the ideal lover . . .

Dexter and Blair are happy! *They* don't have any trouble sleeping, they've got exactly what they want. They . . .

He imagined them with their women in the nearby huts, and his face soured. What had happened to Blair and Dexter was part of why he couldn't sleep.

Blair beat his woman at night. She, of course, loved it. She could not help loving it, just as she could not help enjoying being his slave during the day; serving him breakfast in his hammock in the morning; washing him; dressing him, shaving him and combing his hair; washing his feet at night and drying them using her own blond hair as a towel. Then the daily beating, and to bed. Kelton did not want to think of what Blair did to his woman then.

But he knew that she loved it, as she loved Blair. She loved every minute of it, every blow, every stupid petty indignity. She could not help loving it.

Blair, he could at least dimly understand. To him a woman was merely an animal, something to inflict his will upon to the greatest extent possible—not an uncommon attitude. The lower he made his woman, the higher he made himself. Blair was no monster. On Earth, under normal conditions, with a real woman, he would be held in reasonable check by the force of her personality. But here . . .

Dexter was something else again.

Dexter was regressing, and it was horrible to watch. Dexter's woman woke him in the morning, gently but firmly, pushed him lovingly out of bed, made sure he washed, shaved and brushed his teeth, fed him a nutritious, well-balanced breakfast, a sensible light lunch and an over-indulgent supper. She made sure he got to bed at a reasonable hour and kept him from using the ship's alcohol and tobacco supply.

The thought of the two of them in bed made Kelton bilious. In a very real sense, Dexter was sleeping with the image of his mother. Kelton found it nauseating. He continually had the urge to kick Dexter's woman's teeth down her mealy-mouthed throat.

But, of course, Dexter loved every minute of it.

Kelton felt the woman stir sinuously in her sleep against him. It sent a tremor of pleasure shivering down his spine. Even in her sleep, she knew and played upon every nerve in his body. Making love with her was like playing two-part harmony with a virtuoso; like eating a custom-ordered meal from the finest robot-chef in the Galaxy. She really did know him better than he knew himself. And she loved him quite literally with every fibre of her being.

It would be madness to leave her.

He stroked the small of her back moodily, and she quivered delightfully in her sleep.

It was greater madness to stay.

Even though the planet appeared to be a garden of a world, a real jackpot planet, they had played it by the book. Kelton landed the ship in a large clearing in a forest well south of the equator on the largest continent. Before leaving the ship, they enclosed it in a force-fence, and Blair did a complete atmospheric analysis, while Kelton checked the air for micro-organisms. The ship's robot was sent to scout the area for possible dangerous animals.

There was a saying among Survey men: "Planets are like women. It's not the ugly ones that are dangerous." Lathrop III had been a beautiful planet, and what had eventually happened there was one of the reasons that all Survey ships were now equipped with twenty "Planet Killers"—missiles with hundred-megaton cobalt and sodium jacketed warheads, the "dirtiest" bombs that man made.

But the air checked out perfect, the all-purpose antibiotics and viricides were more than a match for the local micro-organisms, the robot ran into no trouble, and so, on the second day, they went outside.

There were several good reasons why a preliminary Survey team was always made up of three men. First of all, there were three basic specialties needed to make a preliminary evaluation of a planet: geology, ecology and xenology.

But more important, three was a stable number. There would always be a clear majority on any decision. No cliques could form, since the largest possible clique was two, and two was already a majority.

This planet showed no signs of intelligent life, so Blair, the team xenologist, could take it easy. Kelton, the ecologist, and

Dexter, the geologist, would make the reports that would determine whether this planet was worth a full-scale evaluation for colonization.

Kelton's first reaction to the planet was a happy sigh. The atmosphere had a slightly higher oxygen content than Earth's—just enough to make you feel great, without really making you giddy. It smelled clean and fragrant, the smell of growing things uncontaminated by smog, stale hydrocarbons, or any of the other inevitable atmospheric by-products of an industrial civilization.

Kelton felt like a kid in the country.

"Jackpot planet," said Larry Blair. "Ten thousand credit bonus."

"Don't you ever think of anything but money?" snapped Curt Dexter.

Blair leered at him. "There's only one other thing that's *worth* thinking about," he said, "and when you're cooped up in a Survey ship for six months, it isn't very healthy to dwell on *that.*"

Dexter's answer was a scowl. Under ordinary circumstances, Blair and Dexter would probably get along pretty well. But when three men are isolated together for months on end, little things become big things, and friction is inevitable.

But all things considered, Kelton thought, it was a well-balanced team, and a planet like this was just the thing to loosen things up.

Kelton laughed. "Don't count your credits before they're catched, Larry. Just because there are no natives to throw the bull at doesn't mean that this planet's already been evaluated. *Some* of us have to work for a living."

That seemed to break the tension. Even Dexter was smiling.

"Okay, peasants," Blair said. "Curt, you dig for gold, and Doug can dig the animals. *I'll* supervise."

The preliminary work went quite smoothly. Dexter took sample borings of the soil and substrata. Kelton collected specimens and took pictures. Blair helped out some.

The geological report was favorable. The planet's crust contained all the necessary metals for a potential colony's industrial base. Since the planet was rather young, there would be a shortage of fossil fuels, but radioactives were plentiful and coal and oil were far from necessities.

An ecological report, though, must be more detailed. It had been easy enough to determine that the biochemistry of the planet was close enough to Earth's so that the colonists would not have to import a Terran ecology. The local forms of life were quite edible.

But an ecologist must look for more subtle things. Survey records were full of reports on planets with Terrestrial biochemistry that were nevertheless marked off limits. Predators might be too efficient and too big, the local ecologies might be in such delicate balance that a colony would trigger planetwide catastrophe. On some planets, there were key organisms that, while deadly to humans, were also absolutely essential to the planet's food chains and could not be eliminated without destroying the planet's bioforms.

There didn't seem to be anything like that here, but . . .

Kelton checked the slides in the two microscopes again. *It could not be.* Yet there it was.

Two identical cell sections from two seemingly identical female piperlizards, the little insect-eaters which whistled so sweetly at night.

The two lizards were identical, organ for organ.

Yet the cells were different.

The differences were subtle, but under a good microscope, they were obvious. Two females of the same species, outwardly identical. But made up of two different kinds of protoplasm.

Just like the insects.

Just like the landcrocs.

Just like every other organism on the planet that he had studied which was sexually differentiated.

Kelton scratched his head. Functionally speaking, the higher forms had the usual two sexes. But on a cellular level, there was . . . a third sex?

That wasn't the answer either. The males and . . . call it "female A", had identical cellular structure. But "female B" was different. The same species, but different protoplasm.

He grunted unhappily. He knew that it would be impossible to make a positive report until he figured it out. It was far too large an unknown factor. More work was needed. Much more work. He'd have to do a statistical study. What percentage of the females were "type A" and what percentage "type B"?

More important, what did it mean?

There did seem to be a pattern. . . . The cells of the males and "female As" differed among the various species; that was to be expected.

But the "female Bs" of all species had the same cell structure and the same protoplasm.

It was as if they were different phases in the life cycle of the same organism. . . .

An organism that passed through reptile, insect and mammal stages? An organism that at various stages mimicked every other organism on the planet?

It was beginning to rain. The fat drops of water pinged flatly on the great leafbranches that formed the roof and walls of the hut. It was a soft, gentle rain, peaceful, like most everything else on this planet.

Kelton sighed. It would be so easy to spend the rest of my life here, he thought. He felt the reassuring warmth of the woman in his arms. When you come right down to it, what chance would I ever have of finding another woman like her?

A *real* woman like her.

He tried to make himself loathe her. She was an alien lifeform. She wasn't even human. But it would take a good microscope to prove that.

He tried to picture the beginnings of her life: a formless puddle of protoplasm beneath a dead leafbranch on the forest floor. . . .

But it didn't work. When you came right down to it, all women, all men, were born, in the last analysis, of amorphous slime. Did it really matter that others took form in wombs while the woman in his arms had sprung full-grown from a gigantic . . . call it a cocoon . . . ?

With her all-too-human arms around him, with her better-than-human odor enveloping him, it was hard for the biology of the situation to have any real meaning for Kelton.

He remembered finding that first teleplasm nest, under a dead leafbranch. His first reaction, despite his training as a biologist, had been disgust.

There were two stages of the stuff, there on the forest floor: a gray-green puddle of translucent, gelatine-like protoplasm about four feet in diameter; and around its periphery and speckling its surface, cysts, cocoons of various sizes, ranging from pea-size to the size of a large watermelon. It was obvious that the cocoons were made up of the same stuff as the glob.

Kelton radioed for the ship's robot, and twenty minutes later, the mechanism arrived—a caterpillar tank with ten boom-like arms, ending in assorted torches, cutters, scoops, borers and handlers. Kelton ordered the robot to transfer the thing on the ground intact to its specimen cage.

The robot cut a circle in the sod around the glob, about a foot and a half deep, with its cutter-arm. It then inserted a narrow torch-nozzle into the bottom of the groove, swiveled it so that it faced the center of the glob-bearing disc of sod, and under-cut the disc with it. It slipped four handlers under the disc, and lifted it gently through the opening on its back, with the glob still on the sod disc, like a suckling pig on a platter.

Kelton rode the robot back to the ship.

"What in hell is that?" grunted Larry Blair, wrinkling his nose at the glob installed in the specimen cage. "It looks like a dish of jello with an acute case of hives."

"I'm not sure yet," said Kelton. "But it may be the fly in this planet's ointment."

"Huh?"

"Remember when I told you about there being two kinds of females on this planet, type A and type B?"

"Yeah. So . . . ?"

"Well, I did a cell section on one of those cocoons. It turned out to be female B protoplasm."

"So what? So it's a *female B* dish of jello with hives."

"Guess what was inside the cocoon, Larry?"

"How should I know?" said Blair impatiently. "A Kewpie-doll?"

"A female B piperlizard."

Blair goggled. "Huh? You mean that thing hatches out the piperlizards?"

Kelton gestured uneasily at the cocoon covered glob. "Not just piperlizards, Larry," he said. "Insects. Watersnakes. Leafbirds. Landcrocs. Dozens of different species in those cocoons. Every one of them female B."

"I don't get it."

Kelton grimaced. "Don't feel too bad, Larry. *I'm* the ecologist, and I don't know if I get it either. All I have is a half-baked theory. Let's suppose that life started out on this planet as on all other planets—thousands of different species. Then, somehow, something new mutates under this particular sun. A different kind of organism, formless, amorphous like an amoeba, but not microscopic, it's *big*. It has to carve out an ecological niche for itself. It's not a predator. It isn't really a parasite. It isn't a symbiote. First, maybe it starts out mimicking things. Simple organisms. Then there's a new mutation, and the thing becomes . . . not sentient, but *aware*, crudely telepathic, but on a *cellular* level. Call the stuff *teleplasm* now. An entirely different form of life, a new kind of protoplasm."

"You're starting to make me a little sick," said Blair. And he didn't seem to be kidding.

"I don't blame you. This stuff is more than an alien lifeform. It's a whole different concept of life itself. The teleplasm becomes *aware* of other organisms, on a cellular level, on an organic level. Like all organisms, it must compete for food and living space. But in a weird new way. It's amorphous, without a form of its own. It takes the form of organisms around it. Piperlizards. Landcrocs. *Anything*. It has the ability to imitate any lifeform, organ for organ. Now remember, the teleplasm is competing for food. How can it make an easy living?"

"How should I know? I'm no dish of jello."

"Who pays for a wife's meals?"

"Her husband, of— *Oh my God!*"

"Yeah, Larry. That's it. Type B females are teleplasm. They begin life as a glob of goo. Then a male organism blunders by, and the teleplasm somehow 'reads' its image of an ideal mate and imprints the pattern on a part of itself. It forms a cocoon. When the cocoon opens, there's a female insect or landcroc or piperlizard. A type B female. And there's another wrinkle. The type B females are *better* than the natural type As. Before I found the teleplasm, I did a statistical study of the females in this area. *Seventy percent are type B*. The teleplasm is pushing the natural females out."

"Why?"

"Because the teleplasm forms females from the ideal images it gets from the males."

"You mean it sort of custombuilds females to order for the males?"

"That's more or less it. And seven out of ten males seem to prefer 'Brand B'."

"Wow! Hey, too bad it won't work for us!" laughed Blair. "All we'd have to do is concentrate on dreaming up the sexiest dames in the Galaxy, and presto! Out they hatch!"

For the next few days, Blair got plenty of laughs out of that, especially when he tried to needle the dour Dexter into revealing what kind of woman *he'd* be likely to order up from the teleplasm.

But two weeks later, when all the cocoons had hatched out, and the remainder of the teleplasm began to grow and grow, and finally formed three great human-sized cocoons, it stopped being funny.

The brief shower was over, and a cooling breeze set the huge leafbranches of the sailtrees to creaking and groaning. Ordinarily, it was a sound to lull a man back to sleep. . . .

But Kelton knew that he would not sleep again that night. He somehow sensed that this was the night when all his vague uneasiness, all his sense of *wrongness* would coalesce into a decision. The time of temporizing was over.

And deep within him, he already knew what that decision must be, though he refused to admit it to himself, as yet.

Just as the three of them had *known* what waited in those cocoons to be born, long before they hatched. . . .

And when the day finally came, when the cocoon casings began to crack and warp and shrivel, the three of them waited numbly together by the specimen cage, afraid even to think. . . .

Life stirred within the cocoons, stirred and tore at the shriveled envelopes and struggled to be born.

"Should . . . shouldn't we cut them out?" whispered Dexter.

"No," hissed Kelton, with a ferocity that surprised even himself. "I mean . . . I don't think it would be *right*."

"Doug, do you really think that there are . . . *women* in there?" asked Blair.

"Depends on your definition, Larry. But there's nothing in this area whose mates would be as big as those cocoons except *us*."

"But will they be intelligent?" said Dexter.

"Are *any* dames intelligent?" cracked Blair nervously.

"I don't know, Curt," said Kelton, ignoring Blair. "If the teleplasm is really telepathic, then our subconscious image of a woman should be completely reproduced, down to . . ."

The cocoons were parting. The creatures within them threw them aside and stood up.

The men gasped in unison.

One was a bosomy blond, with wide sensual hips and a submissive leer.

Another was dark, fully-built, with an older, calmer, more maternal face on her young-but-somehow-sedate body.

Kelton knew that the third one was his.

She was tall and swarthy, her body an ounce plumper than willowy. Wild black hair cascaded down her shoulders halfway to the small of her back. Her eyes were deep, deep green, large and elfin. They laughed by themselves, and promised things without names.

Her mouth was small, but the lips were full, pursed into a frame for tiny, white feral teeth that she licked sinuously with a small pink tongue.

Kelton felt something turn to liquid fire within him, and his knees began to quiver.

"Larry!" squealed the blond, and threw herself at Blair.

"Curt, little one," sighed the matronly beauty, and enveloped Dexter in a massive hug.

But Kelton barely noticed that his teammates were leaving with their women.

His woman was speaking to him in a voice that was black velvet.

"Hello, Douglas," she whispered. "You've been waiting all your life for me. And I for you."

She rumpled his hair with one perfect hand, and he knew that it was true.

Liquidly, she was in his arms, and he in hers, and her fingers danced a slow tattoo in the pit of his back, and her tongue caressed his knowingly, and her body sidled warm against him, and thought stopped.

They were lying in the grass at the edge of the forest. Kelton had only the most confused memories of the past few hours. They could not have spoken more than a dozen words to each other, but he knew that he was completely, totally, hopelessly in love with this strange, knowing creature.

She seemed to know every inch of his body as though it were

her own; every sensitive area, every little personal idiosyncrasy, the kind of things it should take a woman months to discover about a man: how he loved to have a woman's fingers dancing in the pit of his back, the particular rhythm of his lovemaking, the fact that he liked a woman to keep her eyes open when he kissed her. . . .

Everything.

He cradled her in his arms and inhaled her incredibly sweet perfume. A part of him knew that he was holding something not human, that this fey creature had been born in a cocoon in the specimen cage, that what he should be feeling was revulsion, self-disgust. . . .

But he could not feel it. His body would not accept the reality that this was not a woman, not the most perfect woman that he had ever known. . . .

"Child of my mind. . . ." he mumbled.

"What, Douglas?"

"I said 'child of my mind'. That's you, isn't it?"

She laughed musically. "What a pretty idea," she sighed. "A lovely way of thinking of it. Only I don't feel like a child." She giggled.

He propped himself up on one elbow and stared into her laughing face. "What *do* you feel like?" he said.

"What do you mean, Douglas?"

"I mean, do you understand what . . . er . . . how you came to be. . . ."

She laughed, and kissed him gently on the lips and then on the nose.

"Poor Douglas," she said. "You don't have to worry about hurting me. I know I was not born like other women."

"Then . . . how were you born?"

"Well first, for many years, I was an idea in your mind, a hope, a dream, waiting to be born. I was what you wanted, I was a part of you. And then . . . a *something* happened, and I was made flesh. A dream became a real woman."

"Do you know how . . . ?"

"Douglas! Douglas! I told you not to be afraid of hurting me! I know how I was born. From what you call 'teleplasm'. But I don't *feel* like teleplasm. I feel like a woman. A woman in love. I'm a woman down to the smallest detail. . . ." She giggled. "As you well know, darling. How am I different from other women? Under a microscope, perhaps? Do you plan to make love to me under a microscope?"

He laughed to break the mood. "Well, it *would* be *different*," he said.

"That's my Douglas! That's the man I know and love."

"You really do know me, don't you? Even though you're only a few hours old."

"But Douglas, in another way, I'm as old as you are, and I've known you all your life. I'm what you've always wanted in a woman, and part of what you want is a woman that knows and loves you completely. And now you have it. Now and always."

"I believe you," he said. "I really do. I don't quite understand, but I *believe*. It doesn't matter to you how you were born, does it?"

"No, Douglas. It doesn't matter what I *was*. What counts is what I am. A woman. Your woman, completely and forever."

He took her in his arms, and he kissed her, and once again, he was lost in that sweet madness, and thought stopped.

Soon it would be dawn, and in the light of this alien sun, he would have to act. Of the three men, he knew that he was the only one still capable of making a rational decision.

Theoretically, there was no captain on a Survey ship. It would be ridiculous to name one man official leader over a crew of two. But Survey teams were not put together randomly. Kelton was the most introspective of the three, the man with the most highly developed sense of responsibility, the dominant personality, and he knew it. He could be overruled by the other two, since his position of leadership was purely unofficial. But he had been the leader, and Blair and Dexter tacitly acknowledged it.

But now, Kelton knew, they were no longer a team, but three isolated individuals. The things that had held them together—a job to do, a planet to return to—no longer had meaning.

Of the things that had made three men into a Survey team, only one was left—*the ship*. And it took only one man to run the ship, and all three members of a Survey team were always trained pilots.

But Blair and Dexter would no longer even go near the ship. Indeed, since that day when the women had emerged from the cocoons, they would hardly have anything to do with each other, or with Kelton. Why should they? Dealing with other independent personalities means conflict; it means that you will not always have your way. It means accommodation, compromise.

They've become like children, Kelton thought bitterly. Spoiled brats. They lay around their huts all day, and they have everything they want without lifting a finger, without even an argument. Blair's woman is his slave, and Dexter's is an indulgent mother. Why go back to a life that was less than perfect, to women that made demands, who had minds and drives of their own? They were both contented, and they both planned to spend the rest of their lives here, on this garden of a planet, with their women.

Their perfect women.

It was a great mental effort, but Kelton had finally understood that Blair and Dexter's women *were* perfect, to them, even though they seemed to him like grotesque caricatures of what women should be. But then, the caricatures had been in their minds from the beginning: to Blair, a woman was something less than human, a slave who should be willing to cater to every whim of her lord and master; to Dexter, a woman was something more than human, the source of all satisfaction, all security, the fulfiller of all wants.

There could be no jealousy here. These women were formed to suit every taste and whim of their mates, however childish, however neurotic.

Swapping them would be like swapping toothbrushes.

Kelton knew that, if he wanted it, the ship was his. He could lift-off and leave them, and they wouldn't give a damn. They had no intention of going back to Earth anyway, and they could do nicely without him.

But why do I want to leave? I have the perfect woman too, don't I? To Blair, Woman is Slave. To Dexter, Woman is Mother. What is Woman to me, that I'm not satisfied? It can't be that we can't . . . That was never important to me, personally.

And I only asked the question casually, in the first place. . . .

They had been walking in the cool forest, the great leafbranches swaying ponderously in the breeze, the sun filtering between them, dappling the forest floor with light, when he had asked her.

"No, Douglas," she answered softly. "We can't have children." She frowned. "Does it really matter that much to you?"

"No," he said quite truthfully. "I was really just curious. Scientific curiosity. After all, I am a biologist. How does the . . . er . . . how do you . . . ?"

She laughed warmly. "Douglas, must I always keep telling you that speaking about it doesn't hurt me? I know what I am, and I'm not ashamed. Why should I be?"

"I'm sorry."

"There's nothing to be sorry about. I just want you to feel about it the way I do, for your own sake. To answer your question, I *don't* reproduce. Not in the way you think of it. When you are gone . . . er . . . I mean . . ."

"Now who's afraid to face the truth?" he said gently. "I've no illusion about being immortal. *When I die,* then what?"

She flushed. "When you . . . are no longer with me, I die, in a sense. In a way, it's a beautiful thought. I was born to love you, and when I no longer have you, I will no longer exist in the form that your love gave me. I'll dissolve back into teleplasm, with no memories and no regrets, until someone else, or something else, comes along, and . . ."

Somehow, it hurt him. The idea, not so much that she would outlive him, but that her protoplasm would become so many piperlizards, insects, or whatever else happened along after he was gone. For there would be no other men to form her protoplasm into a woman. He and Dexter and Blair were the only men who would ever see this planet. . . .

Or were they?

Kelton knew Survey doctrine. When a ship did not come back, it was searched for, and the search was not given up until it was found. It might take a year, or a decade, or a century, but Survey would find this planet. It was not a matter of altruism, or protecting its own; if a ship did not come back, it meant that *something* had kept it from returning, and Earth had to know what that something was, before it took more ships, or worse. That something might be a hostile intelligent race, or a deadly lifeform, and Man might be in deadly danger without knowing it, if Survey did not track down all lost ships.

What if they hadn't found out about Lathrop III in time?

Kelton knew that it was a certainty—other men would walk this surface of this planet, sooner or later. It was inevitable.

And for some unfathomable reason, the thought filled him with a nameless dread.

The first red rays of dawn filtered through the leafy walls of the hut. Kelton knew that they would be flashing off the silvery hull of the ship. . . .

Paradise . . . the planet was literally paradise for a man. . . . He kissed his woman gently on the neck. Funny, he thought, none of us have given them names. Why?

He was beginning to understand. . . . The creature sleeping in his arms was not a woman, she was Woman as seen through the eyes of Man, she was *his* personal wish-fulfillment. Her whole life, quite literally, was *him*. She had no independent existence of her own. The proof of it was that when he was gone, she would cease to exist. . . .

And suddenly he understood why Dexter and Blair were completely content, and he was not. To Dexter, Woman was Mother. To Blair, Woman was Slave. Neither concept required that a woman have an independent existence.

But Kelton realized that to him, Woman had always been Mystery.

And a creature of his own mind could hold no mystery for him, only the unsatisfying illusion of it.

Though he loved her, though she loved him, though she was literally perfect, he knew that it could never be enough.

For another word for perfection was death.

Now he fully understood what he had only sensed before. He knew *why* the thought of other men walking this planet filled him with dread. *Seventy percent of the females on this planet were teleplasm.* . . .

The teleplasm was pushing out the real females, the females that produced children. . . .

Now he knew that it was not for himself that he had been afraid, but for the human race.

What would happen when men learned of this planet? What would happen when they took teleplasm back to Earth, as they inevitably would?

What would happen to the *real* women; the women who were more than a reflection of men's desire; the women who had minds and dreams and desires of their own?

Who would father the children of the human race?

How long would there *be* a human race?

He understood, and he knew what he had to do, but there was no comfort in it for him. It was a knife in his heart. For the creature sleeping in his arms knew only that she *felt* like a woman, that she loved him with every fibre of her being.

God help me! he thought forlornly, I love her too. . . .

But he knew what he had to do. Extinction for the human race was too high a price to pay for love. A price that would have to be paid by generations yet unborn, generations that would *never* be born unless. . . .

A part of him had known from the beginning, that the price of paradise was always too high, that if men had the choice, they would choose perfection over reality, even if it meant death in the long run.

And that choice must not be permitted to exist.

Carefully, inchwise, so as not to wake her, so that there need be no good-bys, he disengaged himself from her arms and got up. He dressed himself quickly, and, not daring to look back, he went to the ship.

Kelton put the ship into a ninety-minute polar orbit so that it would eventually pass over the entire planet.

For long minutes, he sat stonily in the pilot's chair, staring at the soft green planet below him.

You can still change your mind, he kept thinking, you can still go back. . . .

And be the *other* kind of murderer. The murderer of the human race.

There was no way out. The teleplasm meant extinction for Mankind. Man and teleplasm could not share the same Galaxy. Other men had faced this decision before, with other lifeforms.

Survey had a nice neutral term for it: "Planetary Sterilization."

It had been done to Tau Ceti II. It had been done to Algol V. It had been done to Lathrop III. Every Survey ship was equipped to do a "Planetary Sterilization."

All he had to do was press the button. The ship's computer would fire the missiles at the proper times. The whole planet would be covered in a nice geometric pattern. Twenty cobalt-sodium warheads were more than enough for a planet of this size.

Forgive me, Blair! Forgive me, Dexter! Forgive me, child of my mind!

He knew that he would never be able to forgive himself.

He pushed the button.

The Equalizer

The Israeli experimental station was small and inconspicuous. It had been carefully planned that way. Five one-story cement-block buildings arranged as the sides of a pentagon, enclosed by a frail, unelectrified fence. True, there were a few soldiers guarding the fence, but this far into the Negev it would have been unusual for them to be absent, even if this were the agricultural station it pretended to be.

A small, innocuous cluster of buildings in the middle of nowhere, surrounded by a sea of rock and sand. A few soldiers, a few scientists, a series of labs—

The Israeli equivalent of the Manhattan Project.

Dr. Sigmund Larus' hands were shaking. But his eyes did not bother to register the tremor; they were fixed on the metal box which sat on the laboratory table.

It was about the size of a small overnight bag, and it weighed considerably less than a hundred pounds.

And this, he thought, is only the prototype—crude, jury-rigged, five times the size that a perfected and miniaturized model would be.

How big was the first atomic bomb, he mused. Measured in the thousands of pounds. Now they had little ones a man could carry.

Larus chewed on his lower lip. What have I done, he thought.

How did it all come to *this?* It began so innocently, with the discovery of enigmatic, quasi-stellar objects far beyond the bounds of the galaxy. What could've been further removed from military consideration?

But these mysterious objects had been found to be giving off literally incredible amounts of energy, more than could possibly be accounted for by any known reaction, including even matter-anti-matter reactions.

It had been such an innocently fascinating problem. One thing led to another. What were these quasi-stellar objects, and perhaps even more important, how were they giving off so much energy?

It had been the most exciting work of his career. His calculations all pointed to only one possible answer, only one reaction could possibly produce energy in such quantities—*the total annihilation of matter.*

The inevitable next question was *how.* What could bring about the total annihilation of matter, the total conversion of matter to energy?

What a question that had been. Larus winced even now as he thought of the torturous months of calculations that had led to his first tentative answer to that question. That first paper had done nothing more than gingerly sketch the requirements for a theoretical field that would cause any matter enclosed in it to be instantly converted entirely to energy. He had never dreamed that such a field could actually be produced electronically, not then—

But *other* people had.

Three papers! Larus thought. Three obscure and largely speculative papers in an astrophysics journal. At the time, I would've been amazed if fifty physicists in the whole world could've understood what I was talking about.

Larus stared at the metal box on the table. The military, he thought grimly, have a way of picking out the essentials in any scientific area. At least what *they* consider the essentials.

One little sentence in one of the papers had brought the Israeli military down on him like a horde of hungry relatives. ". . . Therefore, these equations would indicate that it is theoretically possible to generate enormous quantities of energy at modest cost, since the output would come from the destruction of matter itself, while the input needed to generate such a field would be comparatively insignificant . . ."

Such a vague and general sentence, thought Larus. But in certain minds, it had meant four simple, explicit words:

A Big Cheap Bomb.

Oh, they had been so sly and clever about it. So, Dr. Larus, how would you like a government grant to continue your interesting work on these . . . ah, quasi-stellar objects? And don't you feel that it would help you to understand the physics of these objects if you could produce the field that causes matter to annihilate itself? Well, it's a pleasure to tell you that your government will be proud to contribute to the advancement of . . . er . . . astrophysics. In fact, we'll build you a nice little lab in the middle of the Negev where it's nice and peaceful.

It had all seemed so innocent at the time, a chance to work in peace on a fascinating problem. And the results, after three years of work, were—*this*.

Dr. Larus stared woodenly at the metal box. Stop fooling yourself! he thought. You know what they will call it, you've known for a long time. There's only one name for that little monstrosity. Go ahead, say it out loud.

"The Conversion Bomb," he muttered softly, "the Conversion Bomb."

Within that little box was an explosive force equivalent to a hydrogen bomb.

$E=mc^2$, he thought, Einstein's equation. Poor Einstein, a saintly man who wanted only peace. And now I have made that equation come true, completely true.

The theory is so complex, he thought, but the device is so simple. Once you know how, once you have the blueprints, it's so cheap and simple to make. A pound or so of . . . *anything at all* in the field chamber. Throw the switch, and the field is turned on. Whatever is in the chamber is transformed entirely into energy . . . and hundreds of square miles are destroyed.

So simple . . . Larus had no illusions about how long the secret could be kept, perhaps no one but himself really understood the theory behind the thing, but a . . . a television repairman could build a Bomb from the plans.

And how long had the secret of the atom bomb been kept?

"Dr. Larus," boomed the powerful voice of Colonel Ariah Sharet, and he stalked into the room. "It is done?"

Without waiting for an answer, he bounded to Larus' side. He was a tall, powerful man of thirty-seven, dressed in khaki shirt and shorts. His hair was black and straight, and his coarse skin was deeply tanned. He wore a .45 at his hip.

"It is done," murmured Larus, his frail, old body appearing even smaller than usual beside the robust Sharet.

"It's so *small,*" said Sharet.

"It can be made smaller," sighed Larus. "Much smaller."

"We are saved," exulted Sharet. "Do you realize what you've done, Dr. Larus? You've saved Israel. We know that the Egyptians have missiles, and we can be sure that within the next few years they will have an atomic bomb. Forty million Arabs armed with nuclear missiles against two million of us . . . What chance would we have? We would be slaughtered, driven into the sea. Sooner or later, it would have had to come. But now . . ."

"Now we can drive *them* into the sea?" said Larus. "Now *we* can do the slaughtering?"

"You don't understand the implications of the Conversion Bomb. How much would such a bomb cost to make? If we went into volume production?"

"How much? Two, three thousand pounds at the very most. It's all so simple and cheap, once you know how. Cut-rate annihilation."

"Well, don't you see? We can make *hundreds* of bombs. And they can be made so small, they can literally be delivered by parcel post. As of today, Israel is a world power."

"A world power," sneered Larus. "Two million people, a country so small that a jet can scarcely make a 180° turn without leaving it. A world power indeed. My dear colonel, there are seven hundred million Chinese in the world, over two hundred million Russians, an equal number of Americans, not to mention forty million or so Arabs. This is power."

Colonel Sharet smiled. "As the Americans would say, the Conversion Bomb is 'The Great Equalizer.' What does population, resources, land mean? For a few million pounds, we can have a destructive capacity equal to that of America or Russia, let alone the Arabs. The base of power is now *technology*. One scientific advance like the Conversion Bomb negates any disparity in population or land. Israel *is* now a world power. It is not a dream, it is a cold fact."

"Ah, Colonel, forgive me," sighed Larus, "but you talk like a colonel. So little Israel has developed a Conversion Bomb. So now we are a world power. Shall I recite for you a list of countries that will be able to do what we have done? Sweden, Belgium, Italy,

Brazil, Nigeria, Japan, Indonesia, Turkey . . . on and on and on, down to Costa Rica, Liberia, Laos, Luxemburg, and who knows, some day Monaco, San Marino, Nepal, Bhutan, Sikkim. World power is now a very cheap commodity. It costs only a few million pounds."

Sharet subsided. It was true. "World power" would soon be a meaningless term. *Power* . . . it would mean only the power of every nation to destroy every other.

"You are right," he said, "but even so, we have saved ourselves. At least we will be equal to the Arabs now. We have no desire to conquer, only to *live*. I am a sabra, I have lived my whole life under the guns of the Arabs. Now at least we will know that we will always be as strong as they. We need no longer feel like ants, in perpetual danger of being squashed by elephants."

"I am not a sabra," said Larus. "I have learned in different schools. My degree is from Heidelberg. I have also done post-graduate work in Belsen. Colonel, all men are not like you and me. There are those who would rather kill than live. What would Hitler have done in your fine new world, when every country holds the power to annihilate every other? You know as well as I. He would destroy the world. How many countries are there in the world? Over a hundred. Are you going to tell me that one out of a hundred countries will not produce another would-be dictator? We can both name several madmen ruling countries today who would use Conversion Bombs to destroy the world, out of sheer lust for killing."

"What would you have us do?"

"Forget you ever saw this Bomb!" cried Larus. "Destroy this place. Let me burn my notes and destroy the prototype. Let Man forget this monstrosity, if we are lucky, until he is ready for it, until there are no more nations, but only Humanity."

Sharet frowned. He had expected this. "And what of us? Soon the Arabs will be ready to destroy us. Destroy us they will. It's we or them."

"What are the lives of even two million people, compared to the whole world?" said Larus.

"Do we not have a right to live? Are we all saints? Can you expect us to let them wipe us out, when we have a weapon that can save us?"

Larus sighed. "Could not the same words be as justly spoken

by the Indians, the Pakistanis, the blacks of South Africa, the Tibetans?"

"We have a right to live!" exploded Sharet. "Perhaps the Tibetans and the Angolans and the Cambodians have as much right as we do. Do you think *they* would forget about a weapon that could save them, for the sake of Humanity? *Would our enemies?*"

Larus felt old and used up and defeated. Did Einstein feel this way after Hiroshima, he wondered.

"One favor," he said. "Grant me one favor. Don't send word to Tel Aviv until you've slept on it. *Or tried to*. A small boon to a tired old man?"

Colonel Sharet was not a man without compassion. Nor a man completely without doubts.

"Very well," the colonel said. "I certainly owe you that much."

"You owe it to yourself as well," said Larus.

"Perhaps . . ." muttered Sharet, "perhaps . . ."

Dr. Larus could not sleep, but then, he had not expected to be able to.

He looked up at the black desert sky; the thousands of stars seemed far away and very cold. The landscape was harsh, bare and rocky.

A tough, ruthless, impersonal land, the Negev, he thought. Parched and blazing during the day, cold, bleak and dangerous at night.

He was glad that he was within the fence. The fedayin still prowled the Negev at night. Heat during the day, clandestine assassins at night . . .

He felt more kindly towards Sharet, now. Ariah Sharet had been born and raised in this hard hostile land. It was a land that bred warriors. One had to fight simply to stay alive. A whole life spent with a gun always at your side . . .

No wonder Sharet wants the Bomb! Sooner or later, the enemy *will* become too strong. There are just too many of them, and once they have atomic bombs . . .

But those stars . . . The same stars, he knew, shone down over the Himalayas, over the war-torn rice paddies of Southeast Asia, over the bloodied streets of Budapest . . . A hundred suffering peoples, a hundred just and righteous causes. Do any of them have less right than we to use the Conversion Bomb?

And with dread certainty, he knew it would come to that. This year, an Israeli Conversion Bomb. The word would get out, sooner or later. And the Indians, the Cubans, the Pakistanis, the Angolans, every people that believed they had a wrong to right, an enemy to defend against, a partitioned nation to unite, would build Conversion Bombs . . .

And they'll all be as right as we are. Not more, not less.

A righteous world, armed for Armageddon, every people wanting only to survive, wanting only what was justly theirs. A cache of gunpowder waiting for a spark that must eventually come.

Which aggrieved nation or would-be nation would be Man's executioner? The Israelis? The Kurds? The Ukrainians?

Did it matter? Did it really matter?

Sigmund Larus looked up at the desert stars. Man was so small and puny, and the heavens were so grand.

But Man, small as he was, could blast this planet to a lifeless cinder.

Larus looked up into the heavens, and did something he had not done for twenty years. He prayed.

Ariah Sharet could not sleep either. He was trained in two fields —history and military science—and both preached decisiveness. Yet Sharet could not rid himself of doubt.

As he wandered about the compound, he thought of Larus. By no stretch of the imagination could Larus be considered a traitor. A Jew who had lived through the horrors of Hitler's Europe was *de facto* an Israeli patriot.

And yet, he was willing to see his country destroyed, rather than take the risk of building Conversion Bombs.

A question of backgrounds, Sharet thought. A man is born with a gun in his cradle, and if he is threatened, he kills. Another man learns to live under the heel of an all-powerful tyrant, and when his life is threatened, he meekly submits.

One is called a warrior, and the other a coward . . . *or a saint*.

But where does cowardice begin and saintliness leave off?

A man must fight for his life when attacked, Sharet thought. That much he was certain of.

He looked out over the barren Negev. How many armies had

marched back and forth over these wastelands? Philistines, Phoe-
nicians, Babylonians, Turks, Persians, Egyptians . . . the catalogue
was endless.

And now Larus would have the final absurd horror played out
—let us perish, finally, with our hands folded, while the weapon
that could save us lies unused.

For the sake of Humanity. What kind of Humanity could ask
that?

Sharet stared at the stars, as if in defiance. He knew that he had
made his decision. As long as nations existed, a people had the
right to fight for their survival.

He turned and began to walk back to his room. He knew that
he would sleep now.

As he turned the corner of a building, he saw the figure of Dr.
Larus looking out over the desert.

Well, let him be, Sharet thought, he—

Something had moved along the side of the building to Larus'
back!

It moved again, and now Sharet could see a figure in a burnoose
crouched in the shadow of the building.

Sharet slowly drew his pistol. Suddenly the Arab leaped up and
ran at Larus. Sharet could see a knife gleam in the moonlight.

Larus turned, and screamed in panic.

The Arab was less than five feet from Larus when Sharet shot
him. He fell in a crumpled heap at the scientist's feet.

Larus' hands were shaking again. So close! he thought. He had
seen death before, in the camps, and had been near it himself, but
not this kind of death, not a dagger in the hands of an assassin.

"Filthy scum!" he found himself shouting. "Murderers!"

Sharet is right. No man is obligated to let another slit his throat.
A man must kill, when it means his life . . .

Emotions coursed through his frail old body that he had not
believed himself capable of—feral, visceral emotions; hate, fear,
and the animal hunger for self-preservation.

The tall figure of Ariah Sharet was now standing over the body.
Larus was compelled to agree with the colonel now. Abstract
humanitarianism was one thing . . . violent death was quite
another.

Sharet stood over the dead Arab. He kicked the body over onto
its back.

His stomach twitched as he saw the bloodied face. The Arab was a boy, barely sixteen—a poor ignorant kid. What had he known of why he had died?

Ariah Sharet felt like crying. How many boys like this had died for things they did not even understand? Individuals, as well as peoples had a right to live. He no longer felt like a soldier.

He felt like a killer of children.

"You're right," the two men said simultaneously.

They started at each other's words.

Sharet recovered first.

"I have killed a child," he said. "Funny, how much all children look alike. Arabs, Jews, Russians, Americans. Perhaps *that* is the important thing, not geopolitics, not even peoples. To think that the Conversion Bomb could kill *all* the children."

"And I," replied Larus, "have had a dagger at my throat."

"Well, we have both seen each other's side now," said Sharet.

"So we have. What are we going to do now? Build Conversion Bombs and save ourselves . . . or destroy the prototype and my notes and save the world?"

"I'd like to leave that decision up to you, now," said Colonel Sharet.

Larus laughed humorlessly.

"And I to you, Colonel," he said.

A cold breeze blew in off the Negev. The two men shivered.

"In physics," said Larus, "decisions are so simple. A thing is either right or it is wrong . . ."

"In life," replied Sharet, "things are never simple. A few things we know are right, a few things we know are wrong. But the rest?"

"What is the right decision, Colonel?" asked Larus. "Tell me, if you can, please tell me."

Sharet's face bore the look of the damned.

"There is no right decision," he sighed. "One thing we can be sure of—*whatever we decide will be wrong.*"

And the night seemed to grow darker.

The Last of the Romany

"It's been a long hot journey," said the man with the waxed mustache. "A Collins please, bartender."

The fat bartender reached over to the console, punched the "Collins" button, and asked "Gin, rum, vodka or grahooey?"

"Gin, of course," said the man with the waxed mustache. "A grahooey Collins indeed!" He lit up a large olive-green cigar.

The bartender punched the "gin" button, and tapped the serve bar. The clear plastic container of cloudy liquid popped up through the serving hole in the bar.

The man with the waxed black mustache looked at the drink, and then at the console, and then at the bartender. "Do not think me rude, my friend," he said, "but I've always wondered why there are still bartenders, when anyone could press those silly buttons."

The bartender laughed, a fat good-natured laugh. "Why are there bus drivers on robot buses? Why are there brewers when the beer practically brews itself? I guess the government figures that if everyone who was unnecessary was fired, they'd have a hundred million unemployed on their hands."

The man with the mustache, who called himself Miklos, toyed with the battered guitar, which leaned against the bar. "I'm sorry my friend, for my remark," he said. "Actually, bartenders are still useful. Could I talk to that machine? And they still don't have an automatic bouncer."

"Oh?" said the bartender, leaning close to Miklos. "I was in Tokyo last year, and there they have a great padded hook that drops from the ceiling, grabs a drunk, and heaves him out the door. All untouched by human hands. Ah, science!"

Miklos scowled, and then brightened. "Ah, but the bartender

still must decide who to bounce! A very delicate task, not to be
trusted to a machine. Therefore, a bartender will always be necessary. Another Collins, please."

"Why are you so concerned with my usefulness?" asked the
bartender, punching out another Collins.

The man with the waxed black mustache and the weather-tanned
face became very serious. "It is one of the things I search for in
my travels," he said. "It is very important."

"What is?"

"Men who are still useful," said Miklos. "They are like rare
birds. When I spot one, it makes my whole day. I'm sort of a
people watcher."

"You travel a lot?" asked the bartender, with a little laugh.
"You must be one of the idle rich."

"No," said Miklos without smiling. "It's part of my job to
travel."

"Job? What kind of job? There are no more traveling salesmen,
and you hardly look like a pilot—"

Miklos puffed thoughtfully on his cigar. "It is a hard thing to
explain," he said. "Actually, there are two jobs. But if I succeed
in one, the other is unnecessary. The first job is to search."

"To search for what?"

The man with the waxed mustache picked up his guitar and
fiddled with the strings. "To search," he said, "for the Romany."

"The what?"

"The Romany, man! Gypsies."

The bartender gave him a queer look. "Gypsies? There aren't
any Gypsies left. It wouldn't be permited."

"You're telling me?" said Miklos, sighing. "For fourteen years
I have searched for the Romany. I've hitched, when nobody
hitches, I've bummed when nobody bums. I've looked in fifty
states and six continents. I even went to the Spanish caves, and do
you know what? They have a big mechanical display there now.
Robot Romany! Flamenco machines. The things even pass a metal
hat around. But the Romany are gone. And yet, some day, somewhere . . . Maybe you could . . . perhaps you would . . . ?"

"Me?" said the bartender, drawing away from the man with
the mustache.

"Ah, but of course not. Nobody knows. And of course, everyone thinks I'm crazy. But let me tell you, my friend, crazy is

strictly relative. I think you're all crazy. Nothing personal, you understand. It's this dry, clean, shiny Romany-killing world that's crazy. But come close, and I'll let you in on a secret."

Miklos stuck his face in the bartender's ear. "They have not killed the Romany," he whispered. Then louder: "I am the last Romany. That's the other job, to keep it all alive until I can find them. It's a good joke on the world. They try to kill the Romany, and when they fail, they try harder. But it is good for them that they do not succeed, for it is the Romany that keeps them alive. They don't know it, but when I am gone, they will die. Oh, they'll walk around in their nice, antiseptic cities for a few hundred years before they realize it, but for all practical purposes, they'll be dead."

"Sure," said the bartender. "Sure."

The man with the waxed black mustache frowned heavily. "I'm sorry," he said. "Sometimes I forget that I'm crazy, and then I become crazier. A neat paradox no?"

"You sound like an educated man," said the bartender, "a not-stupid man. How come you can't get a job?"

Miklos raised his head proudly. "Can't get a job! Sir, before I became Miklos, the Last Romany, I was assistant vice president in charge of sales for General Airconditioning. I am a moderately wealthy man. I know what success in this boring world is. You can have it."

"But with your money . . ."

"Bah! I wanted to see the exotic Orient, for example, so what was there? Tokyo was New York, Hong Kong was Chicago, Macao was Philadelphia. Far Samarkand is now a Russian rocket port. It's all gone. The Baghdad of the Caliphs, the China of Kubla Khan, Far Samarkand, Cairo . . . Oh, the cities are still there, but so what? They're all the same, all neat and clean and shiny."

"You ought to be glad," said the bartender. "They cleaned up the opium traffic and the prostitution. They licked malaria and yellow fever—even dysentery. They got the beggars off the streets, and built sanitary markets for the street vendors. I was in Tokyo, as I said, and it's every bit as modern as New York."

Miklos snorted cigar smoke. "And while they were at it, they replaced the Caliphs and Sultans and Khans with City Managers. Feh!"

"Well," said the bartender, "you can't please everybody. Most folks like things the way they are."

"They think they do. Ah well, I've got things to do. Can you tell me where there's a playground?"

"A playground? You wanna play golf or something?"

"No, no, a *children's* playground."

"There's one three blocks west of here," said the bartender, "but what do you want there?"

"It's part of the job, my friend," said Miklos, getting up and hoisting his guitar to his shoulder. "It keeps me from thinking too much and doing too little, and besides, who knows, maybe it does some little good. Good-by." He left the bar whistling a *chardash.*

"A nut," mumbled the bartender, tossing the used containers into the disposal. "Seems harmless enough, though."

The playground was the standard model, one block square, surrounded by a six-foot force-fence, with one entrance on each side. In addition to the usual exponential hopscotch board, force-slides and basketball grid, there was some newer equipment, including a large tri-D, and a robot watchman. Most of the children were seated on benches in front of the tri-D watching "Modern Lives," the playground educational series. They seemed quite bored, except when, as a sop to their frivolity, someone was hit over the head.

The man with the waxed black mustache and the battered guitar walked through the gate. He was noticed only by the robot watchman.

"Sir," rasped the robot, "are you the parent or guardian of any of these children?"

Miklos blew a smoke ring at the robot. "No!"

"Peddlers, beggars, salesmen, roller skates, pets and children over twelve years of age are forbidden in the playground," said the robot.

"I am not a peddler, beggar, salesman, roller skate, bicycle, pet or child over twelve," said Miklos, who knew the routine.

"Are you a sexual deviate?" asked the robot. "Sexual deviates are prohibited from the playground by law, and may be forceably removed."

"I am not a sexual deviate," said the man with the mustache. Predictably, the robot stood there for a moment, relays clicking confusedly, and then rolled away. Miklos entered the playground, threw away his half-smoked cigar, and sprawled himself on the last bench in front of the tri-D.

He strummed a few random chords on the guitar, and then sang a staccato song in Spanish. His voice was harsh, and his playing, at best, passable, but both were loud and enthusiastic, so the total effect was not unpleasing.

A few of the younger children detached themselves from the group around the tri-D and grouped themselves around Miklos' bench. He went through "Santa Anna," some very amateurish flamenco, and an old Israeli marching song. By the end of the marching song, all but the oldest children had gathered around him. He spoke for the first time. "My name is Miklos. Now my friends, I will sing for you a very nice little song about a rather nasty fellow. It is called 'Sam Hall.'"

When he got to the part of the chorus which goes: "You're a buncha bastards all, damn your eyes," the robot came rolling over at top speed, screeching "Obscenity is forbidden in the playground. Forbidden. No child must say naughty words. No obscenity. Will the child who said the bad words please stop."

"I said the bad words, you pile of tin," laughed Miklos.

"Please stop using obscenity," croaked the robot. "Obscenity is forbidden to children."

Miklos lit a cigar and blew a huge puff of smoke at the robot. "I am not a child, you monstrosity. I can say what I please." He grinned at his appreciative audience.

Relays clicked frantically. "Are you a sexual deviate? Are you a beggar, salesman or peddler? Are you a child over twelve?"

"We went through this already. I am none of those things. Get out of here, before I report you for interfering with the civil rights of an adult human."

More relays clicked frantically. There was a slight smell of burning insulation. The robot wheeled off, careening crazily. It stopped about a hundred yards away, and began to mumble to itself.

Miklos laughed, and the children, all of whom were now clustered about him, roared with him.

"And now, my friends," he said, "let us talk of better things: Of

pirates and khans and indians. Of the thousand and three white
elephants of the King of Siam. Of the Seven Cities of Gold, and the
great Caliph Haroun-al-Rashid."

"Have you been to all those, mister?"

"Are you a pirate?"

"What's a caliph?"

Miklos spread his large hands. "Wait, wait, one at a time." He
smiled. "No, I am not a pirate. I am a Romany."

"What's a Ro . . . ?"

"Romany! A gypsy, my young friend. Not so long ago, there
were thousands of us, rolling all over the world in bright red and
yellow wagons, singing and playing and stealing chickens. Now I
am the only one left, but I know all the stories, I know all the
places—"

"You ever steal a chicken, mister?"

"Well . . . No, but I've stowed away on planes, even on a ship
once. Do you know what that would have meant in the days of the
pirates? Sir Henry Morgan would have made me walk the plank!"

"Walk the . . . plank?"

"Yes, he would've stroked his dirty black beard, and said:
'Miklos, ye scurvy bilge-rat, ye'll jump into the drink, and be ate by
the sharks, or I'll run ye through with me cutlass!' "

"Couldn't you call a cop?"

Miklos grimaced and twirled the ends of his mustache. "A cop!
Sir Henry would've ate one of your cops for breakfast. And at that,
he'd be getting off easy. You know what Haroun-al-Rashid
would've done? He'd have his Grand Vizier turn him into a camel!"

An older boy snickered loudly. "Aw, come on, ya can't turn a
cop into a camel."

"I can't, and you can't, and maybe nobody today can. But in
those days, in Baghdad! Why, anyone could!"

Most of the older children wandered away, but a hard core of
six- and seven- and eight-year-olds remained.

"You must believe," said Miklos, "and then you can do these
things. Fifty years ago, you could cross the world with your thumb.
Now they say it's impossible. But, my little friends, I know better.
I have done it. How? Because I am a Romany. I believe, even if
they say I'm crazy."

"Wow mister, Romanies is smart, huh?"

"No smarter than you. In fact, you can only do these things if you're a little stupid. Stupid enough to believe that somewhere, sometime, there still is a Baghdad, and Samarkand is still Far. You must be stupid enough not to care when the police and the Chairmen of the Board say you're crazy. And if you believe hard enough, and are crazy enough . . ."

"What, mister?"

The man with the waxed black mustache sighed, and then he leaned close to the circle of small heads and whispered: "If you believe hard enough, and care long enough, and are crazy enough, and become nice and wicked, then some day you will get to the Spanish Main, and the Seven Cities of gold, and the magic city of Baghdad, where there are no robots or schools, only magicians and wild black horses. And some day, you will see Far Samarkand, shining white and gold and red above the sands of the desert. And, little friends, if you are especially dirty, and never, never wash behind your ears, and only brush your teeth once a day, and don't watch the tri-D, and say four bad words a day for a month, and dream always of the lost far magic places, some day you will wake up, early on a cool autumn morning, and you will be a Romany!"

Miklos picked up the guitar. "And now, my little Romany, we will sing."

And he played the old songs, and sang of the far places until the sweat dripped onto his mustache. Then he pulled out a red bandanna, wiped his face, and played some more.

For two hours, he played and sang, and told the old tales.

He was just finishing the story of Atlantis, when the cop arrived. The cop was dressed in the usual blue tunic and shorts, and the usual scowl. "What the hell's going on here?" he said.

The robot came wheeling over, moaning, "Obscenity is forbidden in the playground. Obscenity is—"

"Shaddap!" said the cop.

The robot shut up.

"All right, bud," said the cop, "what do you think you're doing?"

"Just singing a few songs, and telling a few stories," said the man with the waxed mustache meekly.

"You're disturbing a public playground," said the cop. "I think I'll run you in."

A little sparkle returned to the man with the mustache. "Is that a crime, officer?" he said.

"No, but . . ."

Miklos chewed on his cigar. "Then I guess you'll be on your way," he said.

"Not so fast," said the cop. "I can still run you in for vagrancy."

The man with the mustache grinned, and then permitted himself a large laugh. "I'm afraid not, my friend. No indeed, I'm afraid not." He reached into his pocket and pulled out a roll of wet, soiled bills. He counted out two hundred dollars, and shoved them under the cop's nose. "See, my friend? I am hardly a vagrant. Well, my little friends," he said, turning his back to the cop, "I must be going, before there is any more trouble, and I am tempted to turn this worthy officer of the law into a you-know-what. Good-by, my friends. Remember the Romany."

The children grinned. The cop stood there. The man with the waxed black mustache hoisted his guitar to his shoulder, and slowly walked out of the playground, whistling loudly.

The early morning sun shone in through the large picture window, bathing the bar in bright yellow light. The bar was empty, except for the bartender and a young man with a detached, faraway look. The young man, who was wearing the gold and black uniform of the Space Corps, sat at one end of the bar staring out the window and sipping a beer.

Miklos stepped in, the open door admitting a blast of hot air into the air-conditioned room. "Hello, my friend," he said, sitting down two seats away from the young Spaceman. "A beer, please."

The bartender pressed beer, and the plastic stein appeared in front of Miklos. Miklos took a long drink. "The morning is the best time for a good cold beer," he said. "Too bad so few people recognize its beauties." He glanced at the young man. The Spaceman gave Miklos a funny look, but not one of distaste. He said nothing, and continued to stare out the window.

"Did you find the playground?" asked the bartender. The Spaceman smiled a twisted smile.

"Of course," said Miklos, lighting a cigar. "No trouble at all. That is, except for a cop that tried to chase me away. But he was little trouble." He pointed to his head. "Not too bright, you know."

The Spaceman chuckled softly.

"You still haven't told me what you did there," said the bartender.

The man with the mustache thumped his guitar. "I played this thing, I sang, I told the kids a few stories."

"What for?" asked the bartender.

The young man got up, and sat down next to Miklos. "I know what for, don't I?" he said, smiling.

Miklos laughed. "If you say you do."

"Say," said the bartender, "you're a Spaceman. You been around, no?"

"I suppose I have."

"Well then," said the bartender, "maybe you can help our guitar friend here. He's looking for something."

"Oh?" said the young man with the faraway stare. He seemed to be suppressing something between a snicker and a grin.

"Yeah," said the bartender, laughing, "Gypsies!"

The Spaceman did not laugh. He ignored the bartender, and turned to Miklos. "You are looking for Gypsies?"

"Yes," said Miklos soberly. "Yes, I am looking for Gypsies."

"For the Romany?"

Miklos stared hard at him. "Yes, the Romany."

The Spaceman drank the last of his beer. "It is a hard thing," he said, "to find Romany these days."

"I know, I know," said Miklos, resting his head in his hands. "For fourteen years I have looked. Fourteen years, six continents, and God knows how many countries. It's a long time—a long sweaty time. Perhaps too long, perhaps I am crazy, and there are no more Romany, and perhaps there never will be. Perhaps I should give up, and go back to being a vice president in charge of sales, or go to a psychiatrist, or—"

"I know a place," said the young man.

"A place?"

"A far place," said the Spaceman. "A place that no one has yet seen. Alpha Centauri. Or perhaps Sirus. Or Rigel."

"The stars?" said Miklos. "Nobody's ever been to the stars."

"Indeed," said the young man, smiling, "no one has ever been to the stars. What better place to find the Romany? Out there, in a land that is not yet in the travel tours, a land that no one has ever seen, the kind of land where the Romany have always gone. Somewhere out there, there are cities that put all the legends to shame.

And magic, and wonder . . . The Universe has a billion worlds. Surely, on one of them there are Gypsies, on another Khans, on another ancient Baghdad."

"A very pleasant picture," said Miklos, lighting a cigar, "and probably true. But unfortunately, it's as possible to go to those worlds as it is to visit ancient Baghdad."

"Not quite," said the Spaceman. "On the Moon, they are building a faster-than-light starship. First stop Alpha Centauri. There will be others. Many others."

Miklos stood up. "A starship! Yes! I'll book passage right away. You wouldn't think it, to look at me, but I'm moderately rich." He stared out the window at the sky. "Perhaps I'll find them yet, out there."

"Of course," said the young man, "it's a government project, like the Moon, and Mars and Venus. As they say, there's only room for 'trained experts.'"

"Of course," said Miklos, "of course . . . it's always that way. Always machines, or men like machines, always. But no matter! If those ships exist, there is a way on them. If the stars are there, there's a way to bum your way. If the Romany exist, some day, somewhere, I'll find them." He stood up, and slung his guitar over his shoulder. "I'm off for Canaveral," he said. "And then to the Moon, and then . . . Well, good-by and thanks."

The man with the waxed black mustache strode out into the sunny street.

"Thanks, pal," said the bartender. "You really got rid of that screwball. He was starting to worry me. You really knew what made him tick."

"I ought to," said the Spaceman.

"Whaddaya mean?"

"Well, once there was a kid in Springfield, Ohio, in fact the kid was me. And this kid was like all the other kids in this world, a nice, packaged future member of a nice packaged society. And then one day, maybe eleven years ago, a crazy guy with a mustache blew into town, and told that kid a lot of tall tales about a lot of far places. Something changed in that kid that day—a very small change. But it got bigger and bigger every year, until now that little change is the whole person. And here I am, on my way to Centaurus."

"You mean there really is a starship?"

"There sure is, and you know something? Somehow, some day, in some highly illegal manner, that guy is going to get on it." The Spaceman looked out the window as if he were already on his way to Centaurus.

"What'll they do to him when they find him?" asked the bartender.

The Spaceman looked at him, a strange softness in his eyes.

"Only a certain rare kind of man can go somewhere no one's ever seen. You can't package that kind of man. You can't grow him in controlled schools and mold him on canned dreams. You've got to beat him and kick him and laugh at him and call him crazy. And if someone has whispered certain things in his ear at a critical time, you have a man who will go to the stars."

The young man glared at the bartender.

"What will we say to him, when we find him on the ship? What else, but 'Welcome, Miklos. Welcome home.'"

Technicality

We were pretty well dug in at the base of a long, gently sloping ridge, with six Empie pillboxes guarding the crest, spread kind of thin. This was near the end of the war, when everyone knew that the Empies had had it, but the big boys were still not telling the civvies why. We knew that the ridge was just about all that the Empies had between us and their last real concentration in this part of the state, and tomorrow morning we were going over the top. By this time, the brass had finally got it through their thick skulls that night attacks were just too much to ask from anyone.

Well, up to the lines comes the kid, Barker's replacement, just as the Empies on top of the ridge decide to keep us honest with a brace of barf-bombs. The kid sees those four rockets coming down at us fat and lazy, and he gets the message or at least thinks he does. Without a "Howdy-do" or "Hello, Sarge," he's face downward in the dirt behind me. The wind being in our faces, the Empies have, of course, lobbed the barf-bombs short and the green gas is rolling slowly toward us. We've got maybe a minute, maybe two.

The kid looks up with a face full of mud and he says, "They missed us, huh, Sarge?"

"You have supper yet, kid?"

"Why, yeah, thanks, Sarge. I—"

"Too bad," I have time to say, and then the gut-gas hits, heavy green stuff that works on skin-contact so masks are useless, and we are all too busy gagging and puking to continue the conversation.

A couple of boys in the platoon are still insisting on shooting back up at the Empie emplacements every time they lob something at us, but the Funny Bunnies are way down underground, and when the gas clears enough for me to stop gagging, I chew them out for wasting ammo. Not that they won't go and do the same thing the next time we get fed puke pills. Some jerks just take everything so damned personal.

Well, the kid wipes most of the mud mess off of himself, and you can see that now he is feeling like a real pro. "When do we get to kill us some Empies?" he asks, with what he hopes will impress me as the real gung-ho.

"You might try reporting first, Soldier," I suggest. I am up to my ears with all these Mickey Mice, and I have no energy to do the full-scale sergeant act.

So he tells me that he is Pfc. Tolan, and I tell him how over-joyed I am to see him. Like every other replacement we're getting lately, the kid is just about straight out of high school, and like all civilians, knows next to nothing about the war that's going on all around him. About all the civvies know is that almost two years back, these green characters show up from some place called Tau Ceti, in honest-to-Pete flying saucers. A real live invasion from Outer Space, just like in the movies. Well, to begin with they are mopping the floor with every army on Earth, and they conquer half of good old terra firma. We start using the big stuff, H-bombs even, and then they get real unpleasant. Every time we use even an atomic popgun, three cities get king-size doses of puke gas. Finally, the brass gets the message: the Funny Bunnies will leave the civvies alone as long as we lay off the nuclear stuff. So we find ourselves slogging through the mud just like an old World War II movie, for the sake of the civvies' tender stomachs. Politics!

And do the civvies give a damn now? All they know is that the Empies are leaving *them* alone, and that now, for some reason that no one is really explaining, we are mopping the floor with them. The civvies are all calling the Funny Bunnies "Empies," but maybe one in ten knows that "Empie" comes from "M.P.," and the brass is making sure that no civilian below the Secretary of Defense knows what M.P. stands for. Which is about the only thing about the war that doesn't confirm my pet theory that anything above the rank of Master Sergeant is really a chimpanzee.

So, of course, what the kid asks next is, "What's the secret?"

"I give up, kid. You tell me."

"I mean the Secret Weapon. Everyone says we got a Secret Weapon, ever since last year when we finally started winning. What's the Secret Weapon, Sarge?"

I try not to groan too hard. I point to the kid's autorifle, which at least seems to be in working condition. "You're holding it, kid," I say. "Tomorrow morning, we all go up that hill. All you got to remember is that no matter what, and I mean *no matter what,* you keep running up that hill, and you don't turn back. That's the Secret Weapon, a gun on the end of a pair of legs. And you don't turn back. Turn back, and I blow your brains out, got it?"

The message seems to penetrate. Of course, I don't go around shooting every yuk that turns tail. If I did, I would be shooting about two platoons a week, on the average. But the first time is usually the worst, the one that makes a civvie into a soldier. I figure that, if I can make them more afraid of me than of what's happening to 'em, they got a better chance of sticking it out. Sometimes it even works.

Bright and early the next morning, up we go. We have, of course, not eaten breakfast, and we've emptied our bowels and bladders as thoroughly as possible. I keep the kid as close to me as I can, and I'm doing my best to look ferocious.

We've gone maybe twenty yards when the Empies wake up and start lobbing barf-bombs. Most of the guys are pretty much used to the dry heaves, and so we stumble and retch, but all in all make pretty good time up through the gut-gas. The kid is in a pretty bad way, but he's got guts, and he's even firing his autorifle now and then, trying to look like a soldier. I'm about to tell him to stop wasting ammo, but then I figure, what the hell so he wastes a few rounds, long as it helps keep him going.

We get through the puke-gas, which, of course, is just for openers, and then they really start opening up. Bladderbusters, bowelbillies, itchrays, freezers—just about everything but the heavy stuff. Already, some of the guys have had it, mostly the ones that have been around too long and have been getting flippy anyway.

I glance around at the kid, to see if he has noticed that I am not shooting the tail-turners, but he's far too busy twitching and scratching and shivering to notice anything. But he's still running in the right direction and firing wildly. The kid has guts.

Well, we get halfway up the hill, and the attrition rate is not too bad—more than half of us are still coming. Now we can see the tops of the Empie pillboxes, which are just steel slabs with rocket-ports, raynozzles and gasvents in them. There's one big hatch to each pillbox. All the guts are underground.

Then they start using the Big Stuff.

First, the Aphrogas. Ever try fighting thinking about, feeling about nothing but women—I mean like hitting a Mexican border town after ten years in solitary? Yeah, Aphrogas and then Panic Pills.

I'm scratching and yelling and feeling monsters all around me, like a super case of the d.t.'s, but I'm used to it. I've been in this war a whole six months, see. Well, the platoon is really falling apart now. We've been assigned number two pillbox, and the guys are, as usual, turning tail like polecats. Only me and Anders and Brown and McCuller and Gentry are still coming. And the kid. How about that, I think. That kid really has guts.

Finally, we're maybe fifty yards from the pillbox, and that's within suicide-ray range. Of course we have all had as much hypnoconditioning as we can stand, and as soon as we feel that familiar urge to slit our own throats coming on us, our adrenals cut in, and we go into what the psych-boys call Turnaround, and we're storming up the hill, thinking nothing but Kill! Kill! Kill! Either that, or running for home like scared rabbits.

The little part of me that is not yelling "Kill! Kill! Kill!" is checking the rest of the platoon. Anders and Gentry are running down the hill. Brown has not been able to take enough hypnoconditioning. He's blown his own brains out.

It's me and McCuller and the kid. Kill! Kill! Kill! Up those last fifty yards to the pillbox, and the suicide-ray getting stronger with every yard.

But we've got too much Kill! Kill! in us—me and McCuller and the kid. We scramble up on top of the pillbox lid, up to the hatch, and I pull out a grenade, and they hit us with the last-ditch weapon.

One second it's Kill! Kill! Kill!, and the next we all love the Empies. How could we ever have thought of hurting such nice green little bunnies? Who never hurt anyone. Who love us all, with a great big mother-love. Lovely little Funny Bunnies. . . . Dear little Empies . . .

McCuller sort of slips off the pillbox, blubbering. He has had it. The kid, I guess, has never had a mother. He is just about dragging me, and I wouldn't hurt the dear little Empies for all the world. Dear little enemies. Cute little . . .

With the last bit of resistance that I have left in me, I plant the grenade atop the hatch, grab the kid, and roll us off the pillbox.

Crump! not a big explosion, and most of it is directed downward anyway. The hatch is blown off, the suicide-ray and the love-ray nozzles smashed, and it is all over.

The kid and I rush up to the hatch, and down into the pale, butter-colored light. We're inside a big warm burrow where maybe ten or so little green furry creatures are just standing around on their big haunches next to a lot of now-useless machinery. They have dumpy little bodies like beavers, little heads with long floppy ears, and the saddest expressions in their big brown eyes. They just stand there, not moving, not trying to get away, not doing anything but looking sad and innocent and helpless.

I start firing, and the kid is firing beside me, and in less than a minute there are ten furry little bodies on the ground, all torn to bits and laying in pools of the green stuff the Funny Bunnies have for blood.

It's just me and the kid and all that dead meat. Suddenly, standing there, watching the confused, sad, savage, goofy look on the kid's face and remembering how it was for me when I found out, I know that I have finally had it. I can go up a hill again, through anything they have to throw at me, but I can't shoot any more Funny Bunnies that just stand there, waiting, not doing a thing but looking like your favorite cocker spaniel. I know that they are all crazy fanatics, out to conquer anything that isn't an Empie and that someone has to stop them. But not me, not any more.

"They just stood there . . ." the kid is muttering over and over again. "They just stood there . . ."

I put my arm around the kid's shoulder. The kid had done all right. "Yeah, kid," I say quietly. "They always just stand there. That's why we keep it a secret from the civvies. They would never understand, without coming up a hill against all the hell the Empies dish out, and even then . . ."

I look down at the dead Funny Bunnies. I know I can't kill

them any more, but man oh man, how I hate them. "Know what M.P. stands for, kid?" I say.

"What, Sarge?" he mutters, not realizing that he is about to learn *the* secret.

"Militant Pacifists," I tell him. "They crossed space and conquered half the world before we found out the secret. They're ruthless fanatics, who'll do anything to win, even make men kill themselves. But the Funny Bunnies just can't make themselves do one thing that we do real well, kid. They can't kill. They just never learned how."

The Rules of the Road

The great silver dome sat in the desert at Yucca Flats. It was featureless, save for an innocent-appearing open entranceway, but there was something about it that shrieked: *alien*. The silver shimmer was not quite the shimmer of silver. Rather it was more like the silver of shimmer.

The tanks, machine-gun emplacements and foxholes surrounding the dome confirmed the sense of alienness. The dome was surrounded and cordoned off. Whether it was being guarded or contained was a moot question.

Near the opening in the dome a tent had been pitched. The flag of a three-star general flew from a makeshift flagpole. Inside the tent were a half-dozen canvas folding chairs, an elaborate radio setup, a large map table that seemed to serve no useful function, five assorted colonels, Lieutenant General Richard Brewster —a middle-aged man with the look of an athlete gone to fat—and one lone civilian, looking plucked and out of place amidst all that khaki plumage.

General Brewster eyed the civilian with cold resignation.

"I've lost ten men in there already," he said, in a tone of voice like a poker player describing a particularly bad run of cards.

"Ten men, and we don't know any more than when we started." Brewster stared out the open tent flap at the entrance to the dome. "Only one thing we know," he said. "It's from the stars."

"Interesting," said the civilian flatly. He was a wiry man, not short, not tall. His face showed even more tension than his spare body. His mouth seemed frozen in a perpetual sour sneer, his expression appeared dead and juiceless. Only his large dark eyes betrayed him. They shifted purposefully from focus to focus, absorbing, categorizing, analyzing.

"*Interesting?* Is that all you have to say, Lindstrom? Interesting? It's from the stars, man. We tracked it from beyond the orbit of Pluto. Don't you understand? It's a spaceship from another solar system. It's the key to the stars."

"That's what it is to you," said Lindstrom. "But what is it to whatever sent it here? Are you so sure *they* intend it as a key to the stars? What about those ten men you sent in who never came out? Do you think *they're* so sure it's the key to the stars?"

"What are you leading up to, man?" spat Brewster, with unconcealed distaste.

"Just that you know *nothing* about why that thing came here. Ten men go in, and none of them come out. Maybe it's not here to give us the stars at all. Maybe its purpose is as alien as its manufacture. Or maybe—" Lindstrom paused and allowed himself a grin.

"Maybe it's just a better mousetrap," he said.

"Well," said Brewster, "will you or won't you? If you're trying to point out how dangerous it is, you're wasting your time. I've lost ten men as it is. I know damn well it's dangerous. I've been told you're not afraid of danger. I've been told you *enjoy* it."

Lindstrom laughed brittlely. "In a way," he said. "It's not that I enjoy danger, General. It's just that I need it. The question is, how much do you think you need *me?*"

"What do you mean?"

"I mean two hundred and fifty thousand tax-free dollars. Take it or leave it."

"Payable *if* you succeed in telling us what's inside the dome?"

"What else?"

Brewster nodded. "Okay, you're on."

Bert Lindstrom was aware of his glamor only when he wanted a woman. Then it proved most useful; it was a well-honed, finely-crafted tool. There were plenty of women who could resist the soldier of fortune myth, to be sure, but there were many more who could not. The probabilities were all on his side.

And odds were Bert Lindstrom's religion.

Lindstrom was a calculating man. He would undertake nothing

that did not seem to offer an odds on chance of success. Nothing, from seduction to assassination.

Yet he would never fail to accept a challenge when the odds were in his favor—no matter if he were risking a dime or his life.

For in his system of values, there was no real difference. It was not *what* was being risked that counted, it was the risk itself. His life meant little to him when he was not risking it. Only when he was gambling with his existence did it come to have meaning— then it was the stake, the challenge, the risk.

Lindstrom did not seek death. He risked his life only when he felt that the odds were on his side. He did not seek death, but he had to be near it, he had to risk it, for only at the moment of risk could his life have any meaning.

And this was the best risk in a life of risks. Not necessarily because it was the longest shot of all. Lindstrom had the professional risk-taker's contempt for soldiers who took risks on orders.

That ten soldiers had not come out was a thing of little import.

What was interesting was that the dome from the stars was a total unknown. Even the odds on coming out were incalculable. They might be in his favor, they might not. He was betting his instinctive feelings about himself against a complete unknown.

If he had set up the situation himself in a laboratory he could not have contrived a more perfect risk.

The hot desert wind blew at Lindstrom's back as he approached the entrance to the dome.

The soldiers who had not come out had been armed to the teeth. Therefore Lindstrom was not.

He carried only his old .45, a machete which was more a luck-charm than anything else, a coil of rope, an all-purpose utility knife and a flashlight.

The entrance was little more than a door-sized hole in the material of the dome. Lindstrom peered inside. He could see nothing but blackness. He drew his gun, turned on the flashlight and stepped inside.

As soon as he crossed the threshold, there was light. It did not seem to come from anywhere, it just *was*.

In the pearly luminescence, he could see he was standing at the mouth of a tunnel, a smooth, round, somehow almost colorless tunnel, that curved crazily upwards and leftwards in an arc so steep that it seemed impossible to hold one's footing.

Nevertheless, Lindstrom decided to try to climb it. Although the material of the tunnel seemed glass-smooth, it did not have a low frictional coefficient. It was more like walking on concrete than glass.

Stranger still, although his eyes told him that he was walking up a curve at an impossible angle, his body tilted almost forty degrees from the vertical, his kinesthetic senses told a different story. The force of gravity remained perpendicular to the floor of the tunnel, no matter what angle the tunnel took to the Earth's surface, so that he was walking upright, as if the tunnel had a private gravity all its own.

Lindstrom was somewhat frightened: the instinctual fear of the unknown. This he had, of course, expected. *Fear* meant that there was danger, risk. And risk meant that he was *living*.

The tunnel came to a fork. Decision number one. Had this been the point at which the soldiers had made the wrong calculation? Lindstrom was sure that surviving in the dome was a matter of making the proper calculations, the correct decisions. Either that, or there was no way of surviving. And that was a possibility not worth considering—since if it were true, the game was already lost.

It was like walking on a ledge over a precipice in the dark. You knew that there was a safe path and you knew that there was a point beyond which death lurked. But you had no way of knowing how wide the ledge was, how much margin for error you had.

There was nothing to choose from between the two forks. The one on the right curved up, the one on the left down. Otherwise they were identical. A random choice.

Okay, thought Lindstrom. He hesitated for only a moment, and then, for no reason in particular, took the right-hand turn.

He had only gone a few steps, the intersection was just behind him, when he felt a sudden flash of heat at his back.

He whirled in time to see a solid pillar of fire engulf the crotch of the intersection, the spot where he had stood moments ago pondering his choice.

Lesson number one, he thought. No Hamlets allowed. When faced with a decision, *make it,* one way or the other. Don't temporize, or you'll be vaporized.

The tunnel wound on for an indeterminable distance. Then it ended. Or, from another point of view, took an abrupt ninety-degree turn and became a bottomless, black, circular hole.

Lindstrom shined his light into the hole. The beam petered out in the blackness. The hole seemed made of the same material as the tunnel. There was nothing to secure the rope to.

Now what? thought Lindstrom grimly. And how much time do I have? He remembered the pillar of fire at the fork.

He felt that weird, timeless, floating exhilaration that he only experienced at those times when he knew that death was near, and had the time to comtemplate it.

The hole was like the tunnel. He must go forward, or . . .

Not *like* the tunnel. It *was* the tunnel. Or at least it should be. Fatalistically he dangled his feet into the hole, until his soles contacted its sides. Then he "stood up"—or rather stood *down*.

Quite suddenly, he was standing upright in what had been the hole. Now it was just more of the same tunnel. The thing actually did have a gravity of its own.

Lesson number two, he thought. This place has its own rules. Learn them and obey them.

It was highly probable that none of the soldiers had gotten this far. This was a place that demanded a cold mathematical intimacy with death. It was a place where the greatest risk of all was *not* to take risks.

It was no place for a man under orders.

Lindstrom felt calmer now; he had dared and he had won. The fear that he had left was not a paralyzer, it was a tonic, the satisfied fear that a matador feels when he realizes that he is facing a truly great bull.

He wandered further along the tunnel, and with every passing minute, the calmness he felt he had earned diminished.

This was not ordinary mortal danger—Lindstrom had lived on speaking terms with death too long for mere danger to be extraordinary. It was something far worse. He was thinking too much as he walked, and this was a place that was not to be thought about, because it was a place without rules . . . which is one symptom of madness . . .

There might be no rules, he thought, but there must be a purpose. Something had brought the dome to Earth, something intelligent, and intelligence implies purpose.

But what if it really were just a giant mousetrap?

But that was ridiculous. If they had wanted merely to kill him, they could have done it long ago. The dome was not only their creation, it was a universe in itself. Inside the dome, they could alter the very rules of existence. No, the rules were set up so that it was possible to survive. Fantastically difficult, but *possible*.

That was all he had to cling to. The odds against survival might be astronomical, but survival was at least a possibility.

I can die, he thought. Therefore I can live.

In the distance, around a bend, the tunnel ended. It opened into a large domed chamber. The chamber was lit with the same pearly light as the tunnel, and it seemed to be made of the same substance.

It was a smooth, featureless room. A dead end. It was empty.

A voice that was not a voice nibbled at his mind.

"You have passed the entrance examination," it "said." "Are you ready?"

"Ready for what?"

"Ready."

The single word had many nuances. It seemed to Lindstrom that the voice in his mind was intimate with his entire being. *Ready* . . . Ready was the word that described his entire life. Ready seemed to imply acceptance and belligerence at the same time. Ready to accept possible death, and ready to fight to cling to life. Ready to wait, and ready to make instant decisions.

"Yes," said the voice, "yes."

"Why?" asked Lindstrom. "Why all this? Why . . ."

"Your General Brewster was right," said the voice. "In a way, this is a spaceship. A starship. For your people, it can be the key to the universe. If you are ready. If you can change."

"Change to what?" said Lindstrom.

"Change," said the voice. "Not change to what. Adapt to that which is constantly changing. Live on a tightrope strung over nothingness. Your race is now reaching for the planets of your solar system. A tiny beginning. You have conquered your world by adapting it to your needs. But the universe will not be adapted. An infinity of deaths awaits you out there. Deaths you cannot now even conceive of."

"I've never been afraid of death," snapped Lindstrom.

"You have always been afraid of death," said the voice. "It is your very fear which allows you to face it. But fear is not enough."

"What else is there?"

"You will learn. Here you will learn, or you will die."

"Why? Why?"

"Perhaps you are ready to begin to learn why," said the voice. "Behold the road to the stars."

He was in a place that was terror. It was no place at all. It was everyplace. He was at the same time in a lightless blackness, and the mad dissociated core of a sun. It was a space with no dimensions. It was a space with an infinity of dimensions.

He had no senses. He had senses that could not exist. He tasted color. He saw time raveled like a vast ball of twine about him. He heard the creation of the universe, and he smelt the acrid stench of its eventual death.

Entropy ran forward, backward, in circles. He was bigger than the entire universe; it nestled in his navel. He stood on the nonexistent surfaces of a trillion electrons.

He was an insect, a star, a void, a galaxy.

He screamed and screamed and screamed and screamed . . .

He burned and froze, exploded and imploded, his mind was boiled in alien thoughts unspeakably foul. He rolled in beauty so hideous that he died an infinity of deaths from pleasure . . .

"Stop. Stop. Stop!" His cries echoed from the walls of existence and rebounded back to sting his flesh like a geometrically breeding nest of angry hornets . . .

"Enough," said the voice.

He was back in the featureless chamber.

"W-what . . . *what was it?*"

"That," said the voice, "is the real universe. All else is illusion, a partial truth, the projection in three dimensions of a reality with an infinity of dimensions. *That* is the road to the stars."

"You mean we have to learn to navigate in *that?* To remain sane long enough to find our way? It's impossible!"

"No," said the voice. "That is the real universe. It is not enough to learn to travel through it. You must learn to live in it."

"In it?" exclaimed Lindstrom. "In that madness?"

"It is reality," said the voice. "The universe is not as tidy as you would like it to be. Time is not really a straight line, nor space three-dimensional. It is possible to be all places at once. It is pos-

sible to be all times at once. Your race's view of the universe is
pathetically limited. Limited, perhaps, to preserve your sanity."

Lindstrom felt his mind perched on the edge of a fathomless
abyss. He felt the bonds of reality crumbling about him. What,
after all, *was* reality? Was it really this unspeakable horror, this
mad, murderous confusion . . . ?

"Yes," said the voice, "you are looking down into an abyss. But
you must do more, you must learn to jump willingly into it. In the
real universe, laws of nature are not constant. The rules themselves
vary, according to rules for rules, which in turn vary according to
still higher orders or rules . . ."

"Stop. Stop. No one can cope with a thing like that. I don't
want to know any more. I—"

"The choice is not yours," said the voice. "No human will be
permitted to leave this place unchanged. This chamber is a dead
end. There is no other passage out but the way you came, and
that tunnel is sealed to you forever."

"You mean you intend to keep me a prisoner here for the rest
of my life?"

"No," said the voice. "There is no passage out, but there is a
way out. Either you will learn it, or you will die. We begin."

He was in a space with four dimensions. It hurt his mind.
There was a fourth dimension that was somehow at right angles to
all three normal directions . . .

His body was . . . different. He was enclosed in a cubical box
of some dull metal. Enclosed on all six sides. Slowly the walls of the
box began to contract in on him . . .

He was trapped. He was surrounded on all six sides.

But in *this* space, a cube did not have six sides, it had *thirty-six*.

He did a thing that strained his mind near breaking. He moved
at right angles to all six faces of the contracting cube, simultaneously.

He was out.

And he was a point in a space with no dimensions. He was every
point in the space, since all points coincided.

He was trapped. In a space with no dimensions, there could be
no motion . . .

But *time* existed, and in this place time had three dimensions.

The special point that was Lindstrom wriggled in three temporal dimensions, and became a temporal solid, and thus . . .

He was back in "normal" space-time.

And was whisked into a star-filled blackness . . . But the blazing suns were also the nuclei of the atoms of his body, corresponding, one for one, with each other, macrocosm and microcosm.

He did a thing with his mind for which there are no words, and he was back once more in the featureless chamber . . .

And was transported to even stranger othernesses . . . An infinity of places, dimensions and othernesses for which there are not even the ghosts of concepts.

He felt a strangeness in his mind, a complexity beyond complexity, a revelation of new and unexpected textures in his psyche. Time was flux, space was flux, eternity was a variable.

There came a time when he stood, naked, alone and homesick, on the surface of some far-off planet, looking up at a small star he knew was Sol. He remembered the spaces he had seen—spaces of no dimensions, an infinity of dimensions, spaces that were not spaces, but times.

There *was* a way back to Earth.

He did something with his mind, and the surface of the planet vanished like mist. His body floated in total blackness. He felt it expand and contract rhythmically, from the size of an electron to the size of the universe . . . He caught it in a phase where each of its atoms corresponded to a star in the Galaxy.

Then he let his entire mass slide down the hill of space-time into one of the sun-atoms, the one called "Sol," to one of its electrons called "Earth."

He was back in the chamber.

And he knew the way out.

General Brewster stood outside his tent, staring at the silver dome, and wondering whether it was time to try something else.

"Lindstrom's been in there two days," he said to a nervous-looking colonel. "I think we can assume that whatever happened to the others happened to him."

"What now, sir?"

"I don't know . . . I just don't know. I suppose we could try to blow the thing open, but—"

A man suddenly appeared out of nowhere. He was standing

just outside the dome. He was a wiry man, not short, not tall . . .

"What—it's Lindstrom."

The being that had been Bert Lindstrom began to walk slowly toward the tent. It had two arms, two legs, two eyes, a nose, a mouth. It was, in fact, the perfect image of the man who had entered the dome.

But when Lindstrom was close enough for Brewster to see into his eyes, the general was dreadfully sure that the creature facing him was something other than human.

Dead End

Willy Carson woke up at nine o'clock for no particular reason. But then, there was no particular reason to wake up at any other time, either.

He lay alone in bed for long minutes, feeling the familiar waking-up semi-nausea, feeling, as usual, unable to get up and unwilling to stay in bed. He sighed and reached for the blue pack of cigarettes on the night table. They were marijuana, not tobacco —the government had legalized marijuana in '88, two years after they had legalized prostitution . . . or had prostitution been legalized in '87? Well, what the hell did it matter?

He smoked his usual one cigarette quickly. These days, one was just about enough to get him barely high, sort of hollow and resonant like the first stages of a good beer drunk. He knew that if he smoked much more, it would quickly make him maudlin, and he had had more than enough of *that*.

But the one cigarette was enough to get him out of bed. Just barely.

He dressed quickly, stumbling here and there over his easel, his photoenlarger, his potter's wheel, the assorted odds and ends of dozens of abortive hobbies that littered the bedroom. The bachelor apartment had only three rooms: kitchen-dining room, living room and bedroom. There was no room for all the junk in the kitchen, for some reason he had a compulsion to keep the living room neat, and so the bedroom did double-duty as storeroom by default.

Awakened fully by the motion of dressing, Willy went into the bathroom, rubbed Depilo on his stubble, washed the Depilo and beard off, and combed his thinning hair diffidently.

He went into the kitchen and punched out his usual breakfast on the Autostove—grapefruit, three fried eggs, sausage, toast, coffee. As usual, he swore to go on a diet—next week.

He ate quickly and joylessly, shoved the plastic dishes into the Disposall, and slumped torpidly back in his chair.

Now what? he thought.

For a whole year after he had lost his job, Willy had spent at least five mornings a week looking for work. After all, he had reasoned, I'm a Master Draftsman with a junior college degree, as good a draftsman as there is.

It took him a whole year to finally accept what he had known from the beginning—there just were no more jobs for draftsmen, Master or otherwise. The Draftmaster was just too good; it could do anything a human draftsman could do, it could do it quicker, cheaper, and with no errors. *Draftsman* had joined ditchdigger, machinist, longshoreman, telephone operator, bookkeeper, accountant, pilot, and God-knows-what-else in the ever-growing list of extinct occupations.

Willy had joined the burgeoning ranks of the unemployed and unemployable.

Permanently.

Now what?

He dragged himself out of the kitchen and into the living room. He stared bleakly for a moment at the hi-fi, at the huge cabinet full of records that he hardly ever listened to any more. Resignedly, he flopped down on the couch in front of the huge television screen that was one entire wall of the living room.

"On," he muttered at the T.V.

Instantly, the television screen came to huge, full-colored, jabbering life. It was the morning news.

". . . this increase in the suicide rate is not statistically significant, President Michaelson declared," said the bland, optimistic, not-quite-smiling announcer.

"And now, turning to the world of sports. Only one midweek football game yesterday: New York swamped Cleveland, thirty-eight to fourteen. At the Municipal Arena, up-and-coming young Jackson Davis scored a smashing victory over the veteran Blackie Munroe, two hundred forty-three to one hundred seven. Davis swept boxing, wrestling, judo, medieval swordsmanship, knives and free-for-all. Davis' manager, Lefty Paccelli, is now talking

about a shot at the champion. The champion's manager was inter-
viewed after the match by Bill Faber, WKA-TV Arena reporter—"

"Four," grunted Willy Carson.

Obediently, the television set changed channels.

Picture of a man staggering out of bed, gulping a pill. Then a
cut to the same man turning up his nose at a mouth-watering breakfast.

"Friend," cooed a syrupy voice, "is your present wake-up pill
ruining your appetite? Do you find yourself turning up your nose
at breakfast? Then *you* need Dexayum, the *only* wake-up pill
with an appetite arouser—"

"Drop dead!" grunted Willy.

". . . guaranteed to keep you awake for twelve hours, without
loss of appetite, or your—"

"Off! Off! Off!" Willy shouted the keyword.

The television set shut itself off.

"Five lousy years . . ." Willy muttered. "Five lousy
years. . . ."

Five years, he thought. Five years of collecting $175 a week in
Basic Citizen's Stipend. "B.C.S." Born, collect, stagnate.

How many people were living off B.C.S. now? Willy wondered.
Last figure he remembered hearing was eighty-nine million. By
now, it was probably over a hundred million. Who knew? Who
bothered with the news? What was the point?

Christ! he thought, I'd do *anything* to be working again. Dig
ditches. Shovel manure. Clean toilets.

Fat chance.

When you were automated out of your job, you were out of the
work force. *Period.* The only conceivable direction you could go to
get another job was *up.* You couldn't settle for a less-skilled job,
because such jobs just didn't exist anymore.

And while there were dozens of retraining programs, they were
really just a bunch of sick jokes. Because everyone got as much
education as he could take before he was permitted to add himself
to the Potential Work Force in the first place. You only got a job,
if you qualified for one, after you had reached your education
limit. Which meant that when your job was automated out, you
really couldn't retrain, because you had already had all the training
you could possibly absorb.

So you went on B.C.S. Nobody ever got off B.C.S. It was a dead end. Born. Collect. Stagnate. The world was full of dead ends.

Oh, you were taken care of, and royally. Rent was free. Food was free. Medical care was free. Most of the $175 a week went for entertainment, hobbies, liquor, drugs . . . anything to fill the emptiness, eat up the hours.

But nothing could.

Your marriage blew up in your face. How could two people live together, twenty-four hours every single day, with nothing at all to do but stare stupidly at each other?

Love turned to boredom. Boredom turned to disgust. Disgust turned to hate.

And then you were alone.

Alone with your whole life in front of you. Your whole stupid, empty, meaningless life. . . .

"Damn!" Willy muttered. "Damn! Damn! Damn!"

There were no more idiotic hobbies left to try. There were no drugs that could give life meaning. Television was meaningless images and sounds. Food tasted like sawdust. All the psychoanalysts in the world couldn't adjust a man to living in a vacuum.

Dead end. Dead, dead, dead end.

Once again, Willy found himself thinking about joining a Gang. But the thought only filled him with self-loathing. Once, two years ago, he had even gone so far as to try it. . . .

Most of the men and women in the Gangs had never had a job in their lives. They joined a Gang as kids, and with nothing to take its place, they stayed in the Gang. Middle-aged juvenile delinquents. Just last week, they had arrested twenty people for stomping a man to death.

Eight of them were "students." Seven were middle-aged men collecting B.C.S.

And the other five were collecting Senior Citizen's Stipend. Kill-crazy kids at sixty-plus.

Willy knew that killing had no meaning for him. Just another stupid dead end.

Willy got up. He stood there, immobile, in the middle of the living room, not wanting to stay in the apartment for another moment, but not having anyplace to go, either.

Once again, he toyed with the idea of suicide. Certainly, it was becoming more and more popular. But suicide was just another dead end. Death . . . well, what was death? Only more of the same . . . more *nothing*. Complete nothing. Not very much different, really, from the life he was living. Death was an escape from suffering, but there was no suffering on B.C.S. No pleasure, no pain, no change, no nothing. . . .

He suddenly realized that he might welcome a little suffering. Pain was at least feeling *something*. If you felt pain, at least you had something to look forward to—the time when your suffering would end.

But pain had been abolished, too. . . .

Willy grimaced bleakly. Pain . . . maybe that was it? Maybe if I could just feel a little suffering, he thought despairingly. Maybe then I'd have something to look forward to. Yeah, maybe if I could find a way to suffer. . . .

It wasn't much, but at least it was a purpose. Forlorn, but determined, Willy Carson went forth in search of suffering.

As Willy Carson stood uncertainly on a midtown street, he dully realized that suffering, other than sheer self-torture, was a mighty scarce commodity. Hunger was impossible—food was universally free. You couldn't give your worldly possessions to the poor, for there were no poor. You couldn't lead a life of self-sacrifice; there was no one who needed your sacrifice. . . .

Hordes of well-fed, well-clothed, well-housed people swirled slowly about Willy. There was no hustle, no rushing, for no one had anything very urgent to do. A benign sun shone down on the spotless city through the illusive shimmer of the Climatescreen. Climate control had eliminated even unpleasant weather.

Willy did not have the faintest idea of where to find suffering. Unless. . . .

The Wilderness! The Middle American Wilderness Area. . . . A hundred square miles of carefully preserved natural terrain. No Autostoves there. No Climatescreen. No rent-free apartments. No nothing.

Feeling an approximation of excitement for the first time in years, Willy raced to the nearest stripway. He boarded the moving strip and made his way to the middle express lane.

The border of the Wilderness Area was less than an hour away by express stripway. In an hour, he would be in the Wilderness

Area, away from B.C.S., away from civilization, away from *every-thing*. . . .

The border of the Middle American Wilderness Area was a steel wall ten feet high and stretching beyond the horizon in either direction.

The stripway deposited Willy by an entrance to the Wilderness Area. The entrance was a plain metal door in the wall. On the left side of the door was a speaker-grill; on the right was a small slot in the wall.

Willy walked up to the door and tried to open it. It was shut tight.

"Welcome to the Middle American Wilderness Area," said a flat mechanical voice coming from the speaker-grill. "One hundred square miles of pure natural countryside provided by your government for the enjoyment of the citizen."

There was a metallic click, and something dropped into the slot to the right of the door. Willy went over and picked it up. It was a small metal bracelet with a red button set in its center like a jewel. It was hinged in two places so that it could be clamped over the wrist and fastened by a handcuff-like clasp at the bottom.

"You will find your Safetybracelet in the right-hand slot," said the speaker-grill. "Put it around your wrist and close it. It will remain locked around your wrist until you leave the Middle American Wilderness Area. It contains a small radio transmitter. This safety device insures that the citizen will suffer no discomfort in the Wilderness Area. Should you suffer discomfort, or should you become lost, merely press the red button on the Safety-bracelet, and a Retrieval Robot will immediately be summoned to your aid."

"But I don't want this thing!" Willy shouted at the speaker-grill. "I want to be on my own. Open the door!"

But of course, the entrance was pre-programmed and deaf.

"The entrance to the Wilderness Area will be opened as soon as the clasp of the Safetybracelet is locked around your wrist. This is to insure that no citizen wanders into the Wilderness Area unprotected. Have a pleasant stay!"

Willy cursed the unhearing mechanism. What the hell, he finally thought, nobody says I *have* to press the button, do they?

He put on the Safetybracelet. Instantly, the door opened.

Willy Carson stepped through into the Middle American Wilderness Area. The door closed behind him.

Rolling green hills studded with woods stretched before him as far as the eye could see. The only visible metal was the wall behind him and the bracelet on his wrist.

Willy inhaled the open country air. All the old books had promised that the wild, free country air would somehow be cleaner, tastier than the air of the cities. But Willy was disappointed. There just was no difference in the air of the Wilderness Area. Those books had been written in the days before Climatecontrol, in the days when cities were filled with smog, industrial wastes and gasoline fumes. Now the air in the cities was as fresh and pure as any country air, which of course meant that the country air was no more zestful than the air of the cities.

Willy suddenly had a vision of a man running carefree and laughing through green fields. Even though he recognized it as part of a television commercial, here he was, and there was the green open countryside. . . .

He began to run. He ran about twenty yards into the Wilderness Area, stumbling over roots, little rocks, clumps of weeds. Thirty yards, and he was panting heavily. Forty, and his legs began to feel leaden and disembodied. Fifty, and a sharp pain began in his lungs.

He flopped down heavily in the grass, lying on his back and panting.

Boy, am I out of shape! he thought. He tried to remember a time when he had been in shape, but he could not. Well, what the hell, who *was* in shape these days? Only a few professional athletes. What was the point in physical strength when there was no such thing as manual labor anymore, when there were stripways to take you anywhere you wanted to go?

Now that he was catching his breath, Willy became aware of the myriad little pebbles, lumps and indentations in the ground he was lying on. It was not very comfortable, certainly not as comfortable as the couch in his apartment.

He scrambled to his feet, brushing himself off. He noticed in annoyance that his shirt was marked with green grass stains, his pants soiled with brown earth.

"Damn!" he muttered. "There goes a good shirt and a good pair of pants!"

Still annoyed at his soiled clothing, he began walking farther away from the wall towards the nearest clump of woods.

It was dark and damp and rather cool in the woods. In fact, it was downright chilly. Willy wished he had thought to bring a jacket along. But then, who ever bothered with jackets in Climate-screened cities?

Shivering slightly, he looked about. There were trees and bushes and a little half-dried-up stream. There were rocks sweating moisture, and there were rocks with green moss growing on them. There was damp brown earth and patches of rotting dead leaves. A few birds sang in the trees. There was silence, lots and lots of silence, more silence than Willy ever remembered experiencing. It was so quiet you could hear it.

So this is a wilderness . . . Willy thought. Woods . . . grass . . . quiet. . . .

Now what?

There was no ready answer to the question. He was alone in the woods. No television, no hi-fi, no Arena to go to, no nothing.

So what do you do in the woods? Willy thought awkwardly.

Idly, he began to walk, aimlessly, deeper into the woods. It really *was* chilly. Best to keep moving.

Willy just kept walking. What else was there to do, really? He walked on and on, listening to the birds, looking at trees and rocks and bushes, bushes, rocks and trees. He found that he could really feel nothing but boredom.

He remembered some of the books he had read, that month or so when he had decided that the thing to do was read. Those jerks had written all kinds of stuff about the beauty of nature, how wonderful it was to be alone with the trees and the grass and the animals. Come to think of it, he thought, I haven't seen any animals at all, except for a few lousy birds.

Big deal. Birds. Trees. Grass. Rocks. So what?

Well, at least I'm free out here, he told himself. Yeah, that's it, *freedom!*

I'm free! I'm free to . . . to . . . to do *what?* Just *free,* I guess.

Some of those writers made a big deal about being free, too. But what in hell were they talking about, really?

I guess freedom means not having to do anything you don't want to do, he mused.

But hell, he thought, who does? Who has to do anything he doesn't want to do? Not on B.C.S. You never have to do anything you don't want to do. . . .

Well then, maybe it's more than that. Maybe freedom is being able to do what you *do* want to do.

So what do I want to do? That's easy! Willy thought bitterly. I want a job. I want to work. And that's the one thing in the world I *can't* do. I can't do it in the city, and I can't do it here either. . . .

As he walked on, Willy was becoming less and less concerned with abstract musings, and more and more aware of something much more prosaic—it was time for lunch. He was beginning to get hungry. Damn, he thought, now why didn't I think to bring some food along?

He eyed the red button on the Safetybracelet. I can always call for the Retrieval Robot, he thought. It'd probably even have some food along with it, just in case. . . .

"No!" he shouted. "That's not what I came out here for!"

Okay Willy, he told himself, so you're hungry. Isn't that what you wanted in the first place? To *feel* something for a change?

So now you *do* feel something. You feel hungry. Do you good!

Now Willy had something to do, something meaningful—get some food.

So how do you get food in the woods? he wondered. Kill a rabbit or something, I suppose.

But he hadn't seen a rabbit or anything else. And how do you kill a rabbit? Hit it with a rock, maybe?

Willy realized that he had never killed anything in his life, and that he did not have the slightest idea of how to go about doing it, not without a gun. And maybe not *with* a gun, either.

And what would he do with a dead rabbit, even if he had one? Eat it raw?

He didn't think he could ever get *that* hungry. So I'd have to cook it, he thought. Now how do you cook a rabbit?

I guess you just spit it on a piece of wood and roast it over a fire. But how do you build a fire? With self-lighting cigarettes, no one carried matches or a lighter anymore, and how else could you start a fire?

Well, hunting sure is out! he thought.

And now he was *really* getting hungry. Willy hadn't missed a meal as long as he could remember, and he had never been *really* hungry before.

It wasn't the way he had imagined it at all. It was like a big hollow in his guts, and it sort of hurt. It almost really *did* hurt.

And now that he was suffering at last, he found that it didn't make him feel any more alive at all. It was just plain unpleasant.

He stopped walking and once again he considered the red button on the Safetybracelet. It would be the easiest thing in the world to push it. Then he wouldn't have to be hungry anymore. And he didn't *want* to be hungry.

No! No! At least I'll get back to the city on my own!

Yeah, that's it. I'll go back to the entrance. I'll go home and have a good meal.

Now let's see, the wall is . . . *where?*

Willy looked around. He was surrounded by trees and rocks and bushes, bushes, rocks and trees. He couldn't see the wall. He couldn't see the horizon. He couldn't see anything but trees and rocks and bushes.

Where the hell am I? he thought.

He began to walk, faster and faster. He had no idea in which direction the wall was, but he had to get to it! He had to do something! He would *not* press the button! He would make it on his own.

For hours, Willy blundered about in the woods, as his hunger became an ache, then a dull throb, and finally a pain, a real, burning hunger-pang in his stomach.

Willy was hungry. He was hungry and lost and cold and he didn't like it one bit.

"I won't! I won't! I won't!" he muttered continually as he staggered through the woods.

I won't press the button! I'll make it back on my own!

Then it started to rain.

At first it was just the patter of raindrops on the leafy roof of the woods. Then it started to come down harder and harder and harder.

The trees became soaked, and the raindrops began to penetrate the treetops. They began to hit Willy, big, fat, cold raindrops. And the trees began to drop their overload of moisture on him.

Willy, who had lived his life in the protected, Climatecontrolled cities, had never been caught in the rain before. He did not at all enjoy the new experience.

It rained and rained and rained. Willy's clothes became saturated. His hair became wet and matted, and water dripped down his forehead and into his eyebrows. Cold water.

Willy was soaked. It was getting colder.

He sat down on a big, flat rock. The rock was wet. He felt it through the seat of his sodden pants. He was wet, he was cold, he was tired, and he was very hungry.

He was thoroughly miserable.

He was as miserable as he had been back in his apartment, maybe more miserable. There was no meaning in being cold or wet or hungry.

Willy Carson had found suffering. It didn't make him feel any happier at all. It didn't fill any of the empty places in his life. It just made a few new ones.

With a little sighing sob of resignation, he pressed the red button on his Safetybracelet. Soon, very soon, the Retrieval Robot would arrive and take him back to the city.

It would take him back to his apartment, back to his Autostove, his hobbies, his long pointless days and empty nights. Back to the endless, meaningless years that would stretch on and on and on. . . .

But now Willy wanted to go back, back to the same old empty dead end that was his existence. It would be no less empty, no less futile.

But Willy had learned one inevitable, brutal lesson: suffering too, was meaningless, suffering too, was a pointless dead end.

And as he heard the whir of helicopter blades approaching, one forlorn, bitter realization filled his being with final despair:

Pain too, hurt.

A Night in Elf Hill

Dear Fred:

Yeah, it's your brother Spence after all these years, and of course I'm yelling for help. Just spare me the I-told-you-sos and the psychiatrist's pounce. So I'm a black sheep and a miscreant and a neurotic personality. We never could quite stand eachother even when we were kids, and when you became a shrink and I Shipped Out, that really tore it. The reality of inner space versus the escapism of outer space, maturity versus perpetual adolescence, isn't that what you said? Sometimes I think you were born speaking that jargon, and if you'll pardon my saying so, I still think it's horse-hockey.

But the bitch is that now I find myself urgently in need of your brand of horse-hockey. I've got something I've got to tell to somebody, something that's been eating me up for a year, something way over my head. Something you only tell a brother or a shrink —and for all your squareness, Fred, at least you're both.

I suppose I've got you good and confused by now, just like in the bad old days, but I hope I've got you as intrigued as bugged.

Don't go putting things in my mouth, though; I've got no regrets. Seventeen years in space, and I don't regret a minute of it. But you never could understand that. Remember? I'd tell you about the kick of five new planets every year, of a new woman on every one of 'em, of the greener grass just beyond the planet beyond the next one, and what I'd get from you is long lectures on "flight from reality" and "compulsive satyrism." The only reason I'm raking up these tired old coals, *Herr Doktor,* is that it all bears on the problem that I'm going to do my damndest to try and dump in your lap.

Yeah, space is my oyster, always has been, always will be—and that's my only regret. The knowledge that eighteen years of it is all I can ever have.

You know how the time limit on Merchant Service Papers works, or at least you should, since shrinks like you stuck us with the system. When you apply for Papers, they give you a solid week of physical and mental examinations, everything in the book and some things that aren't, and they tell you just how long they figure you can stand the Jumping in and out of sub-space, the accelerations, the pressures, the tensions. They tell you how long, and they put it down on your Papers. This man is certified for eighteen years in space and not a millisecond longer. The moving finger writes, and all that. . . . Actually, I've got no fair reason to complain: eighteen years is Good Time. The average is closer to fifteen.

It's a nice safe system. No one suddenly goes ape and wrecks a ship, like in the bad old days. No spacer, shipping far beyond his endurance, comes home a shattered hulk from Farside Syndrome anymore.

Yeah, a good, safe, secure system. The only thing wrong with it is that you know you have that date hanging over your head, and you know that under the rules the day will come when you start collecting that Mustering Out Pension (a nice piece of change every year as long as you live—even to a high-priced shrink like you, Fred), and get that last free ride to the planet of your choice.

Sure, you think it's a sweet set-up. *You* would. Eighteen years of your life in return for financial security in perpetuity. Why don't you go to Port Kennedy and take a good hard look at all those old men sitting in the sun, living off their nice fat pensions and watching the ships taking off for the stars like one-eyed cats peeping in a seafood store? Old men of thirty-five or forty. Ask *them* if it's such a sweet set-up! How would you like to be put out to pasture when you're forty? After eighteen years, what do you have to live for *but* the next planet? That last free ride back to Earth is the sickest joke there is. It's not for me. In the bad old days, they let you ship out till it killed you, and ask any of the hulks that haunt Port Kennedy if that wasn't the more merciful way.

Man, I'm sure glad this is a letter, because I can all but hear you bellowing "I told you so." What was it you used to call Shipping Out, "A night in Elf Hill"? Where a man goes into the

hall of the elves for one night of partying, and the next day, when
he comes out, a hundred years have passed, and he's an old, old
man and his life is over. . . . I can hear you telling me that I can't
find myself by searching the Galaxy, that I've got to look within,
and now look at you, Spence, you're a hollow shell, a thirty-eight-
year-old adolescent. I can see you shaking your head with infinite
sadness and infinite wisdom, and you should be glad this isn't face-
to-face too, 'cause I'd kick your sanctimonious teeth down your
throat, and you know that I always could lick you.

Suffice it to say that unless you can come up with some pearl
of wisdom from out of your bottomless pit of middle-aged
maturity, and don't get me wrong, Fred, I hope to God you can,
when I'm Mustered Out next year, that last trip won't be back to
Earth. It'll be to Mindalla.

I know, I know, you never heard of Mindalla. Who has? It's
a nothing little planet orbiting a G-4 sun. Colonized about a
century ago. Maybe fifteen million yokums living off a piddling
mining industry on one continent. That's Mindalla. Ten thousand
mudballs just like it scattered all over the Galaxy. But I'm afraid,
really afraid, that unless you can stop me, I'm going back. Going
back to stay.

I made my first planetfall on Mindalla a little over a year ago,
on a freighter from Sidewinder, carrying the kind of cargo we just
don't talk about. Fortunately, it's a big, big Galaxy, and there are
so many planets in it that you never have to go back to a single one,
even if your Papers go all the way to the twenty-year maximum.

And so, I believed at the time, this would be my first and last
visit to Mindalla. I mean, when you've been in space as long as I
have, seen hundreds of cities on hundreds of planets—G'dana,
Hespa, the Ruby Beach of Modow, the whole wild lot—Mindalla
is strictly nowheresville.

The population is small, there's only one town with nerve
enough to call itself a city, the outback has been pretty thoroughly
explored by air, no interesting local beasties, no natives. And the
colony is just not old enough to have really marinated, if you dig,
become decadent enough to appeal to my peculiar tastes. . . .
But let's not get into *that*.

Still, like it or not, I had three days on this mudball, and I knew
from long experience that a planet's just too big a place to be a

total nonentity. That's why I went into space in the first place; that's where it's really at. Not all that crap about "the vast spaces between the stars." Space itself is creation's most total bore. What makes a man Ship Out is just being a kid on Earth, and looking up at all those stars, and knowing that they all own whole worlds, and that each of 'em *is* a world, as full of surprises as Earth was when Adam and his chick got themselves booted out of Eden. I guess that's it—you're got to dig surprises. Man like me *hates* security as much as you love it.

So I knew there had to be *something* for me on Mindalla, a new taste, a new sound, a new woman. A nice surprise. . . .

Well, I wandered from bar to bar, my usual S.O.P., and to make a long, tedious story short, I came up with only two little goodies, and one of 'em seemed to be just a fairy story at first.

But the second concerned the Race With No Name. The Race had left one of its weird ruins on Mindalla.

Even *you* must know about the Race With No Name. Billions of years ago, before Man was even a far-distant gleam in some dinosaur's eye, before the 'Bodas or the Dreers, or any of the other races that are around today ever existed, the Race With No Name owned this Galaxy, from the Center clear to the Magellanic Clouds. A billion years ago, they disappeared, died out, or migrated elsewhere, or God-knows-what, leaving nothing but ruins on thousands of planets. If you can call lumps of some metal that assays out stainless steel but hasn't rusted at all in a billion years "ruins." A lump of the stuff here, a whole mountain of it there, weathered to dust by a billion years of time and wind, twenty or so Artifacts that no one understands, scattered throughout the known Galaxy—the Race With No Name.

But you know that. What you don't know is what the Race means to spacers. It's our own private little nightmare that somewhere, somehow, some of 'em are still around, and that one day we're going to run into them, in sub-space, or some forgotten planet on the Rim. . . . A race a billion years gone, a race that was young when the Galaxy was coalescing, a race that had as much in common with us as we do with worms. . . . A race that we can't be sure doesn't still exist, somewhere. . . .

And the Race With No Name left a few lumps of metal on Mindalla, as they did on thousands of other planets. Nothing unusual. . . . But then there was that local fairy story. . . .

It seems that a few decades ago, a Mindallan who had been a spacer settled down on his pension near something called the Great Swamp. Apparently, he wigged out—was known to rave about someplace in the Swamp that was the "most beautiful city in the Galaxy." Of course, there was no such thing in the Swamp. And one day, he just disappeared and they never found his body. The locals claimed that other men had disappeared into the Great Swamp, but nobody I talked to could name names.

Just the usual crock, eh? But the Race With No Name had left a ruin on Mindalla, and when you added that to the fairy story, you came up with something that smelled of Artifact.

I guess they've found maybe two dozen intact Artifacts of the Race With No Name. I lose count. There's the Solid Hole on Beauchamp, the Time Trap on Flor Del Cielo, the Sub-Space Block on Misty, that horrible thing they haven't even named on Channing, the thing that turns living creatures inside out. . . . No one knows what any of the damned things really are, and I suppose we never will. Maybe I *hope* we never will.

But I got the smell of Artifact on Mindalla. Somewhere in that swamp was . . . *something*. No matter how many men have died, or worse, because of them, I still never heard of a spacer who could resist the lure of discovering an Artifact. Don't ask me why. Why do people pick at scabs, *Herr Doktor?*

So I rented a flitter, bought some tinned food, leased an energy-rifle which everyone assured me was about as necessary as a Conversion Bomb, and set out for the Great Swamp.

The Swamp was where it was supposed to be—about four hundred miles east of the city. "Great Swamp" turned out to be local hyperbole, of course—you could lose it in the Everglades.

I set the flitter down in a clearing near the center of the Swamp. The clearing was ringed with trees—something between palms and mangroves: gnarled, ringed trunks, big, bright-green, feathery leaves. The ground was coal-black, the way it sometimes is around a volcano on Earth, only here it was soggy, half-mud, interlaced with hundreds of sluggish little streams. In short, a swamp.

I put a small radio direction finder in my pocket, turned on the flitter's beacon, hoisted my small pack, slung the energy-rifle over my shoulder and set off rather noisily to get the lay of the land.

One weird thing—the trees were lousy with a kind of feathery stuff like Spanish moss, long globs of it hanging everywhere. It was a deep, deep red, and it gave you the feeling that you were walking through perpetual sunset. Kind of eerie, maybe, but also sort of soothing.

Quite a few critters around—ugly little lumpy fish like mudpuppies in the streams, small six-legged blue lizards all over the place, octopoid things swinging in the trees by their tentacles like monkeys—but nothing big enough to worry about, even without the rifle.

Actually, I suppose you'd go for the place—you always were a nature nut, and this swamp had what you'd call atmosphere, what with that red moss all over everything and the black soil, and those octopoids in the trees, covered with a golden fuzz and gabbling like turkeys. Now you know me, Fred, I'm strictly a city boy, my idea of beauty is Greater New York, or Bay City, or Riallo. But I must admit that I sort of dug the place. It put me at ease, it even smelled kind of sweet and musky as I went deeper into it.

And of course, that's when I should've started to sweat. I don't care how tame a planet is, it just shouldn't *seem* harmless if it isn't Earth. Every planet is different from every other in thousands of ways, and at least *one* of those differences should be the kind that makes a man look behind him. Besides, every other extraterrestrial swamp I've ever seen stank like an open cesspool.

Well I must've just wandered around for hours before I felt . . . How can I describe it? A kind of scratchy shiver in my head, like running a broken fingernail down a piece of slate. An awful feeling, but it just came and went in a moment, and all of a sudden, things got kind of dreamy-like.

The moss seemed to get thicker, the light richer, heavier. And all of a sudden, the air was full of tiny, neon-colored birds, no bigger than beetles, like a whole aquarium full of flying tropical fish, and they almost seemed to be whistling in harmony.

I went on in a kind of daze, and that scratchy feeling came and went again, and a very funny thing happened. I found myself remembering all kinds of things: women I had known, the taste of Blandi wine and fried prawns, the smell of Shondor aphrofume, the sun flashing on the Ruby Beach, the carnival feel of Riallo. . . . Good things, a whole lifefull of good things, all whipping through my mind like someone had recorded the best moments of my life on tape and was playing the whole tape back, a hundred times normal speed.

It was like being high on mescal and bhang and duprish all at once, and I got flashes of *that* too, I mean memories of what being high was really like, mixed in with the rest of it.

I forgot everything—the reason I was in the Swamp, the fact that I had to be back on the ship in two days, even my depression at my impending Mustering Out. I just wandered around reliving the best moments of my life at breakneck speed.

And then I felt that awful, nerve-tingling feeling again, stronger this time. It seemed to last for hours, and then it was gone again, and. . . .

I was standing on top of a little hill. And there below me, where it just couldn't possibly be, was a city. *The* city. The city the Mindallan spacer had raved about. And he had been dead right. It *was* the most beautiful place in the Galaxy.

I've seen a thousand cities on hundreds of planets. I've seen Riallo on Topaz which makes Greater New York look like a dirty little milltown. Fred, this place made Riallo look like a cluster of mud huts.

Translucent towers of emerald a mile high, piercing the clouds like artificial mountains, hundreds of them, and the streets of the city wound around their feet, streets jammed with buildings from a hundred planets and cultures—Argolian force-pavillions, mosques, Boharaanan fhars, skyscrapers, stadia, ziggurats—all shimmering and flickering in the ever-changing light that seemed to come from the towers, that made the sky above the city a great rainbow aurora.

A river separated the foot of my hill from the city. A bridge crossed the river, and a road crossed the bridge. The road was a ribbon of burnished silver. The bridge was a single, arching, dazzling living crystal that might've been diamond. The river was a flow of liquid gold.

The Capital city of the Universe. Utterly stupifying, utterly impossible . . . and yet, I had that, what do you call it, *déjà vu* feeling that I had somehow seen it before.

What can I say, Fred? I must've been out of my head. It couldn't be there, but it was, and I couldn't even think of all the impossibilities of the situation, the sheer insanity of it all. I ran down that hill like a sex-starved hermit towards a Mexican border town, down the silver road, across the diamond bridge, and I was *there*, totally *there*.

Ever been in Rio at the height of Carnival? Ever spent Mardi Gras in Old New Orleans? Ever heard of how Riallo becomes one great citywide party on Settling Day Eve? Well triple that. Raise it to its own power, take a big drag of opium, and man, you won't even come close.

It just sucked me in—*whoosh!* The streets were simply boiling with people and beings. Golden Women from Topaz, tall green Jungle Masters from Mizzan, Steppenvolke from Siegfried dressed in clinging mirror-suits, lemur-faced Cheeringbodas, women with their hair piled into nests for shimmering Grellan Glass Butterflies. . . . Beings from a thousand planets, all babbling, laughing. . . . Carnival sounds; laughter, singing, music. Carnival smells; perfume, frying food, hashish smoke, wine, women.

I felt as if I had stepped into the Arabian Nights. Any minute, a flying carpet might float by. I felt as if I had been searching for this place, this huge Carnival, this moment in time, all my life. I wanted to laugh and scream and cry.

And then I felt that itching in my mind again, and I saw *her* coming towards me, straight towards me through that packed throng.

She was wearing those now-opaque, now-transparent golden robes from Topaz. She was almost my height, had exotic oriental features but bone-white skin. Luminous emerald hair cascaded onto her shoulders. She had a slim-but-full body, and through a momentary transparency in her robes, I saw that her nipples were an impossible blood-red, matching the color of her small, full lips.

She was like no woman anyone had ever seen, and yet as she stood before me, I had that uncanny *déjà vu* feeling again. I knew her, but from where? Ridiculous! How could any man forget a woman like *this?*

She touched my hand, and a thrill went through me like a jolt from a Pleasurebox. *"Hello,"* she said, and the sound of her voice turned my knees to jello. "I've been waiting for you. We've all been waiting, a long, long time. Just for you. Come! Come join the carnival!"

"What . . . ? Uh . . . ? How . . . ?" I stammered like some poleaxed yokum. *Me,* Fred, old Supercharged Spence!

She laughed, reached up, curled her hands around my neck and kissed me. Her mouth was warm and open, and the taste of her breath made me forget everything. I moved my body against her, asking *the* question, and she answered me with a counter-pressure that was more than a compliance, more certain than an open invitation.

She snaked her hands down my neck, over my shoulders, across my chest, and took both my hands in hers. She nodded towards the choked, swirling streets. "Come on," she said. "The best night of your life is waiting for you, and the darkness is just beginning."

"How long . . . ? How long does all this go on?" I somehow managed to say.

She laughed, a long, wild laugh that made me burn and made me shiver. "Forever!" she cried maniacally. "For you, this can be the night that lasts forever!"

And before I could say a word, before I could tell whether I was eager or afraid, she tugged at my hands, and we were off into the carnivaling city together.

It was dusk—I don't know what time it was by the revolution of Mindalla, but in that impossible city it was a winey, misty, red dusk, and dusk it remained as long as I stayed there, a heady night that always seemed about to fall.

She led me through the streets, through the laughing, packed streets, past knots of humans and 'Bodas and Dreers, open stands offering food and wine and drugs from all over the Galaxy, and finally into . . . a house? a room? a place?

A great round hall, the "walls" a circle of marble columns, past which I caught glimpses of other halls, and rooms, and passageways beyond, that seemed to go on and on and on, a labyrinth of rooms and hallways packed with people and beings and tables bearing food and drink, an endless, continuous party that wound through the hall, and the rooms beyond, and perhaps the entire city, without limits, without end.

We ate from tables piled with the delicacies of scores of cultures, dozens of worlds: caviar, mulgish, roast boar, shar-shu-ding, pilaf, cheeses, cakes, breads, majoun. . . . And strangely, my hunger, though never sharp, lasted through it all, through a feast that seemed to go on for hours.

We drifted from crowded room to packed courtyard. A dark chamber where naked women danced to the pounding beat of African drums. . . . An open court by the golden river where we sat on white sands, inhaling *moutar* from Topaz, and watched the

Golden Ones do their insidious Water Dance. . . . A neon-lit
room where weirdly-dressed kids danced to the music of an ancient Terran rock band. . . .

The amorphous building seemed to be the city itself, and the
city was one wild carnival of food and music and dancing, swirling, laughing, and completely carrying me away. It seemed that I
had but to think of something—a certain food, a wine I remembered, a music I had heard of, and it was *there,* anything I ever
wanted, ever could want.

And when the time came when there was only *one* more thing
I wanted, we turned a corner, stepped through a doorway,
and. . . .

We were suddenly alone. We were floating in a dark chamber,
floating in nothing at all. A velvet, buoying nothing, softer, somehow than free-fall itself. She threw aside her robes, and all at once
her body seemed to glow with a warm, golden light. She plucked
at my clothes, and then I was naked too, and my body was glowing from within like hers.

When we made love, it seemed as if we were alone in the whole
universe, the light of our bodies the only light there was. She was
perfect . . . and I was *better.* You know me, Fred, so you know
what I mean when I say it was the best I had ever had, and the
best I had ever been. It made me forget every woman I had ever
known.

And afterward, I wasn't tired at all—I was full of vitamins and
ready for another night of partying. So we laughed and kissed,
and it was back to that endless, fantastic party.

And this time around, I felt that the eyes of every woman there
were on me. Ever have that feeling? I suppose *you* never have,
Fred. But I felt like the cock of the walk; I somehow knew that
any woman there I wanted would be mine, and glad to be of service. But it only made me eager for another go at the chick with
the white, white skin and the green hair. I somehow knew that I
would have plenty of time to sample the rest of them, all the time
in the world. . . .

So the spirit moved me again, and we were alone again. We
swam nude in a pool of golden water heated to blood-heat under
a huge silver moon (on moonless Mindalla), and then we
stretched out on a lawn of bright green grass while a warm, per-

fumed breeze swiftly dried our bodies. I reached out, touched one perfect breast. . . .

"Spence . . ." she moaned.

It brought me short. I suddenly went cold. I had never told her my name. That one impossibility somehow reminded me that I was in the middle of a swamp, a swamp where there *was* no city, where. . . . I was afraid, furious and afraid.

I pulled my hand away. "Who are you?" I snapped. "What is—?"

She leaned toward me, kissed me, and the question seemed stupid, trivial. . . .

But something in me was still fighting it. I shoved her away. "What the hell is all this? What's going on here?"

She looked at me, a strange, pleading look in her eyes. She laughed a wicked, sensual laugh. "Do you *really* have to know?" she sighed.

But I wasn't buying. *Something* was being done to me, and I had to know what.

"Tell me!" I roared. "Tell me or—"

She began to cry, wilt, whimper. I felt like a heartless monster. "If you insist . . ." she said, "I've got to tell you. But don't insist —take my word for it, Spence, you won't like what you hear. What do you care what we are, where you are? Look around you, smell the air, hear the music, touch my body. Do you want to lose all this? Can any place be like this for you again? Will you ever have another night like this, ever, ever?"

I felt a terrible, aching sadness. I knew she was right, knew that this moment, right now, this night and no other, past or future was the best I could ever know. I was a spacer with less than two years left on my Papers, and suddenly I felt like an old, old man—from this moment, the rest of my life could only be a long, gray downhill slide to nothingness.

"It doesn't have to be," she said, as if reading my mind. "This moment, this night, this place, this carnival, never has to end. Not for you. Forever, Spence. It can last forever, and forever is a long, long time. . . ."

"Tell me!" I screamed, shaking her shoulders, driven by some savage compulsion, perhaps the knowledge that I was being offered something that in another moment I would be powerless to resist.

Suddenly, a terrible pain sheered through my head, and the city, the pool, *her,* flickered for a moment and were gone.

I was lying on the moist black swamp earth. I was dressed. My clothes were clammy, my stomach ached with hunger. It was night.

And I was alone.

Then I heard a voice in my mind, a cold, chitinous voice like a million crabs clicking their claws in my head. "A billion years," the voice said, and the very sound, the sandpaper feel of it, filled me with dread. "A billion years is a long time to be alone, unused, discarded like a broken toy."

"Who . . . what are you? Her . . . ? The city . . . ?"

"You . . ." the voice in my mind rasped. "Mostly you, a little of me. I looked into your mind, read your memories, your desires, things you didn't even know yourself, and I gave it to you. What you wanted, what you *really* wanted. It was easy. That's what I was . . . *made* for doing. A billion years ago."

"All an illusion?" I stammered. "Just a reflection of my dreams?"

The voice laughed, a hideous, crawling mental sound that set every nerve in my body screaming. "You underestimate the subtlety of the Masters," the voice said. "Those you call the Race With No Name. No mere wish-fulfillment for them. Every world in this Galaxy was theirs, but it was not enough for *them.* They craved new worlds, subjective worlds, worlds that lived and breathed and reflected their private whims, but worlds that were still apart from their minds, worlds that held surprises for their dirty, jaded minds. None of them mere dreams, but none of them real."

"But you . . . you're real! You're talking to me now!"

"I'm real," the voice said, words dripping sour acid. "You would call me an . . . *Artifact*. They created me out of metal and force . . . and things you could never understand. They gave me the power to read the innermost thoughts and desires of all sentient beings, the power to spin dreams, beautiful dreams without end. A toy, just a toy. But they wanted more, they wanted passion. So they made me sentient, a living, caring thing, a thing with a will and only one motivation—the passion to please a sentient being, any sentient being. And then, a billion years ago, they left for I know not where, and they left me here to rot, flung aside when they no longer were amused by their toy. They left me here to rot and suffer and yearn to please a sentient being. For a billion years, a billion empty years till humans came to this planet."

I shivered in the warm night, felt monstrous things staring at me from out of the black, black night, from out of the unthinkable, distant past.

"But . . . you're not a woman?" I said.

"I can give you every woman you could ever learn to want," the voice said.

"I . . . I want to see you. . . ." I stammered.

"I cannot disobey the order of a sentient being," the voice said. "No matter how much I want to. . . ."

There was a movement in the trees, and I saw a dark shape, a slithering, metallic thing, a lump of darkness blacker than the night. . . . A wet sound. . . . A cold, cold wind across my face, a vortex of . . . of something my eyes could not focus on. I felt myself falling into a black, black pool, eaten alive by green squamous things. . . .

I screamed and screamed and screamed.

And all at once, I was standing in the middle of the diamond bridge, and *she* was standing before me.

"I can't keep you from going," she said. She kissed me and gestured toward the great emerald spires, the carnival that went on and on and on. . . .

"All yours, Spence," she said. "Your own private heaven. A universe all for you, a universe that was made for you. Think of it—being made love to by a whole universe. A night of pleasure that never ends. Forever, Spence, a special kind of forever."

"What . . . what kind of forever?"

She laughed, touched me lightly on the lips. "What does it matter?" she said. "A second, an hour, a day, a year, a billion years. If it *seems* like forever, it *is* forever, isn't it, Spence? And I can make it seem like forever. You know I can. I can't keep you from going . . . but can *you* keep you from coming back?"

Then she was gone, and the city was gone, and I was alone in the silence of the Swamp. I stumbled forward a few steps, and my feet clattered against something in the dark, something hard and round. I reached down, touched it, and pulled my hand back.

It was a skull. A human skull. I remembered the Mindallan

spacer, and I felt the gnawing hunger in my guts, and I remembered that in the city I had eaten and eaten and eaten. . . .

What kind of forever?

Now you know why I'm writing to you, Fred. Soon my Papers will expire, and I'll have to pick one lousy planet out of a whole Galaxy on which to spend the rest of my life . . . thirty, forty, fifty years of . . . of nothing. Or a whole universe that can be mine for a day or a week or a year that will seem like forever.

Please Fred, talk me out of it! Say something, anything, that will make it seem wrong. But make it good, brother mine, make it good. Say something, anything, that will keep me from going back to Mindalla.

Spence

Deathwatch

The old man's breathing was shallow now, dry and brittle, each breath an effort of no little significance. His head rested on the pillow like a dried and shriveled nut on a napkin.

The man standing at the foot of the bed stared impassively into indefinite space. His strong, unlined face showed no emotion—though there was a strange look, indeed, about his eyes, a deep, ageless resignation that seemed grossly out of place on a face that could be no more than twenty-five.

The woman leaning her head on his shoulder had long, thick, honey-colored hair framing a young face wet with tears. Now and then a sob would wrack her body, and the man would stroke her hair with near-mechanical tenderness. He would pass his tongue slowly over his lips as if searching for words of comfort.

But there were no words and there was no comfort. The only sound in the room was the rasping breath of the old man in the bed sighing the dregs of his life away . . .

He smiled happily at his wife as she cuddled the newborn baby in her arms. He was, like all babies to all parents, a beautiful baby: weight, nine pounds; skin, ruddy; voice, excellent.

A son, he thought. *My* son. Secretly, he was relieved. While the doctors had assured them that there was no reason in the world why they could not have children, he had always had that inane, irrational feeling that he would never really be able to *know* that it was true until this moment, when he could actually reach out and touch his son.

He chucked the baby under the chin, and it cooed satisfactorily. All was right with the world . . .

Until a half hour later, when the doctor told him the truth about his child. The invisible but inescapable truth.

It took him a while to fully understand. And when he finally did, his first thought was: How will I tell *her?*

To his great relief and mystification, his wife took it better than he did. At least she seemed to. Or was it merely that built-in anesthetic that women seem to have that lets them blot out any tragedy that is far enough in the past or far enough into the indefinite future?

Whatever it was, he was grateful for it. Bad enough for a man to have to look ahead decades into the future and face the inevitable, to have to live with the thought of it long before the reality itself . . .

For a woman, *let her just have her son.*

He was a boy, just like any other boy, wasn't he? Like every other normal boy. He would learn to walk, to talk, to play with other children. He'd probably have the mumps, and maybe chickenpox, too. There'd be good report cards and bad ones, he'd come home with black eyes and skinned knees . . .

Not a monster. A boy like any other boy. A woman could forget. A woman could lose herself in just being a mother.

But for how long could he make himself feel like a father?

The mutation was called immortality, perhaps inaccurately, since it would take forever to know whether it was really possible to live forever.

Nevertheless, men and women began to be born who did not grow old and die.

Not that they were invulnerable; they simply did not age. A balance was struck in their systems at about the age of twenty, and from that age on, the body renewed itself; nervous system, circulatory system, endocrine system, digestive system—all retained their youthful vigor indefinitely.

They were not supermen. They could succumb to the usual diseases. They were just as prone to accidents as other men. They were neither better nor wiser. The mutation, like most other successful mutations, was a narrow one—it produced otherwise ordinary human beings who would not age.

The why of the mutation was, of course, one of those basically unanswerable riddles of evolution. Why do men have no tails? Why do birds have wings? Why intelligence itself?

Immortality was just one more in nature's endless series of experiments. Like all the others, it was, in itself, neither a gift nor a curse. It was whatever men would make of it.

And what it would make of men.

He tried earnestly to be a good father. He was not gruff with his son—if anything, he was too gentle, for he could not look at that boyish face without a pang of regret, without a feeling of sadness.

He did try his best. He tried to be a companion to his son: fishing trips, camping, games—they did the usual father-son things together. And later on, he tried to be his son's confidant, to share his dreams and yearnings and trials. He tried as few fathers try.

But it all fell flat.

Because it was all mechanical, it was all hypocritical. For there was one thing he could not bring himself to try, there was one thing he could not bear.

He could not let himself love his son.

And though he would scarcely admit it, even to himself, he was relieved when his son graduated from college and took a job 3000 miles away across the continent. It was as if half of a great weight were lifted from his shoulders; as if a dagger that had been hanging directly over his head had been moved across the room.

His wife took it like all mothers take it—it hurt to have a continent between her son and herself, but the hurt would grow numb with time . . .

The immortality mutation bred true. It would be passed along from generation to generation like any other dominant gene. Two immortals could produce immortal children, just as two dark-haired people produce dark-haired children.

The immortals would breed as fast as ordinary men, and since youth and potency would be theirs forever, they would be able to produce an unlimited number of offspring in their millennial life spans.

Since the immortals, in the long run, could easily outbreed mortals, the entire human race would someday be heir to the gift of immortality. In the long run.

In the short run . . .

Their son wrote home, and when he did, the answering letters were invariably written by his mother and countersigned, unread, by his father.

There were trips home every year or so, visits that his mother waited eagerly for and that his father dreaded. There was no hostility between father and son, but there was no warmth either—neither genuine pleasure at meeting nor sorrow at parting . . .

He knew that he had closed his son out of his heart. It was a cold, calculating thing to do. He knew that, too.

But he knew that he *had* to do it, for the sake of his own sanity, to be a rock that his wife could lean on . . .

It was a sacrifice, and it was not without its cost. Something within him seemed to shrivel and die. Pity, compassion, love, became academic, ersatz emotions to him. They could not move him—it was as if they were being described to him by somebody else.

And occasionally he found himself lying awake next to his sleeping wife, in the loneliest hours of the night, and wishing that he could cry at least one real tear.

Just one . . .

The laws of genetics are statistical—the coldest form of mathematics. A dominant gene, like the immortality gene, breeds more or less true. Immortality was dominant, death was becoming recessive.

But recessive does not necessarily mean extinct.

Every so often—and the frequency may be calculated by the laws of genetics—two dark-haired people produce a blond, two healthy people a diabetic, two ordinary people a genius or an immortal, two immortals . . .

The old man's breath was stilled now. His heart gave one last futile flutter and gave up the fight.

Now there were only two lives in the room, two lives that would go on and on and on and on . . .

The man searched his heart futilely for some hint of genuine pain, some real and human emotion beyond the bitterness that weighed him down. But it was an old bitterness, the bitterness between father and son that was the fault of neither . . .

The woman left his side and tenderly, with the tears streaming down her creamy cheeks, she stroked the white mane of the dead old man.

With a trembling sob, she pressed her soft smooth skin against the wrinkled leather of his cheek.

And, finally, after long cold decades, a dam within her husband burst, and the torrent of sternly suppressed love and sorrow flooded the lowlands of his soul.

Two lone and perfect tears escaped his still-impassive eyes as he watched his wife touch her warm young lips to that age-wrecked face.

And kiss their son goodbye.

The Ersatz Ego

My name is Dr. Harvey Sanders. Perhaps you've heard of me. Probably not.

I have never sought publicity. Indeed, I shun it. My work is what counts.

It is not spectacular work. It makes no headlines. Yet, in its way, it is making a profound revolution in this country. Not merely a social revolution, but a revolution in the American psyche itself.

I am a psychiatrist. I adjust men's minds. I adjust them so that they in turn will be able to adjust to social change.

To *any* social change. I make people happy. Happy under virtually any social conditions.

I have all the accepted degrees from all the accepted universities. But I learned how to make men happy in a very special school —let's call it the University of North Korea.

My professor of psychology at this unique institution was a Major Sung ping Lee. Sung ping Lee, as far as I know, did not have any of the accepted degrees from any of the accepted universities. But don't let anyone tell you that Major Sung was not one hell of a psychologist.

I enrolled in the university two days after the Chinese "volunteers" swept south across the Yalu River. I was, at the time, a Captain in the United States Army. I was to become Guinea Pig 537.

Major Sung was in full control of the situation from the beginning.

"Captain Sanders," he said, as I sat before him in the bare preliminary interrogation room, "I see that you are a trained psychiatrist. Tell me, Captain, do you propose to give us nothing but your name, rank and serial number?"

"You know the rules of the Geneva Convention as well as I do, Major."

But instead of making threats, Major Sung beamed. *"Excellent,"* he said. "What a shame if you had chosen to be cooperative at the start! Our experiment would've become rather pointless. And what a pity *that* would've been. As it is, I can see that we will have a most interesting time together."

Sung rose to his feet and placed his shiny, smiling face inches from mine.

"Tell me, Captain," he said softly, "do you believe in God?"

"What?" I mumbled.

"Oh come now, Captain. Surely you will not be giving away any military secrets by answering *that* question."

"Uh . . . I suppose not. Very well, Major. Let us say for the sake of argument that I do *not* believe in God." I smiled. I felt sure I had given him the opposite of what he had expected.

Once again, I was surprised.

"Perfect!" said Sung. "I can see that you will be an ideal subject. Captain, let me assure you that by the end of this month, you most certainly *will* believe in God."

"What?"

"Look at my face, Captain. Today it appears to you as the face of a man, an enemy. *In a month, you will recognize it as the face of God.* That will be all for today, Captain Sanders."

Early the next morning, I was taken to a different room. Once again, it was bare and Spartan—one chair, and a padded couch, complete with restraints, and sitting next to it, something which looked vaguely like an electroshock therapy apparatus.

Sung was waiting for me.

"Ah, Captain Sanders!" he said. "Today we begin our experiment. Tell me, Captain, what do you think that device is?"

"Some new kind of electroshock apparatus?"

"Very good, Captain. A close guess. So you have some acquaintance with electroshock therapy?"

"Enough to know that if you're planning to torture me with that thing, you're wasting your time. Electroshock therapy works by inducing a current directly in the brain. The brain has no pain receptors. You can give me just enough current to knock me out, or enough to kill me, but you can't make me feel pain. It's physiologically impossible."

Sung laughed. "Such lack of subtlety!" he said. "Captain, there are tortures and tortures. Not all of them involve brute pain. Have you ever read a serious study of torture?"

"Torture? What is there to say about torture? You induce pain in the subject until he submits to your will."

"Ah, but Captain, surely you realize that there is psychic pain as well as physiological pain. Even subconscious pain. Tell me, Captain, you have been using electroshock therapy in the West for a good many years; how does it work?"

"Why, you induce a current—"

"No! No!" said Sung. "I mean how does it *really* work? Just how does a current induced in the brain bring about psychological change?"

I shrugged. No one really knew the answer to that one.

"Consider Pavlov," said Sung.

"What about Pavlov?"

Sung grinned. "Pavlov proved that it is the presence of a stimulus, positive or negative, that counts. Pain is a negative stimulus, but that doesn't mean that every negative stimulus must involve pain. Now this device," he said, pointing at the strange-looking electrical apparatus, "is something like an electroshock apparatus. It induces a small current in the brain, but never more than just enough to cause a momentary blackout. A pure negative stimulus, so to speak. No pain at all involved."

"That's all it does?"

"That's all. But as you will discover, it is quite sufficient."

He said something in Chinese, or maybe Korean, and the guards grabbed me and threw me down on the couch. They strapped me in, and Sung attached a set of electrodes to my head.

"Very well," he said. "Now we begin. And let us begin at the beginning—name, rank and serial number."

He stepped over to the control console and fiddled with it for a few moments.

"Ah! Now then, your name?"

He threw a switch and I blacked out. No pain, no nothing. Just unconsciousness.

When I came to, it could've been a minute, or an hour later. I had no way of knowing.

"Ah!" said Sung. "You are awake. Now then, let us understand each other. Your name is not Harvey Sanders. You do not have a name."

"Name?" he said.

"Ha—"

Blackness.

Awareness returned. Sung stared in my face. "Name?"

Blackness.

"Name?"

Blackness.

"Name?"

Blackness.

How many times it happened, I can't remember. Ten? Twenty? A hundred?

Finally, there came a time. . . .

"Name?" said Sung. And there was no blackness. Only . . . only. . . .

"Come now. I promise you there will be no more shocks. Tell me now, Captain, what is your name?"

"Captain. . . . Captain. . . ."

"Come now, Captain, surely you have a name? *Everyone* has a name."

"Of course. Only . . ."

"Only *what?*"

"I can't . . . I. . . . *I have no name.*"

"Good, Excellent. But surely you have a rank?"

"Captain, United States Army."

Blackness.

"Rank?"

Blackness.

"Rank?"

Blackness.

I don't think it took very many blackouts for me to lose my rank. After all, a *name* is something you live with all your life.

"Very good," said Sung finally. "But we must have something to call you, eh? Hmmm . . . Guinea Pig! That's it. Guinea Pig 537. Now then, what is your serial number?"

I honestly couldn't remember.

"Come now, Guinea Pig 537, no serial number?"

I lay there numbly. I was . . . *no one.* . . . I was . . . a man!
I was . . . what did he call me, Guinea Pig 537?

Sung studied my face intently.

"Excellent!" he said. "You are a fine subject, Guinea Pig 537.
You have earned your evening meal. Take him back to his cell
now."

That night, I lay on the hard bed, trying to remember.

A name. . . . A name was the thing one was called. It had two
parts. One part told what family you came from. I knew what a
family was. I had one. There was my mother, and my father, who
was dead, and my brother Bill, and my sister Eileen. . . .

And me. My name was. . . .

Was. . . .

Guinea Pig 537.

No! That wasn't my real name. Sung had called me that, but it
wasn't my name. I knew, because my name was . . . it was. . . .
Blankness.

*   *   *

"Ah, good morning, Guinea Pig 537!" said Sung. "I hope you
slept well. We have a busy day ahead of us."

I struggled with the straps, but it was no use.

"Now then," said Sung, "where are you from? Where were you
born?"

"New York, New York!" I shouted in defiance. It was a name,
a label, a place to cling to.

Blackness.

"Where were you born?"

Blackness.

I lost my birthplace, my age, and my country that day. I was
a man. I existed. I had come to this place—*Korea*—to fight a war.
I had been captured somewhere below the Yalu River. . . . I
had that much. . . .

For a while.

Day after day, Major Sung ping Lee chipped away at the collection of nomenclature and memories that was *me.* More and
more surrendered and passed into oblivion. My infancy, my childhood, my adolescence. . . .

And all without a twinge of pain. "The brain has no pain receptors," I had told him.

"There is torture and torture," Sung had said.

And finally, the ultimate day came.

"Guinea Pig 537!" barked Sung. "Who are you?"

Blankness.

"Where are you?"

Blankness.

"What are you?"

Something bubbled into consciousness in my blighted mind.

"I am!" I shouted. "I am! I am! I am! I am!"

Sung smiled slowly. "At last," he said. "The final delusion. Very well. What are you?"

"I am!"

Blackness.

"What are you?"

"I am!"

Blackness.

"What are you?"

"I am. . . ."

Blackness.

"What are you?"

Nothingness. Featureless billows of black in a field that was black. Blankness. Oblivion. *Nothingness.* Pure, undiluted primeval nothingness.

Finally, after aeons of nothingness, millennia of chaos, a voice:

"We have torn it down," said the voice. "Now we begin to *create.*"

"Who am I?" said the voice. Blankness.

"I will tell you," said the voice.

"I am God."

"God . . . ," I mumbled. "God . . . there is . . . God. . . ."

"I am the Lord. Do not be afraid. I shall create for you a cosmos. I shall create for you a personality," said the voice. It chuckled. "Perhaps not *quite* in my own image."

"God. . . . God is with me. . . ."

"Let there be light."

And there was light. A soft yellow light. It was a face. The face of Sung ping Lee.

"Would you like a name?" said the face of God.

"Name. . . ."

"I shall give you a name. Let us call you *Harvey*. Harvey Sanders. What is your name?"

"Harvey Sanders. . . . Oh, thank you! Thank you, God. Harvey Sanders! Harvey Sanders! My name is Harvey Sanders!"

"You are a man," said God.

"A man! A man!"

I was a man. My name was Harvey Sanders. I was a man named Harvey Sanders. God had made me a man and given me a name.

God was good. I loved God.

Now the days with Major Sung were no longer torture. I was literally in the presence of my maker . . . in fact, I was being *made*.

I was a man named Harvey Sanders.

I was Captain Harvey Sanders.

I was Captain Harvey Sanders of the United States Army.

I was Captain Harvey Sanders who had been born in New York.

I was Captain Harvey Sanders, *psychiatrist*.

Day by day, week by week, I grew. I can remember it all, or at least most of it. I remember getting my name, and my rank, and my country, and my family. My infancy, my childhood, my adolescence, the years in college. . . .

Brick by brick, memory by memory, Major Sung ping Lee built up a replica of the personality he had destroyed; carefully, almost lovingly, like an expert restoring some ancient tapestry.

Why all this was done, I still cannot understand. Sung learned nothing of importance from me, since there was nothing important that I knew. Did he do it just for his own sadistic amusement? But that makes no sense either. There was no pain at all.

And if it was an important experiment, why did he let me remember how he did it, when he could've obliterated the memory completely?

The Communists, we are told, never do anything without a reason. I wonder. . . .

There was a time, I think, when I did know the answer. I vaguely remember Sung telling me something, something ugly, and laughing. I remember feeling fear, and hate. . . .

There is a whole week that I do not remember, the week when

he told me . . . whatever that fiendish *something* was. Sung *made*
me forget. It was not very difficult.

He left me with only one sentence out of that whole week in
my memory. Did he do it to taunt me? It seems so meaningless:
"The subtlest weapon is a sword that thinks it's a plowshare." Now
what could he have meant by that?

At any rate, he was finally finished. The day came when I
walked out of that room the same man that I had been so many
weeks before. At least, I feel that I am the same man. There is, of
course, no way to be sure. The Harvey Sanders who first met Sung
ping Lee was obliterated. Completely. Perhaps there are some
small differences.

But of course, I shall never know.

I never saw Major Sung again. A few years later, the war was
over.

And I was repatriated.

Of course, I was gone over by Army psychiatrists before I was
discharged. But it was really all quite superficial—more of an ex-
tended coffee-klatch than a rigorous psychological examination.
After all, I was one of them, a member of the club, so to speak.

Still, there was that one peculiar incident. . . .

I was speaking with a Colonel Destry, the head of the processing
center, and a psychiatrist who I respected professionally. He had
asked me about the methods of the camp interrogators. Understand, I had not told anyone of Major Sung. First of all, I was not
likely to be believed, and secondly, if I *was* believed, I might very
well spend the next few years under observation. The Army might
conceivably be quite reluctant to release a man who had been
taken apart and put back together again by the Chinese.

Still, at that point, I really did want to get it off my chest, and
Destry seemed like a man I could talk to.

"Well," I began, "one of the interrogators, a man called S—"
The strangest thing happened. *I could not pronounce Sung's name.*
The word stuck in my throat like a piece of wet dough. Understand, I *knew* the name I wanted to say, and I knew how to say
it. But I just *couldn't. Something* was blocking me.

"Yes Captain?" said Destry, looking somewhat perplexed.

"Er . . . one of the interrogators, *Major Su Ling,*" I said,
dredging the fictitious name up from somewhere, "used a—"

The Ersatz Ego

Again, there was a block. I could not describe Sung's apparatus or what happened in that room. I remembered it all, except, of course, for that week I've mentioned, and yet something was stopping me from speaking about it. *Had I been conditioned against it?*

Destry eyed me in a very peculiar manner, as well he might.

"He used a rubber hose, and beat the bottom of my feet with it, and. . . ." And I reeled off a whole catalogue of non-existent atrocities and tortures until I was sure Destry was satisfied.

Now perhaps you are thinking that I should've found some way of telling someone about Sung. That's all very well from your point of view. Yes, I admit that the episode worried me a bit at the time.

No doubt about it, Sung had conditioned me against revealing anything about what had happened. But after all, it was an experiment, wasn't it? I can certainly understand his wanting to keep it secret.

And from my point of view, . . . well if I wanted to be discharged from the Army, I had to keep my mouth shut.

So, after a few more preliminaries, I was discharged.

As a young psychiatrist just starting out, I got a job in a large public mental institution. Electroshock therapy was a fairly common practice in the hospital, and for obvious reasons, I became engrossed in the subject.

Quite frankly, no one in the United States seemed to know as much about the subject as Major Sung did. For decades, shock therapy had been used on certain difficult cases. A large percentage seemed untouched by the therapy. About an equal percentage showed some improvement. A smaller number were "cured," at least overtly.

But no one really knew *why*. They knew that electroshock therapy had certain results—they could observe them. *How* it worked was a mystery, and until that mystery was solved, there was no real way of increasing the rate of cures. You just plugged a patient in and hoped.

But I knew *how* and I knew *why*.

One of the more reasonable hypotheses had been that the electroshock acted as a negative stimulus, suppressing the disturbing psychic elements, driving them deep down into the subconscious, so that the overt behavior of the patient improved. But this was not really a cure. The disease, the conflict, was still there, lurking somewhere in the subconscious.

What I had been taught by Major Sung was that whole diseased aspects of a personality, *indeed, the disturbed personality itself,* could be destroyed. By proper use of electroshock, the disturbed personality could be broken down into primeval formlessness, and then rebuilt.

And who knew this better than I?

It would be pointless to recount the trials and tribulations of my long, careful campaign to put my method into practice. The problem was that I dared not tell anyone that I had experimental proof, that I *was* experimental proof.

A plan was even then, in the beginning, forming in my mind. This new technique could be more than a cure for mental illness, it could cure *social* neuroses as well. . . .

But I had to go slow. Build up my professional reputation in the conventional way. Publish a tentative paper on the history of shock therapy; then the beginnings of my new theory; then a subtle piece on the psychology of brainwashing; step by step, I led the proper people down the path from what they knew to what *I* knew.

Without any particular step being too big, too radical, without any big jolts along the way. . . .

And finally, as I had planned, as I had spent years pointing towards, the day came. I was asked to apply my theory to a patient.

I was asked. That was important. I had never demanded the right to use my new therapy. It was much better to wait to be asked. That way, I could be sure that the profession was ready to accept it, without undue clamor. I wanted no publicity . . . the plan that had been forming in my mind, the plan for a better society, demanded discreetness.

But the day did finally come.

It was a boy named Tom. Of course, that isn't his real name. Ethics of the profession, you know.

Tom was twenty, withdrawn, rebellious, hostile, suicidal. A hard-core, severe neurotic. He had been given up on by three analytical therapists, and the new therapy seemed the only alternative.

It was decided that I should be given the chance.

142

Like so many other neurotics in this country, Tom had been rather brilliant. Learned to read at three, out of high school at fifteen . . . almost a prodigy.

And like so many other intelligent young people, unwilling to conform to the will of society. A runaway as a boy, a delinquent as an adolescent, a severe neurotic as a young man.

At eighteen, he had tried to kill himself for the first time. He tried several more times before he was committed to an institution.

In so many ways, a typical case.

Which was why I was so interested in applying my therapy to Tom in the first place—his *was* a typical case. Typical of what I had come to consider "the American Neurosis."

Naturally, generalizations do not apply to all individuals within a culture, but in general, certain nations seem to develop more or less prevalent attitudes among their citizens—call them national neuroses. The German is obsessed with a drive for meticulous order. The Oriental, at least until very recently, worshipped the past. The Russians are afflicted with social paranoia and xenophobia.

And the American is a rebel.

Most Americans of any intelligence have always, in one way or another, been rebels against society. The American fears order. He distrusts control.

And, at the bottom, he is unwilling to put his faith in authority and society. *Any* authority, *any* social order.

The American sees himself as a unique individual. Rules are for others, not for him. He has built a whole philosophy around this unrealistic attitude.

Of course, if you look at it logically, this *is* an unrealistic attitude. It is really society which counts. Men who continually flout the current social order, whatever it may be, will be continually kicked in the teeth by reality.

In short, they end up as unhappy neurotics.

Like Tom.

One thing that must be said for the Communists; they understand the relationship between the individual and society. Society, being the sum of all individuals, is more important than any of them. When an individual starts to believe that he is more important than his society, he begins to become a neurotic.

And he ends up like Tom.

I certainly don't want you to get the wrong idea, though. I'm no Communist. After all, I fought in a war against them, didn't I? I was a prisoner of the Communists, was I not?

At any rate, you can see the significance of Tom's case as a test. If I could cure Tom's neurosis, if I could mold a new personality for him that would willingly conform to the social order, that would accept authority, then I would eventually be able to do the same for the millions of other Americans afflicted with this disease of individualism. Perhaps you find this thought repulsive. It's understandable. After all, you too, to some degree or other, are afflicted.

But try to look at it rationally. What is so wrong about the individual living for the good of society? What is really so sacred about the "rights of the individual"? *What* rights?

The right to be a neurotic? The right to be unhappy?

The important thing is for the individual to accept the rules of the society he lives in. No matter what they happen to be. Ideology aside, the man who *willingly* accepts order, control, rules, will stay happy, no matter what conditions he finds himself living under. He will be free of neuroses.

And is there anything that's *really* worth being unhappy for?

So perhaps you think that there is. "Dignity," you may say, "freedom," "honor," "Democracy". . . . Are these really anything more than empty words?

Now you think that they are worth being unhappy for.

But then, you haven't been cured yet, have you?

I knew what I had to do. I had been planning this moment for years. I would cure Tom. I would erase his previous personality entirely, and build a new, healthy personality in its place.

A whole *new* personality, a personality that would think it was the same Tom as before, *but* that would really be an entirely *new ego*.

I remember him lying there, thin and drawn. There was a strange look in his eyes, a look that was sullen and resigned.

"Tom," I said, "I'm going to help you."

"You're going to help me," he said. He said it like a machine. Or did the very flatness of his tone constitute an insult?

No matter. I was ready to begin.

"What is your name?"

Shock.

"What is your name?"

Shock.

"What is your name?"

Just as Major Sung had led me down the path to dissolution, I led Tom. Not, of course, for the same unfathomable purpose. As the days and weeks passed, name, family, memory dissolved, and as it had come to me, the ultimate moment came to Tom.

"What are you?"

"I am!"

Shock.

"What are you?"

"I am. . . ."

Shock.

"What are you?"

Blankness.

He lay there, his eyes passively closed, dreaming the truly innocent dreams of the foetus.

Lying there on the table before me was a raw, formless . . . *ego* would be too structured a term. . . . The primeval id, or something even more primitive, without memory, form, or even desire. Human clay, waiting for my hands.

For a moment, I knew what it felt like to be God.

For one ridiculous moment, I thought of Sung. And I thought of myself, years ago, lying there, like Tom was lying there now, formless human clay. . . .

Finally, this inevitable moment of doubt passed.

"You hear me," I said.

"Hear. . . ."

"Do you know who I am?"

"Who you are. . . ."

I took a deep breath. Now I would take the first step down a long road, the road back for people like Tom, the road to a healthier, better-adjusted American psyche. . . .

"I am God," I said.

That was many years ago. Tom was the first. It was a complete success.

After Tom, there were others, thousands of others. And now, other psychiatrists, by the hundreds, are learning the method.

American society is now in the process of being quietly transformed. Actually, it is not merely society which is being changed, it is the nature of the American psyche itself.

The new American will be a very different breed. He will be happy.

He will be happy no matter what changes his society undergoes in the future. His content will come from within, it will be unshakable. He will be able to adapt, indeed, he will not even be conscious of adapting. It will be as natural as breathing.

All he will require will be some social order to conform to. *What* that social order will be will not be significant. Ideology will no longer be important to him.

When he reads in his history books (if he bothers to trouble himself with such things at all) about the great and meaningless ideological conflicts of the twentieth century, it will all be nonsense to him.

Whatever ideology eventually triumphs—democracy, socialism, fascism, communism, some new ism as yet unborn—he will accept it without question; he will accept it with enthusiasm.

And whoever his rulers may be, he will be happy.

And the sweet irony of it all is that all this will come about as the result of a pointless experiment in a Korean prisoner of war camp. Truly, this is one of those rare cases when a sword has really been turned into a plowshare, is it not?

Not that I don't have personal doubts, once in a while. After all, I'm human, am I not?

It's really quite silly to worry about Major Sung, and the first crude beginnings of my technique, isn't it?

After all, all that is in the past. The Korean War is long over.

And we won that war. . . . .

Didn't we?

Neutral Ground

A bolt of jagged blue lightning rent the rolling red clouds, leaving a gash of orange-yellow in its wake that faded in a few moments and then disappeared.

Visual effect? Tyson wondered. Just some kind of after-image, or did the lightning or whatever it was cause some kind of unstable chemical change in the atmosphere?

He willed his disembodied ego forward, toward the base of the sheer black cliffs that towered in the distance, hard and majestic over the endless, featureless yellow sands.

There was a . . . *something* lurking by the cliffs. Tyson was viscerally sure of it. It was the same something that he had felt briefly before, in three of the other Places. He felt a curious mixture of fear and curiosity at the texture of the somethingness in his mind . . .

Something, call it curiosity perhaps, was pulling him toward the cliffs. But there was also a force in his mind holding him back, a force that increased in direct proportion to his nearness to the cliffs. He recognized the repelling force for what it was—fear.

He had felt the fear before, three times before, the same three times he had felt the presence of the something. He had felt it in the Place that was all stars and hardened brown lava fields, in the Place where ten great suns illuminated an endless, blinding plain of glare ice, in the Place of thousand-foot-tall trees.

The fear was fear of the unknown something. It was not fear of the unknown as such, for all Voyages were into the unknown, and no Voyager had yet experienced the same Place twice.

It was the alienness of the something, an alienness that was as foreign to the Places as Tyson was. He could feel it, and it was that awareness which filled him with cold dread. What waited at the base of the black cliffs was no more a part of this reality than he was.

Mentally gritting his non-corporeal teeth, the point of view that was Tyson willed itself once more toward the cliffs. The yellow sands flowed under him, from the point of view of a man walking, though in the Places Tyson had neither feet nor legs. It was as if his ego were clinging desperately to the ghost of *bodyness,* though Tyson's body was far, far away.

Yet the closer he came, the slower he moved, for the fear was building up with his approach like the bow-wave of a boat moving not through water but through some thick syrup. . . .

Now the sands seemed to grow misty, vague, like melting mists. The black cliffs seemed to evaporate into billows of black smoke. . . . The smoke began to drift, dissipate. . . .

He knew the signs well. He was coming out of it. Another Voyage, another Place. . . . Another encounter with the *something.* . . .

There was blackness, emptiness, a swirl of omnidirectional motion. . . .

Burt Tyson felt the soft foam rubber of the couch beneath his limp body. Sensation was returning to his limbs and trunk in a pins-and-needles tingle.

He opened his eyes. Yarmolinski's long, perpetually worried face was staring down at him.

"You all right, Burt?" Yarmolinski said mechanically.

"Of course, Ralph," Tyson said with a little smile, feeling control of the muscles of his face coming back to him. "Never lost a Voyager yet, have we?"

"Not *yet,*" Yarmolinski said with a sly grin. Yarmolinski was such a notorious pessimist that it had become a standing Project joke, even to Yarmolinski himself.

"Cheer up, Ralph," Tyson said. "There's always a first time. We'll have a disaster for you yet."

Now Tyson felt himself regaining full control of his body. He sat up shakily on the couch and dangled his legs over the edge, wiggling his feet experimentally.

"What was it like this time?" Yarmolinski asked, turning on the tape recorder.

"Pretty simple one," Tyson said. "Red clouds, yellow desert, black cliffs. No vegetation, no life of any kind. . . ."

"Sounds like it might be the same Place Jack went to on his last Voyage, though of course, there's no way to be sure. . . ."

"Ralph . . . ?"

"What's the matter, Burt?" Yarmolinski, seeing the sudden shadow cross Tyson's face.

"*It* was there again," Tyson said softly.

"Did you see anything?"

"No."

"Hear anything?"

"You never hear anything."

"Smell it? Taste it? Feel it?"

"No!" Tyson snapped. "Hell, Ralph, it was just *there*. You have to be a Voyager yourself to understand. It was just there. There was me, and there was the Place, and there was *something* that was neither part of me nor part of the Place. That's all I can tell you about it because that's all I know."

"Have any ideas what it might be?"

"Hell man, we don't even know what the Places are! Planets? Other dimensions? Other times? So how can anyone even guess at what *it* might be?"

"Take it easy, Burt. After all, you know you're always jumpy afterwards. It's just one of the side effects."

"Not this time, Ralph. Look, I've been on what, thirty-six Voyages now. Thirty-two of 'em have been normal Voyages—if you can use such an idiotic word to describe a Voyage—bur four times out of thirty-six, I've run into this *something*. Maybe not the same something each time, but anyway the same *kind* of something. It's *not* just nerves. When I'm there, I feel that finding that something is the most important part of the Voyage, and yet somehow, I can't bring myself to. . . ."

"You're afraid of it, aren't you?" Yarmolinski said evenly.

Tyson sighed. "Give me a cigarette, will you?" he said. Yarmolinski handed him a cigarette and lit it for him. Tyson took a quick puff and exhaled it through his nose.

"Yeah, Ralph," he said, "I'm afraid of it. I don't know why, but I am."

"I've got a theory," Yarmolinski said. "Want to hear it?"

"Go ahead, Ralph."

"Okay. Let's assume that the Places have no objective existence. No one has really been able to prove otherwise. The Psychion-36 makes hidden segments of the Voyager's own subconsciousness accessible to him. The Voyager 'visits' his own mind. Well, then the *something* might very well be something in your subconsciousness that you are afraid to face. Every human being has things like that in his subconscious mind. It would explain the fear. It would explain why the fear grows more intense the closer you get to it—there's a very similar effect in psychoanalysis. The closer a patient gets to the core of his neurosis, the more he fears it and the harder it becomes to approach."

"Very pretty," Tyson said. "The only thing wrong is your basic assumption—that the Places are figments of Voyagers' minds. I'm not saying the Places exist, in the same way that this couch, or the Earth exists, but they *can't* just be personal hallucinations. If they were, how do you explain the fact that different Voyagers seem to have visited the same Places?"

"*Seem* is the word, Burt. Since there's no way for Voyagers to objectively record what they see, we can't be *positive* that any two Voyagers have experienced the same Place."

"You're entitled to your theory, Ralph," Tyson said, "and I'm entitled to mine. Maybe the something is another Voyager . . . ?"

"Impossible! There are only seventeen Voyagers in the Project, and we *never* put more than one under at the same time."

"Sure," said Tyson, "but what if the Places are in *another* time? What if they're all in the *same* time? Then two Voyagers, even though they were put under at different times here, *could* meet in the same Place, would *have to* meet if they voyaged to the same place. . . ."

"Sounds kind of far-fetched," Yarmolinski said, "but it is just as logical as my idea. But then why the fear?"

"Maybe because we just don't *know* that it's another Voyager. All we sense is that there's something alien around, alien to the Place, and because we don't expect another Voyager, alien to us as well."

"Seems to me," Yarmolinski said, "that you're making assumptions about the Places as questionable as mine. It all seems to depend on what the Places really are, and that, no one knows."

"Well," Tyson sighed tiredly, "that's what Project Voyage is about in the first place, now isn't it?"

Just what is Project Voyage really all about. . . . ? Burt Tyson thought as he washed his fatigue away in the near-boiling shower.

The trouble seemed to be that the Project just grew; it had no real goal, unless you could call Voyaging itself a goal. The real goal, Tyson thought, should be to find out exactly what Voyaging was, what the Places were, but no one even knew how to go about asking those questions.

All that anyone really knew about Voyaging was how to do it . . .

Voyaging had been discovered by sheer chance. Psychion-36 was one of dozens of still enigmatic so-called "consciousness-expanding" drugs developed in the late sixties and early seventies. People who took Psychion-36 experienced hallucinations, as they did under many similar drugs. But Psychion-36 hallucinations were like no others. They were Voyages.

They traversed a short period of blackout to awake as disembodied egos in the Places. While their bodies lay in inert trances lasting for about an hour, their minds wandered through fantastic landscapes. And what was different about these hallucinations, what had made Project Voyage imperative, was that, although no one Voyager had yet visited the same Place twice, there was strong evidence that different Voyagers had been to the same Places.

Tyson rinsed himself with warm water and turned the cold tap on full blast for a minute or so. He was beginning to feel more like himself. Voyaging always took a lot out of him.

Trouble is, he thought as he dried himself, there's no common ground between the Places and reality, no point of tangency, no way to relate the two levels of existence. The Places might be anywhere, any dimension, any time. . . . or sheer hallucination. . . .

Everyone in the Project had a minimum of one pet theory. The only thing the theories had in common was that none of them could be proved or disproved.

And now there was a . . . *something,* or a class of similar somethings that were appearing in the same Places with Voyagers with greater and greater frequency. First on only one in thirty Voyages, then one in twenty, one in ten. . . . It was as if there were some weird kind of kinship drawing Voyagers and . . . *somethings* together, as if the unknown mechanism in the human mind that chose the Place for any given Voyage was acquiring a

bias for Places where the somethings lurked, where the somethings lurked and filled the Voyagers with a nameless fear. . . .

"You sure you want to Voyage again so soon?" Yarmolinski
said again, as Tyson settled himself on the foam-rubber couch.

"I feel fine, Ralph," Tyson replied, "and I want to find *it*. I have
a feeling that I'll meet it again. . . . And I somehow sense that
those somethings, whatever they are, are more important than the
Places, or Voyaging itself. I've got to find out what they are."

"I hope you're not going in over your head, Burt," Yarmolinski
said. "What happens if you *do* make contact with it? What if it's
dangerous?"

"For crying out loud!" Tyson laughed. "How in blazes can it
really be dangerous? My body is right here the whole time, under
your mother-hen care. How can anything harm me in any of the
Places when I'm not really there?"

"Who knows?"

"Stop it Ralph, or you'll have me acting as paranoid as you do.
Let's get on with it."

Yarmolinski shrugged, swabbed Tyson's arm with alcohol, and
injected the Psychion-36 into the vein in the pit of Tyson's elbow.

Tyson closed his eyes. He felt the feeling retreating from his
toes and fingers . . . his legs and arms . . . his pelvis . . . his
chest . . . his neck . . .

He was a disembodied mind, a sightless, soundless, sensationless point of view floating in a sea of nothingness. . . .

The Voyage began.

The blackness became blacker than black. The soundlessness
roared in his non-existent ears. There was a feeling of swift motion in all directions at once. . . .

Then, quite suddenly, the darkness dissolved. He was in a
Place.

It was a Place of gently rolling green hills and valleys stretching
to the horizon in all directions. The sky was a strikingly Earthlike
blue, but there were three suns in it, blue, yellow, red.

Tyson moved his point of view closer to the ground, like a man
bending. Although he had no body, his point of view was limited
to what his corporeal body could do. He could not fly above ob-
stacles any more than he could on Earth. Moving about in the
Places was, in a sense, much like walking—your conscious mind

willed you in a certain direction, and mechanisms which you were but dimly aware of translated, in some unknown manner, will into act. Somehow, in the Places, the mind translated what would ordinarily be a desire to walk or run or bend into an equivalent displacement of point of view.

Now Tyson could see that the green of the rolling countryside was not that of grass. The ground was covered, every square inch of it as far as he could see, with a luxuriant coat of green moss less than a half-inch thick.

Tyson went up gentle hills, down into little valleys. This was certainly one of the more monotonous of the Places, nothing but moss and sky, sky and moss. . . .

As Tyson shifted his point of view aimlessly about, he noticed that there seemed to be black spots scattered at very wide intervals on the mossy plain. He willed himself over to the nearest one.

It was a hole. It was a perfectly circular hole perhaps twenty feet in diameter. It seemed to have no bottom, at least not as far as Tyson could tell. Had he a body, and had he something to drop, he might've tested the hole's depth, but he had neither.

This sure is a strange one . . . Tyson thought. Almost like some weird pool table. Green moss and holes. . . .

But then, all Places had their own brand of weirdness. Each was an adventure. That was the lure of Voyaging. . . .

Aimlessly, Tyson moved on. There was not very much to explore in this Place. Everything was all the same. . . . Perhaps over the horizon . . . ?

Tyson passed close by another hole.

Suddenly a gibbering dread filled his mind. *It* was there. In the black depths of the hole a something lurked. *The* something.

Tyson fought with his own mind as it demanded: escape! escape! This was as close as he had ever been to it, as close, so far as he knew, as any Voyager had been. . . .

The fear he felt was shattering, total, unbearable. Tyson screamed silently in the depths of his mind. He screamed and screamed and screamed, but this time he was determined to stand his ground.

He forced himself to the edge of the yawning hole, at the bottom of which *it* waited. He looked down, down into the blackness. He saw nothing, but the horrible, objectless dread tore irresistibly at his will.

Tyson flinched back. Then he forced himself forward. Again the fear slammed him back.

Again he pressed forward, fighting a battle with madness in his own mind. He had to face it, he *had* to.

Slowly, haltingly, agonizingly, he felt *it* begin to rise up out of the depths of the pit.

Alien, terrible, he felt it rise. The entire Place seemed flooded with primal dread. It was too much; no man could face *this*.

Tyson fled. He fled over the mossy hills, down the green valleys. Mindlessly, panic-stricken, the ego that was Burt Tyson fled. *It* followed.

He could feel the something pursuing. He could feel the alienness clawing at his mind. He could feel a half-formed desire emanating from it. Something vague, almost pleading, yet totally fearful. Tyson fled.

A tiny lost portion of his mind remembered Tyson's resolve, wanted to stop, to turn, to face that which followed. . . . But the fear was too much, the resolve seemed something far, far away and long centuries ago. Tyson fled, he willed his ego over hills, down valleys, as fast as a man could run. He wished forlornly that the unguessable laws of Voyaging did not limit his speed to human capabilities, but it was in vain. Even the fatigue of running was beginning to overcome him, completing the Earthly illusion.

No! No! No! Tyson screamed in his mind.

It was gaining. What would happen if it caught him? What nameless horrors could it inflict, what terrible death . . . ?

Tyson tried to tell himself that his body was safe in the Voyage Room with Yarmolinski. But he could not make himself believe that there had ever been anywhere but the Place, the green moss, the hills and valleys, the holes, and *it* gaining on him, *always gaining*.

Then, finally, the green moss began to blur. The hills grew misty. The suns began to flicker, to gutter and go out. . . .

The Voyage was finally ending. With only moments to spare, with *it* almost upon him, the Voyage was finally ending. . . .

Thank you! Tyson thought, as he felt the blackness enveloping him. Oh, thank you . . . thank you . . . thank you. . . .

"Thank you! Thank you!" Tyson screamed.

"Burt! Burt! Calm down. It's over. It's me, Ralph." Yarmolinski shook Tyson's trembling body. Tyson opened his eyes. They were wild with terror.

"Take it easy, Burt, take it easy. . . ." Yarmolinski soothed. He lit a cigarette and pressed it between Tyson's trembling lips.

"Ralph . . . Ralph. . . ." Tyson took long, hurried drags on the cigarette.

"You okay now?" Yarmolinski finally said.

"Yeah," Tyson grunted. "I'm all right now . . . Lord. . . ."

"What happened?"

"There was an—*it* there again, Ralph. This time, it almost . . . caught me. It was nearly on top of me when the Voyage ended."

"Burt," Yarmolinski said softly. "You think maybe you've had it? You've been on thirty-seven Voyages now, more than anyone else. You've run into this thing five times, also more than any other Voyager. Maybe there's some kind of limit to how many Voyages a man can stand. Maybe you've reached your limit."

Tyson stared silently at the ceiling for long moments, watching the cigarette smoke curl lazily upwards.

"No Ralph," he finally said. "No! We've got to find out what this thing is. We can't keep running from it. *I* can't keep running. Sooner or later, someone has to face it and find out."

"Why you?"

"Because I've run into it more than any other Voyager. You said so yourself. Now I've had it happen twice in a row. I think that I must be somehow becoming a magnet for it . . . or vice versa, or maybe both. Maybe it has something to do with my brainwave pattern, or maybe it's just because I've had more Voyages than any one else. Whatever the reason, I think that I'll run into it almost every time out now. Someone has to stand and face it, and since I'm the most likely Voyager to run into it on any given Voyage, it might as well be me."

"But what happens if you *do* face it?" Yarmolinski asked.

"I don't know . . ." Tyson said. "I just don't know. And *that's* what I have to find out, I guess."

"You know what curiosity did to the cat."

"Good old cheerful Ralph," Tyson laughed shortly. "Makes me feel better already, knowing that at least you're your old optimistic self. Talking about curiosity, I almost get the feeling that it's curious about *us*. If only I had stood my ground. If only I weren't so damned afraid. . . ."

"But you *were* afraid, Burt. Maybe you had good cause. What if the Voyage hadn't ended when it did?"

"What if—?" Tyson shuddered. If the Voyage hadn't ended, *it* would've caught up with him. It had been gaining. Another few minutes in the Place, and . . .

That was it!

"What's on your mind, Burt?"

Tyson exhaled a great puff of smoke. "I've got an idea, Ralph . . ." he said slowly. "It scares the hell out of me, but I'm sure it would work. If I can bring myself to do it. . . . If I've got that much guts."

"Want to tell me, Burt?"

"Not yet," said Tyson. "Schedule me for another Voyage to-morrow. I'll tell you then, if I still want to go through with it. Otherwise . . . well, it's not the sort of thing one man has the right to suggest to another."

"You're absolutely sure you want to go through with this?" Yarmolinski said, as he swabbed Tyson's arm with alcohol. "Remember, there'll be no way to change your mind."

"I'm sure," Tyson said grimly. "It's the only way. I've got to be *forced* to face it. I'll never be able to do it otherwise. So, an hour after the Voyage begins, you give me a second shot of Psychion-36. Double the time of the Voyage. If we'd have done it last time, it would've caught up with me, and . . ."

"And what? That's just it, Burt, we don't know—"

"Please, Ralph! That's the whole point. We don't know what the Places are, and we don't know what *it* is. This is the only way to find out. Get on with it!"

Yarmolinski shrugged. "It's your funeral," he said, as he injected the first shot of Psychion-36 into Tyson's arm.

Tyson felt the familiar numbness inching towards his head from his extremities. There seemed to be a numbness in his mind as well, the numbness of fear, the fear of fear itself . . .

He closed his eyes, trying to purge himself of fear, letting his mind plunge into the growing, deepening blackness, the endless, swirling sensationless chaos. . . .

There was the familiar moment of unguessable motion, and the Voyage began.

The Place was a great, high-walled crater of smooth, black vol-

canic glass. Tyson found his ego in the middle of the crater, the
rim wall stretching up high and smooth and shiny-black all around
him. A great yellow sun blazed overhead, yet the sky was dead,
space-black. If such criteria applied to the Places, this one must
be airless.

This was the most desolate Place he had yet seen. Black, featureless volcanic glass, black sky, harsh sun. A Place without pity.
A Place without refuge.

Grimly, without bothering to explore the Place at all, Tyson
waited. He waited for *it*. He waited under the cold black sky, the
harsh yellow light. He waited, alone, fearful. He waited. . . .

Then all at once, he felt *its* presence. He felt the fear, the nameless, reasonless dread. It was in the crater with him, transparent
to all senses, but unmistakably *there*.

The fear was terrible, demanding, unfaceable. He wavered for a
moment, a small portion of his mind trying to convince the rest
of him that there was nothing to be afraid of, that he could not die
here, in the unreality of a Place, that his body was safe back in the
Voyage Room under the watchful care of Ralph Yarmolinski. . . .

But the rational being that had made the decision to face *it* was
long ago and far away, flayed into panic by bottomless terror. Tyson fled. He fled to the far wall of the crater. Madly, senselessly,
forgetting the immutable laws of the Places which forbade to his
detached ego any motion impossible to his body, he tried to force
himself into the air and up over the sheer crater wall. But, of
course, it was futile. The unbreakable illusion of *bodyness,* which
had been a link with sanity on previous Voyages, now was the final
piece of an inescapable trap.

He felt *it* approaching. There was nothing to be seen, but he
sensed it approaching, in a curiously jerky, hesitant manner.

He fled around the base of the crater wall. It hesitated, then
followed. Round and round, Tyson whirled, circling the base of
the smooth crater wall as if caught on some mad monstrous merry-
go-round.

Wait . . . wait . . . something seemed to wail shrilly in his
mind, in between waves of visceral fear.

Tyson dully tried to marshal his courage, to turn and face the
thing, which now almost seemed to be pleading: *wait . . . wait.*

. . . But it was no use. No degree of curiosity could overcome the senseless terror.

Tyson fled. The gleaming black wall of the crater became a dazzling blur as he whirled mindlessly around it, as the *something* gained slowly but inexorably on him, as waves of fear breached his mind.

Round and round for an eternity . . . and it was almost upon him now. Another few moments, and . . .

Then the crater began to dissolve, to grow vague, to flicker.

The drug was wearing off! The Voyage was ending!

Tyson gibbered with relief. In a moment, the Voyage would be over. He would be back, safe in the Voyage Room . . . but there seemed to be something he had forgotten. . . .

Suddenly, he remembered. The second shot of Psychion-36! Yarmolinski was going to give him another shot!

The flickering stopped. Once again, the volcanic glass of the crater was cold and hard and terribly substantial. Yarmolinski had given him the second shot. The Voyage would last another hour.

He was trapped. Irrevocably trapped.

And *it* was almost upon him.

I'm trapped! Tyson thought. There's no way out . . . no place to hide . . . no escape. . . . Well, if this must be it, he told himself savagely, at least let me face it like a man, not a whining dog!

He stopped. Tremendous tides of fear roiled his being as he felt it approach.

Then *it* hesitated. It stopped. It retreated. It began to move forward again, and once more hesitated. Again it retreated.

The fear became more intense, overwhelming.

Then Tyson suddenly understood. It was not his fear alone that he was feeling.

It was afraid of him, too.

It was radiating fear as he must be. The two of them were feeding each other's terror.

Of course! Tyson thought. I'm as alien to it as it is to me!

Tyson felt a sudden pang of empathy for the something, whatever it was, that was transparent to all his normal senses. Whatever it is, he thought, I'm scaring it as much as it's scaring me.

As if in response, the atmosphere of terror seemed to wane.

Before he could change his mind, purposely leaving himself no room for second thoughts, Tyson rushed forward to meet it.

He saw nothing, heard nothing, felt nothing, but there was a soundless scream that was both his and its.

And there, in a Place that might or might not be real, the two disembodied minds that were Tyson and the stranger occupied the same locus and merged.

Who? Who? Who? a thing screeched in his mind, a thing alive with strangeness and fear.

Me! Me! Me! Tyson thought back in panic and revulsion.

Who? Who? Who? Who are you? Who are you? What are you? What are you?

The alienness was like a reptile stench in his mind. . . . But he fought his instinctive dread. It must be as bad for the thing as for himself.

Voyager! he thought at it. Voyager! From another . . . time? place? dimension? reality? Who are you?

Yes, thought the stranger, calmer, but still unalterably alien. *Yes . . . Voyager . . . traveler . . . explorer into the unknown. . . . I too am . . . Voyager . . . traveler . . . explorer. Why do you fear me? I mean you no harm.*

Why do *you* fear me? Tyson thought back, almost mirthfully.

I do not know. I do not know. Perhaps because I feel your fear.

That is why *I* fear you, Tyson thought. Then, suddenly, impulsively: We are fellow . . . Voyagers, explorers, adventurers. . . . We should not fear each other.

No, thought the stranger, calmer, almost wistfully, *we should not fear each other.*

You are a stranger here too? Tyson thought. This is not your world?

No. Not my world. Perhaps not even my Galaxy. Perhaps not even my universe.

Not mine either, thought Tyson, with a growing sense of sympathy for the alien. I have been to many such Places.

I too.

What are the Places? Tyson asked hopefully. Do you know?

No. Do you?

No, thought Tyson. We do not know. Some of us have thought that they might simply be hallucinations of our own minds, but now that we have met, that obviously cannot be.

Some of us thought the same, replied the alien. *Not those of us who are Travelers, though. Perhaps the Places are in another universe, another time. . . . We visit them through the medium of a drug. We do not know how it works.*

Nor do we, Tyson thought. The Places are a mystery.

Yes.

The Places are not of your universe?

How can we know? Perhaps they are planets orbiting other suns in our own Galaxy. We cannot know, for we have not yet visited other suns with our bodies.

Nor have we, Tyson answered. Perhaps . . . perhaps, he thought, with growing excitement, perhaps we live in the same Galaxy!

Perhaps, answered the alien. *I would like to think so. But how can we know? All we know is that our two races have met, here in this Place that is alien to both of us, here where both of us are minds without bodies, in a place that may not even exist. But we have met. Our minds have contacted each other, though our bodies are still chained to our planets.*

I am glad that we have met, Tyson thought. Our peoples can be friends.

Yes, answered the alien, *friends. Friends against the unknown.*

Perhaps, thought Tyson, feeling a strange new emotion that was both fear and hope, perhaps our peoples will meet someday, when we both go to the stars. Perhaps someday we will stand on the ground of each other's planets.

Perhaps, replied the alien. *Perhaps, if we live in the same universe.* Then, somehow sadly, filled with loss; *But how can we ever know?*

The Places! Tyson thought. Our peoples have passed each other before in the Places, like fearful animals in the dark. But now there need be no more fear. We will meet again . . . in the Places, whether they are real or not. The Places will be our meeting ground, until someday, perhaps, our ships meet each other in our own universe. . . .

Yes, thought the stranger, no longer quite an alien, *in the Places. In the Places where we are both aliens, we will have a meeting ground. We will meet again.*

Perhaps, together, some day, we will learn what the Places really are, Tyson thought.

Yes, thought the stranger, his mind seeming to grow faint and dim in Tyson's, *yes, together. It is a good thought. This Place is fading now. The drug is wearing off. I am returning to my own world. Goodby . . . goodby . . . goodby till we meet again . . . in the Places . . . goodby . . . goodby. . . .*

Goodby, Tyson thought. Goodby, fellow Voyager.

The stranger was gone. Once more, Tyson was alone in the Place, waiting for the Psychion-36 to wear off, waiting to return to an Earth that would no longer be quite the same.

He was alone, but not in the same sense as he had been before. Somewhere, sometime, in some universe, there were other intelligent beings, beings that could be as much friends as aliens.

In this Place, in this enigmatic reality that might or might not be real, two races had contacted each other for the first time, a contact so tenuous, so tentative, that all each had learned was that the other existed. It was not very much.

But it was a beginning.

Once More, With Feeling

Sausalito, California, United States of America, 1967. The hour after dusk: the sky a crystalline blue-black, the lightscape of San Francisco across the obsidian waters of the Bay something straight off an old picture-postcard, the nightly tongue of fog just now pouring through the Golden Gate, the slow-motion ghost of an enormous breaker.

Major Jase Stone, USAF, stood on the end of a short wooden pier looking out on the fog-bank as it advanced on San Francisco and listening to the slap-slap of the wavelets against the hulls of the pleasure boats moored in the marina. Stone was twenty-seven but he looked a well-preserved thirty-five in the bulky sweater and white duck pants; in uniform the etched angles in his face and the steel walls behind his eyes would seem routine, but in mufti he looked like a man who had seen too much of the underside of the world too soon.

Well here I am, he thought. Was it worth it? He thought cynically of the Congressional Medal of Honor tucked beneath the pile of new civilian shirts in the dresser drawer of the room he had rented overlooking the Bay. A piece of metal and cloth gingerbread, awarded for dedication to the art of killing above and beyond the call of duty, perhaps beyond reason. A stupid thing, perhaps a wicked thing to risk your life for—but the three weeks in a rest area of your choosing that went with it under the new rules, that made it seem worth the gamble, worth the human lives that had paid for every second of this furlough in blood.

Back there, the killing and the screaming women and the craters and the fog that killed. And here, now, a clean night sky unsullied by the contrails of rockets, and the fog was cool and bracing and smelled of the sea.

Wouldn't you?

Stone shook the fireball visions out of his mind's eye, turned, walked slowly off the pier and back towards the center of town where the lights were smoky jewels in the thickening fog and people laughed and smiled in the streets around him. He was suddenly seized by a frightening vision of hyper-reality: the warm brick-reds and wood-browns of the buildings, the deep blue-black of the sky, the romantic patina of the fog, seemed too perfect to be real, like the technicolor of a movie. The San Francisco-Gothic buildings seemed studiedly quaint and the young girl across the street with her long slim legs and flowing blonde hair was a creature of Central Casting.

Stone shuddered but the illusion would not dissolve—and *was* it illusion when there was another reality where fireballs shattered the sky and urchins darted from one heap of rubble to the next in search of a scrap of garbage or a dead dog?

Time to get drunk, Jase boy, he told himself. Time to really tie one on and soak the damned war out of your brain for three weeks. And for chrissakes, don't let it get maudlin! A few good stiff ones, and then find yourself a nice chick and let her show you just how real she really is.

Down the block was a medium-sized bar. No crowd outside, but as he neared it, he could hear a satisfying buzz of talk from within and he saw a man leave with a big-eyed girl and it looked like a good omen and so he stepped through the psuedo-antique swinging doors and into the smoke inside.

To his left was a series of wooden tables crowded with couples and groups of couples mostly in their twenties and thirties, real cozy-like, and again that awful feeling of unreality as if they were extras hired to produce the proper atmosphere and Stone shivered. To his right was the bar with high wooden stools along it. At the far end of the bar, a man in his forties was hustling a girl in her early twenties. The rest of the stools were empty.

Stone sat down on the stool nearest the door and ordered bourbon, neat.

He drank it quickly, felt the warmth of the liquor begin to melt him into the unreality of the bar, ordered another and sipped at this one slowly, savoring the acrid, very real bite of the whiskey across his tongue. He began to relax. Sausalito, California, USA, 1967, a good old American bar—and the specter of that other reality within him began to fade as he willed himself into the ambience of here, now.

A sudden breeze caused him to look over his shoulder at the doorway where a girl stood uncertainly paused at the threshold of the bar. Her tight full body seemed somehow costumed in the black stretch-pants and short suede jacket. Her red hair fell in billows to her shoulders. Their eyes met and something passingly strange seemed to happen: the reality of the bar faded again and as they looked through the smoke at each other there seemed to be an instant and long-standing bond between them, as if both knew they were the only real people in a world of wraiths.

Without taking her eyes off him, she sat down on the stool next to his, propped her face in one hand as she leaned her elbow on the bar, studied him with hot, feral eyes.

"*Yeah,*" he said.

"I have the feeling you are a stranger in this place," she said as if they had been talking for hours. There was an expectant tension in her voice that he couldn't fathom but that rippled the flesh of his thighs.

"What makes you say that?" he asked.

"I'm a stranger here too. How do you say, it takes one to know one, no? Something about the way you look, detached, you know? Almost disdainful of . . . all this."

"I'm . . . a soldier," Stone said. "A soldier on leave. Sorry to hear it shows."

"Ah, a soldier!" she said. Her eyes gleamed, then banked, and Stone thought: *Jesus,* without being sure how he meant it.

"You like soldiers?" he said, putting a testing edge on the words.

"I don't know. I've never met one before." And the weird intensity, the almost manic earnestness coming off her as she stared at him like some exotic animal convinced him she was not putting him on.

"Never met a soldier before? Where the hell you been keeping yourself, baby?"

She seemed to hesitate before answering, as if about to say one thing, thinking better of it, then saying another: "Why is that so important to you?"

Far too earnest a response, and Stone laughed to show her how important it wasn't. But then he found the vehemence in his own voice betraying . . . almost betraying it all:

"Because I'd like to take a good look at someplace where there's no soldiers, no armies, no killing, no—"

"You've been in a war!" she whispered. There was something positively obscene in the way she said it.

"That turns you on too?" he said, finding himself both repelled and attracted by this strange, somehow naively-feral creature.

Something guarded came into her eyes, and at that moment Stone lost all illusions as to who was picking up whom. "What's wrong?" she said. "You think I am some kind of . . . what is the old term, 'camp-follower,' that is it?"

"That's a polite word for it."

She laughed. The laugh was strained. "No," she said, "I am like you, a . . . tourist, no? You see, I admit it openly, I am a tourist from a boring place looking for the exciting, the exotic. And there was that about you, excitement, a kind of aura of romance, you know. I didn't know what it was until you told me you were a soldier. I've never met a soldier before; it is the idea that excites me. You know, being in the same room with a man who has lived by killing and bravery, who may tomorrow himself be—" She cut herself off at that, but the look on her face told Stone it was quite deliberate.

"You're pretty weird, baby," he said. "You must come from a pretty far-out place."

She frowned. "You would find it strange, yes," she said. "But not exciting at all. Very boring, controlled, how do you say it, *sterile*. No place for an exciting man such as yourself. But I am a boring woman from a boring place; let's talk about you, much more exciting, no? I don't even know your name."

"Major Jase Stone, USAF," he said. The chick was clearly off her nut. But there was something tantalizing about it, titillating. He wondered what it would be like to make love to this girl. What form would her kinkiness take in bed?

"USAF," she said hesitantly. "Air Force of the United States, no? Ah, an officer in the fabled Air Force of the United States! I'm excited to know you, Major Stone. I am Tanya Grouzenko."

A chill went through Stone. "A Russian name?" he said.

"My father is Russian, my mother a North American. Why do

you . . . ? Ah yes! The . . . what is it called, 'Frozen War'?"

"Cold War," Stone said. "It's been in all the papers."

"So you fight the Cold War . . . ?" she asked rhetorically. Stone opened his mouth, abruptly realized he could not say what he was about to say, shut it. The moment passed as she smiled, paused, said: "Does that make you a cold warrior?"

The best Stone could manage was a coughing laugh. "Touché, baby," he said.

Her eyes were gleaming. "Why not?" she said.

"Come again?"

"Aren't you getting a little ahead of things, Major?"

Stone blinked at the three consecutive non-sequiturs. Or *were* they non-sequiturs? Or was he so hung up and out of practice that he couldn't pick up on a perfectly good invitation?

"Are you trying to tell me something?" he asked lamely.

"I'm trying to *ask* you something."

"Ask me what?"

"Is there someplace nearby where you could, how do you say, make love to me, Major Stone?"

The room was small, cozy you might say if you were thinking that way—a bed, a dresser, a night table, the big bay window, and just enough floor space to walk around in—and it was paneled in ersatz knotty-pine. Tanya rushed inside as if she owned the place as Stone opened the door for her, threw off her jacket, tossed it on the dresser, kicked off her shoes, grabbed his hand and pulled him to the window, where she stared out at San Francisco, wavering through the fog, her face hidden from him.

"Ah, so perfect!" she sighed. "San Francisco, California, United States of America, 1967, the most beautiful city on the North American continent in the period, indeed. And Tanya Grouzenko, here with Major Jase Stone of the Air Force of the United States of America! Ah, it is like. . . ."

She turned to him, layed a warm palm against his cheek. Her eyes were shining, and she looked incongruously like some romantic schoolgirl—which certainly didn't jibe with the no-nonsense way she had picked him up. On the way to the room, Stone had almost managed to convince himself that she was simply some kind of nympho, a little too kinky maybe, but just what he needed: a nice uncomplicated roll in the hay. But now

. . . there was something at the center of whatever made this girl tick that just didn't add up; a void, a mystery. And it had a sick, almost sinister smell to it.

"Major," she said softly, "you have fought in a war, yes? You will fight again?"

"Three weeks' leave and then back to. . . ." He grimaced, let it hang as visions of refugees and rotten flesh and fireballs flickered through his mind. Screams and dying women.

For some reason, this reaction seemed to be just what she wanted.

"Ah," she sighed, "so this is but a short moment of calm between battles for you? The water and the sky and the fog to soothe you, and a woman to make you forget and then—the war. Back to the front, no? To kill or be killed! So sad, so tragic, so. . . ."

Stone was about to say something really nasty about sadists and ghouls when—

She ripped open her white blouse (a ludicrously theatrical gesture, even to the sound of tearing cloth simulated by the velcro fastener as it parted), tore it off and threw it to the floor with a florid flourish, hurled herself into his arms, her warm bare breasts pressed against him, began nuzzling his ear and whispering: "Forget, my Major, forget the killing and the danger . . . Let me give . . . give . . . give. . . ."

Stone wavered on the edge of tossing her away and laughing or maybe puking, possibly both—what insane crap filled the head of this crazy chick?—but her hands were moving all over his body and her tongue was in his ear and she was grinding her body against him in almost a caricature of passion, and once she had bowled him over backwards onto the bed, he stopped thinking and let reflexes take over. . . .

It was short and she was very noisy about it and dug her long nails into his back at the climax and he was physically satisfied almost before he knew what had happened.

Afterward, they lay naked on the bed, she utterly sated, her eyes heavily-lidded, languid, he with nerves rubbed raw, having found nothing more than sheer physical relief without a shade of human connection, feeling like some kind of walking dildo and hating the girl without quite knowing why.

"Ah," she murmured dreamily, "just as I had always imagined. . . ."

"You're not going to try and tell me you were a virgin!" he snapped.

She propped herself up, stared at him, and there was something somehow incredibly old, decayed, in her eyes that made his stomach twitch. "Virgin!" she laughed. "How quaint! I have tasted . . . things you cannot even begin to imagine, Major. But yes, you know, in a way, it was as delicious as . . . losing one's virginity. Never before have I felt what I felt with you."

"So now I'm supposed to be Superman?"

"Superman? Super . . . ? Ah, the American folk-hero, no? I don't understand—the myth started as a children's story, did it not? You mean it had some sexual implications?"

Shards of a whole were beginning to come together in Stone's mind. *Had* sexual implications . . . *fabled Air Force of the United States. . . . Frozen War. . . . I am like you, a . . . tourist, no . . . ?* But from where?

Or when?

He reached out, grabbed her throat between the thumb and forefinger of one hand, pulled her face to within a few inches of his. He reached for the killer inside, painted it across the features of his face. Tanya sighed; the fear that suddenly came into her eyes was overlaid with musky arousal.

"Why—?"

"Take a good look baby," he said coldly. "I'm a soldier, that means I know how to kill. That means I *will* kill if I need to."

Her body undulated towards him; her arms snaked around him; her fingernails lightly raked the skin of his bare back. "Yes," she crooned, "yes, yes, yes. . . ."

Viciously, he backhanded her across the face with his free hand. She moaned. Her eyes grew hotter. Her synapses were all crossed —no way to turn this crazy chick off!

"*When are you from?*" Stone suddenly roared, inches from her face.

"Twenty-one fifty—" she blurted, then caught herself. She stared at him in bewilderment. "How did you . . . ?"

"Never mind. I know, that's good enough. When?"

"Twenty-one fifty-seven," she said softly. Then a trace of viciousness came into her voice. "From your future, you understand that? A time-tourist, yes. I could tell your fortune, Major. You would not like that at all. Not at all."

"Try me," Stone said.

She pulled away from his grasp. He let her go.

"Talk," Stone said. "So you're a time-tourist. Why here? Why now? Why me?"

She laughed. "Ah, you think I am some kind of . . . how do you say, Mata Hari, a temporal spy, yes? How delicious! I wish that my life was that exciting. No, I am a simple tourist, I'm afraid. Why now? Why here? Why you? Because, my Major, this is a romantic city in a romantic era. The World Union of Soviet Socialist States in 2157, that is a dull place in a dull time. Inhabited by dull men. Bureaucrats, party officials like my father, technicians. A sterile, controlled, predictable world order built on the ashes. And you—a man of passion, a primitive, so exciting! And the romance of making love to a Major in the Air Force of the United States of America, soldier of the last great lost cause, so romantic, so tragic, so utterly delicious!"

"Lost cause?" Stone said shrilly.

"Yes, my Major, the cause of your country, of your children, was lost. Over a hundred years before I was born. The Big War, the nuclear holocaust. Ah yes, you Americans fought valiantly! Moscow, Leningrad, Odessa, Kiev, Novosibirsk and a hundred other Russian cities destroyed. A hundred million Russians incinerated! But a hundred and seventy million Americans died in the destruction of your cities—New York, Chicago, Los Angeles, all of them. And here . . . San Francisco, too. We destroyed you. We won the war. And we built the new world on the ashes of the old. The scars are gone, even in the hearts of the descendants of the Americans that survived. The World Union of Soviet Socialist States *is* the world, a dull world, passionless, predictable, totally controlled. The World Union of Soviet Socialist Boredom! During the war, time-travel was developed, of a kind: at great expense one can be thrust into the past and held there for a few weeks. Soon I will snap back to my boring world like a bug on the end of a stretched rubber band. I will not horrify you with what I had to do to arrange this trip. But it was worth it. I will remember you always."

A tremendous killing urge came upon Stone; he grabbed her by the throat and began to squeeze. Abruptly, he stopped, released her. There was something better, more fitting, a foulness to match her own. *Lost cause . . . lost cause. . . .*

He bolted from the bed, very conscious of his own muscles moving beneath his skin, rummaged through a dresser drawer and extracted the Congressional Medal of Honor, in its leather-covered case.

He took the medal from its case. She cringed as he threw it at her and it hit her on her beautiful right breast. She picked it up and studied it listlessly. He stood over the bed, said: "Do you know what that is?"

She hesitated, then said: "Your Congressional Medal of Honor, no? The highest decoration your country awarded. I have seen pictures. Impressive, yes, but—"

"Moscow," he said.

"I don't understand."

"They don't give out those things lightly," he said. "Not since what's left of Congress decided that a time-furlough should be part of the deal. As you said, time-travel is very expensive."

She stared up at him; comprehension was beginning to dawn in her eyes. "You mean you . . . ?"

"From 1993, baby. It wasn't easy to get these three weeks. I'm a big hero back there. A lone flight over enemy territory, one fifty-megaton bomb—and pow! Give my regards to Moscow! That's me, old Jase Stone, the man who got Moscow. Eight million Russians died so I could have a vacation in 1967, so you could have the pleasure of making it with the romantic hero of a lost cause. How's *that* grab you, baby?"

She looked up at him, her eyes like saucers. "You hate me, is that it?" she said. "And you want me to hate you."

"Don't you understand what I'm saying?" he screamed. "Eight million people, *your* people! I killed them! I'm soaked in their blood! Every minute that you've spent with me was bought with a thousand Russian lives! Doesn't that mean anything to you, you bloody bitch? Can't you feel anything?"

In her eyes, a stinking madness. She sat up on the bed, leaned her face up at him, began to stroke her own body with her long, supple hands. "Like Genghis Khan," she purred, "like some glorious barbarian bathing in the blood of his enemies. . . . Oh, oh, I feel, my Major, I feel, I feel! Burn and pillage and rape! We defeated you! You're doomed! Hate me! Hate me! Hate me! Show me how much you hate me! Burn and kill and rape! Burn and kill and rape! Hate me! Hate me! Hate me! Hate me to death!"

A fireball exploded behind Stone's eyes, a nuclear inferno of rage and hate surged through his muscles and he began to slap her, again, and again, and again, the sting of his palms against her flesh shooting up his arms into his brain, roiling images of shattered skys, screaming women and her face, her stinking ghoulish face as she moaned and writhed under his blows in infuriating ecstasy.

She began to curse and scream in Russian, clawed at him with her long nails. Then, with an amazingly athletic movement, she wrapped her legs around him, pulled him down on top of her, and he couldn't stop himself, every thrust of his body against hers was a sword-thrust, every moan of passion a cry of agony—damn you! damn you! damn you!

Afterward, just before he kicked her out of the room, she had told him: "You were magnificent, my Major. You hate so fiercely!"

He stood, still naked, staring out the window at the shimmering lights of San Francisco, peaceful and serene under the crystal dome of the black night sky—like an old picture postcard.

The sky, like a fragile bowl of black glass, about to shard into a million brittle fragments.

It's a Bird! It's a Plane!

Dr. Felix Funck fumblingly fitted yet another spool onto the tape recorder hidden in the middle drawer of his desk as the luscious Miss Jones ushered in yet another one. Dr. Funck stared wistfully for a long moment at Miss Jones, whose white nurse's smock advertised the contents most effectively without revealing any of the more intimate and interesting details. If only x-ray vision were really possible and not part of the infernal Syndrome. . . .

Get a hold of yourself, Funck, get a hold of yourself! Felix Funck told himself for the seventeenth time that day.

He sighed, resigned himself, and said to the earnest-looking young man whom Miss Jones had brought to his office, "Please sit down, Mr . . . ?"

"Kent, Doctor," said the young man, seating himself primly on the edge of the overstuffed chair in front of Funck's desk. "Clark Kent!"

Dr. Funck grimaced, then smiled wanly. "Why not?" he said, studying the young man's appearance. The young man wore an archaic blue double-breasted suit and steel-rimmed glasses. His hair was steel-blue.

"Tell me . . . Mr. Kent," he said, "do you by some chance know where you are?"

"Certainly, Doctor," replied Clark Kent crisply. "I'm in a large public mental hospital in New York City!"

"Very good, Mr. Kent. And do you know why you're here?"

"I think so, Dr. Funck!" said Clark Kent. "I'm suffering from partial amnesia! I don't remember how or when I came to New York!"

"You mean you don't remember your past life?" asked Dr. Felix Funck.

"Not at all, Doctor!" said Clark Kent. "I remember everything up till three days ago when I found myself suddenly in New York! And I remember the last three days here! But I don't remember how I got here!"

"Well then, where did you live before you found yourself in New York, Mr. Kent?"

"Metropolis!" said Clark Kent. "I remember that very well! I'm a reporter for the Metropolis *Daily Planet!* That is, I am if Mr. White hasn't fired me for not showing up for three days! You must help me, Dr. Funck! I must return to Metropolis immediately!"

"Well then you should just hop the next plane for home," suggested Dr. Funck.

"There don't seem to be any flights from New York to Metropolis!" exclaimed Clark Kent. "No buses or trains either! I couldn't even find a copy of the *Daily Planet* at the Times Square newsstand! I can't even remember where Metropolis is! It's as if some evil force has removed all traces of Metropolis from the face of the Earth! That's my problem, Dr. Funck! I've got to get back to Metropolis, but I don't know how!"

"Tell me, Mr. Kent," said Funck slowly, "just why is it so imperative that you return to Metropolis immediately?"

"Well . . . uh . . . there's my job!" Clark Kent said uneasily. "Perry White must be furious by now! And there's my girl, Lois Lane! Well, maybe she's not my girl yet, but I'm hoping!"

Dr. Felix Funck grinned conspiratorially. "Isn't there some more pressing reason, Mr. Kent?" he said. "Something perhaps having to do with your Secret Identity?"

"S-secret Identity?" stammered Clark Kent. "I don't know what you're talking about, Dr. Funck!"

"Aw come on, Clark!" Felix Funck said. "Lots of people have Secret Identities. I've got one myself. Tell me yours, and I'll tell you mine. You can trust me, Clark. Hippocratic Oath, and like that. Your secret is safe with me."

"*Secret?* What secret are you talking about?"

"Come, come, Mr. Kent!" Funck snapped. "If you want help, you'll have to come clean with me. Don't give me any of that meek, mild-mannered reporter jazz. I know who you really are, Mr. Kent."

"I'm Clark Kent, meek, mild-mannered reporter for the Metropolis *Daily Planet!*" insisted Clark Kent.

Dr. Felix Funck reached into a desk drawer and produced a small chunk of rock coated with green paint. "Who is in reality, Superman," he exclaimed, "faster than a speeding bullet, more powerful than a locomotive, able to leap tall buildings at a single bound! Do you know what this is?" he shrieked, thrusting the green rock in the face of the hapless Clark Kent. "It's Kryptonite, that's what it is, genuine, government-inspected Kryptonite! How's *that* grab you, Superman?"

Clark Kent, who is in reality the Man of Steel, tried to say something, but before he could utter a sound, he lapsed into unconsciousness.

Dr. Felix Funck reached across his desk and unbuttoned Clark Kent's shirt. Sure enough, underneath his street clothing, Kent was wearing a pair of moth-eaten longjohns dyed blue, on the chest of which a rude cloth "S" had been crudely sewn.

"Classic case . . ." Dr. Funck muttered to himself. "Right out of a textbook. Even lost his imaginary powers when I showed him the phony Kryptonite. Another job for Supershrink!"

Get a hold of yourself, Funck, get a hold of yourself! Dr. Felix Funck told himself again.

Shaking his head, he rang for the orderlies.

After the orderlies had removed Clark Kent #758, Dr. Felix Funck pulled a stack of comic books out of a desk drawer, spread them out across the desktop, stared woodenly at them and moaned.

The Superman Syndrome was getting totally out of hand. In this one hospital alone, there are already 758 classified cases of Superman Syndrome, he thought forlornly, and lord knows how many Supernuts in the receiving ward awaiting classification.

"Why? Why? Why?" Funck muttered, tearing at his rapidly thinning hair.

The basic, fundamental, inescapable, incurable reason, he knew was, of course, that the world was full of Clark Kents. Meek, mild-mannered men. Born losers. None of them, of course, had self-images of themselves as nebbishes. Every mouse has to think of himself as a lion. Everyone has a Secret Identity, a dream image of himself, possessed of fantastic powers, able to cope with normally impossible situations. . . .

Even psychiatrists had Secret Identities, Funck thought abstractedly. After all, who but Supershrink himself could cope with a ward full of Supermen?

Supershrink! More powerful than a raving psychotic! Able to diagnose whole neuroses in a single session! Faster than Freud! Abler than Adler! Who, disguised as Dr. Felix Funck, balding, harried head of the Superman Syndrome ward of a great metropolitan booby-hatch, fights a never-ending war for Adjustment, Neo-Freudian Analysis, Fee-splitting, and the American Way!

Get a hold of yourself, Funck, get a hold of yourself!

There's a little Clark Kent in the best of us, Funck thought.

That's why Superman had long since passed into folklore. Superman and his alter ego Clark Kent were the perfect, bald statement of the human dilemma (Kent) and the corresponding wish-fulfillment (The Man of Steel). It was normal for kids to assimilate the synthetic myth into their grubby little ids. But it was also normal for them to outgrow it. A few childhood schizoid tendencies never hurt anyone. All kids are a little loco in the coco, Funck reasoned sagely.

If only someone had shot Andy Warhol before it was too late!

That's what opened the whole fetid can of worms, Funck thought—the Pop Art craze. Suddenly, comic books were no longer greasy kid stuff. Suddenly, comic books were Art with a big, fat capital "A." They were hip, they were in, so-called adults were no longer ashamed to snatch them away from the brats and read the things themselves.

All over America, meek, mild-mannered men went back and relived their youths through comic books. Thousands of meek, mild-mannered slobs were once more coming to identify with the meek, mild-mannered reporter of the Metropolis *Daily Planet*. It was like going home again. Superman was the perfect wish-fulfillment figure. No one doubted that he could pulverize 007, leap over a traffic jam on the Long Island Expressway in a single bound, see through women's clothing with his x-ray vision, and *voilá,* the Superman Syndrome!

Step one: the meek, mild-mannered victim identified with that prototype of all *schlemiels,* Clark Kent.

Step two: they began to see themselves more and more as Clark Kent; began to dream of themselves as Superman.

Step three: a moment of intense frustration, a rebuff from some

Lois Lane figure, a dressing-down from some irate Perry White surrogate, and something snapped, and they were in the clutches of the Superman Syndrome.

Usually, it started covertly. The victim procured a pair of long-johns, dyed them blue, sewed an "S" on them, and took to wearing the costume under his street clothes occasionally, in times of stress.

But once the first fatal step was taken, the Superman Syndrome was irreversible. The victim took to wearing the costume all the time. Sooner or later, the stress and strain of reality became too much, and a fugue-state resulted. During the fugue, the victim dyed his hair Superman steel-blue, bought a blue double-breasted suit and steel-rimmed glasses, forgot who he was, and woke up one morning with a set of memories straight out of the comic book. He *was* Clark Kent, and he had to get back to Metropolis.

Bad enough for thousands of nuts to waltz around thinking they were Clark Kent. The horrible part was that Clark Kent was the Man of Steel. Which meant that thousands of grown men were jumping off buildings, trying to stop locomotives with their bare hands, tackling armed criminals in the streets and otherwise contriving to commit *hara-kiri.*

What was worse, there were so many Supernuts popping up all over the place that everyone in the country had seen Superman at least once by now, and enough of them had managed to pull off some feat of daring—saving a little old lady from a gang of muggers, foiling an inexpert bank robbery simply by getting underfoot —that it was fast becoming impossible to convince people that there *wasn't* a Superman.

And the more people became convinced that there was a Superman, the more people fell victim to the Syndrome, the more people became convinced. . . .

Funck groaned aloud. There was even a well-known television commentator who jokingly suggested that maybe Superman *was* real, and the nuts were the people who thought he wasn't.

Could it be? Funck wondered. If sanity was defined as the norm, the mental state of the majority of the population, and the majority of the population believed in Superman, then maybe anyone who *didn't* believe in Superman had a screw loose. . . .

If the nuts were sane, and the sane people were really nuts, and the nuts were the majority, then the truth would have to be. . . .

"Get a hold of yourself, Funck!" Dr. Felix Funck shouted aloud. "There is no Superman! There is no Superman!"

Funck scooped the comics back into the drawer and pressed a button on his intercom.

"You may send in the next Supertwitch, Miss Jones," he said.

Luscious Miss Jones seemed to be blushing as she ushered the next patient into Dr. Funck's office.

There was something unsettling about this one, Funck decided instantly. He had the usual glasses and the usual blue double-breasted suit, but on him they looked almost good. He was built like a brick outhouse, and the steel-blue dye job on his hair looked most professional. Funck smelled money. One of the powers of Supershrink, after all was the uncanny ability to instantly calculate a potential patient's bank balance. Maybe there would be some way to grab this one for a private patient. . . .

"Have a seat, Mr. Kent," Dr. Funck said. "You are Clark Kent, aren't you?"

Clark Kent sat down on the edge of the chair, his broad back ramrod-straight. "Why, yes, Doctor!" he said. "How did you know?"

"I've seen your stuff in the Metropolis *Daily Planet,* Mr. Kent," Funck said. Got to really humor this one, he thought. There's money here. That dye job's so good it must've set him back fifty bucks! *Indeed* a job for Supershrink! "Well just what seems to be the trouble, Mr. Kent?" he said.

"It's my memory, Doctor!" said Clark Kent. "I seem to be suffering from a strange form of amnesia!"

"So-o . . ." said Felix Funck soothingly. "Could it possibly be that . . . that you suddenly found yourself in New York without knowing how you got here, Mr. Kent?" he said.

"Why that's amazing!" exclaimed Clark Kent. "You're one hundred percent correct!"

"And could it also be," suggested Felix Funck, "that you feel you must return to Metropolis immediately? That, however, you can find no plane or train or bus that goes there? That you cannot find a copy of the *Daily Planet* at the out-of-town newsstands? That, in fact, you cannot even remember where Metropolis is?"

Clark Kent's eyes bugged. "Fantastic!" he exclaimed. "How could you know all that? Can it be that you are no ordinary psychiatrist, Dr. Funck? Can it be that Dr. Felix Funck, balding, harried head of a ward in a great metropolitan booby-hatch is in reality . . . *Supershrink?*"

"Ak!" said Dr. Felix Funck.

"Don't worry, Dr. Funck," Clark Kent said in a warm, comradely tone, "your secret is safe with me! We superheroes have got to stick together, right?"

"Guk!" said Dr. Felix Funck. How could he possibly know? he thought. Why, he'd have to be . . . *ulp!* That was ridiculous. Get a hold of yourself, Funck, get a hold of yourself! Who's the psychiatrist here, anyway?

"So you know that Felix Funck is Supershrink, eh?" he said shrewdly. "Then you must also know that you can conceal nothing from me. That I know your Secret Identity too."

"*Secret Identity?*" said Clark Kent piously. "Who me? Why everyone knows that I'm just a meek, mild-mannered reporter for a great metropolitan—"

With a savage whoop, Dr. Felix Funck suddenly lept halfway across his desk and ripped open the shirt of the dumbfounded Clark Kent, revealing a skin-tight blue uniform with a red "S" insignia emblazoned on the chest. Top-notch job of tailoring too, Funck thought approvingly.

"Aha!" exclaimed Funck. "So Clark Kent, meek, mild-mannered reporter, is, in reality, *Superman!*"

"So my secret is out!" Clark Kent said stoically. "I sure hope you believe in Truth, Justice and the American way!"

"Don't worry, Clark old man. Your secret is safe with me. We superheroes have got to stick together, right?"

"Absolutely!" said Clark Kent. "Now about my problem, Doctor . . ."

"Problem?"

"How am I going to get back to Metropolis?" asked Clark Kent. "By now, the forces of evil must be having a field day!"

"Look," said Dr. Funck. "First of all, there is no Metropolis, no *Daily Planet,* no Lois Lane, no Perry White, and *no Superman.* It's all a comic book, friend."

Clark Kent stared at Dr. Funck worriedly. "Are you feeling all right, Doctor?" he asked solicitously. "Sure you haven't been working too hard? Everybody knows there's a Superman! Tell me, Dr. Funck, when did you first notice this strange malady? Could it be that some childhood trauma has caused you to deny my existence? Maybe your mother—"

"Leave my mother out of this!" shrieked Felix Funck. "Who's the psychiatrist here, anyway? I don't want to hear any dirty stories about my mother. There is no Superman, you're not him, and I can prove it!"

Clark Kent nodded his head benignly. "Sure you can, Dr. Funck!" he soothed.

"Look! Look! If you were Superman you wouldn't have any problem. You'd—" Funck glanced nervously about his office. It was on the tenth floor. It had one window. The window had steel bars an inch and a quarter thick. He can't hurt himself, Funck thought. Why not? Make him face reality, and break the delusion!

"You were saying, Doctor?" said Clark Kent.

"If you were Superman, you wouldn't have to worry about trains or planes or buses. You can fly, eh? You can bend steel in your bare hands? Well then why don't you just rip the bars off the window and fly back to Metropolis?"

"Why . . . why you're absolutely right!" exclaimed Clark Kent. "Of course!"

"Ah . . ." said Funck. "So you see you have been the victim of a delusion. Progress, progress. But don't think you've been completely cured yet. Even Supershrink isn't *that* good. This will require many hours of private consultation, at the modest hourly rate of a mere fifty dollars. We must uncover the basic psychosomatic causes for the—"

"What are you talking about?" exclaimed Clark Kent, leaping up from the chair and shucking his suit with blinding speed, revealing a full-scale Superman costume, replete with expensive-looking scarlet cape which Funck eyed greedily.

He bounded to the window. "Of course!" said Superman. "I can bend steel in my bare hands!" So saying, he bent the inch-and-a-quarter steel bar in his bare hands like so many lengths of licorice whip, ripped them aside and lept to the windowsill.

"Thanks for everything, Dr. Funck!" he said. "Up! Up! And away!" He flung out his arms and lept from the tenth-floor window.

Horrified, Funck bounded to the window and peered out, expecting to see an awful mess on the crowded sidewalk below. Instead:

A rapidly-dwindling caped figure soared out over the New York skyline. From the crowded street below, shrill cries drifted up to the ears of Dr. Felix Funck.

"Look! Up there in the sky!"

"It's a bird!"

"It's a plane!"

"It's SUPERMAN!!"

Dr. Felix Funck watched the Man of Steel execute a smart left bank and turn due west at the Empire State Building. For a short moment, Dr. Funck was stunned, nonplussed. Then he realized what had happened and what he had to do.

"He's nuts!" Felix Funck shouted. "The man is crazy! He's got a screw loose! He thinks he's Superman, and he's so crazy that he *is* Superman! The man needs help! *This* is a job for SUPER-SHRINK!"

So saying, Dr. Felix Funck bounded to the windowsill, doffed his street clothes, revealing a gleaming skin-tight red suit with a large blue "S" emblazoned across it, and lept out the window screaming "Wait for me, Superman, you pathetic neurotic, you, wait for me!"

Dr. Felix Funck, who is, after all, in reality Supershrink, turned due west and headed out across the Hudson for Metropolis, somewhere beyond Secaucus, New Jersey.

Interplanetary flight having been perfected, the planets and moons of the Sol system having been colonized, Man turned his attention to the stars.

And ran into a stone wall.

After three decades of trying, scientists reluctantly concluded that a faster-than-light drive was an impossibility, at least within the realm of any known theory of the Universe. They gave up.

But a government does not give up so easily, especially a unified government which already controls the entire habitat of the human race. *Most* especially a psychologically and sociologically enlightened government which sees the handwriting on the wall, and has already noticed the first signs of racial claustrophobia—an objectless sense of frustrated rage, increases in senseless crimes, proliferation of perversions and vices of every kind. Like grape juice sealed in a bottle, the human race had begun to ferment.

Therefore, the Solar Government took a slightly different point of view towards interstellar travel—Man *must* go to the stars. Period. Therefore, Man *will* go to the stars.

If the speed of light could not be exceeded, then Man would go to the stars within that limit.

When a government with tens of billions of dollars to spend becomes monomaniacal, Great Things can be accomplished. Also, unfortunately, Unspeakable Horrors.

Stage One: A drive was developed which could propel a spaceship at half the speed of light. This was merely a matter of technological concentration, and several billion dollars.

Stage Two: A ship was built around the drive, and outfitted with every conceivable safety device. A laser-beam communication system was installed, so that Sol could keep in contact with the ship all the way to Centaurus. A crew of ten carefully screened, psyched and trained near-supermen was selected, and the ship was launched on a sixteen-year round-trip to Centaurus.

It never came back.

Two years out, the ten near-supermen became ten raving maniacs.

But the Solar Government did not give up. The next ship contained five near-supermen, and five near-superwomen.

They only lasted for a year and a half.

The Solar Government intensified the screening process. The next ship was manned by ten bona-fide supermen.

They stayed sane for nearly three years.

The Solar Government sent out a ship containing five supermen and five superwomen. In two years, they had ten super-lunatics.

The psychologists came to the unstartling conclusion that even the cream of humanity, in a sexually balanced crew, could not stand up psychologically to sixteen years in a small steel womb, surrounded by billions of cubic miles of nothing.

One would have expected reasonable men to have given up.

Not the Solar Government. Monomania had produced Great Things, in the form of a c/2 drive. It now proceeded to produce Unspeakable Horrors.

The cream of the race has failed, reasoned the Solar Government, therefore, we will give the dregs a chance.

The fifth ship was manned by homosexuals. They lasted only six months. A ship full of lesbians bettered that by only two weeks.

Number Seven was manned by schizophrenics. Since they were *already* mad, they did not go crazy. Nevertheless, they did not come back. Number Eight was catatonics. Nine was paranoids. Ten was sadists. Eleven was masochists. Twelve was a mixed crew of sadists and masochists. No luck.

Maybe it was because thirteen was still a mystic number, or maybe it was merely that the Solar Government was running out of ideas. At any rate, ship Number Thirteen was the longest shot of all.

Background: From the beginnings of Man, it had been known that certain plants—mushrooms, certain cacti—produced intense hallucinations. In the mid-twentieth century, scientists—and others less scientifically minded—had begun to extract those hallucino-

182   SUBJECTIVITY

genic compounds, chiefly mescalin and pcilicibin. The next step was the synthesis of hallucinogens—L.S.D. 25 was the first, and it was far more powerful than the extracts.

In the next few centuries, more and more different hallucinogens were synthesized—L.S.D. 105, Johannic acid, huxleyon, baronite.

So by the time the Solar Government had decided that the crew of ship Number Thirteen would attempt to cope with the terrible reality of interstellar space by denying that reality, they had quite an assortment of hallucinogens to choose from.

The one they chose was a new, as-yet-untested ("Two experiments for the price of one," explained economy-minded officials) and unbelievably complex compound tentatively called Omnidrene.

Omnidrene was what the name implied—a hallucinogen with all the properties of the others, some which had proven to be all its own, and some which were as yet unknown. As ten micrograms was one day's dose for the average man, it was the ideal hallucinogen for a starship.

So they sealed five men and five women—they had given up on sexually unbalanced crews—in ship Number Thirteen, along with half a ton of Omnidrene and their fondest wishes, pointed the ship towards Centaurus, and prayed for a miracle.

In a way they could not possibly have foreseen, they got it.

As starship Thirteen passed the orbit of Pluto, a meeting was held, since this could be considered the beginning of interstellar space.

The ship was reasonably large—ten small private cabins, a bridge that would only be used for planetfalls, large storage areas, and a big common room, where the crew had gathered.

They were sitting in All-Purpose Lounges, arranged in a circle. A few had their Lounges at full recline, but most preferred the upright position.

Oliver Brunei, the nominal captain, had just opened the first case of Omnidrene, and taken out a bottle of the tiny pills.

"This, fellow inmates," he said, "is Omnidrene. The time has come for us to indulge. The automatics are all set, we won't have to do a thing we don't want to for the next eight years."

He poured ten of the tiny blue pills into the palm of his right hand. "On Earth, they used to have some kind of traditional ceremony when a person crossed the equator for the first time. Since we are crossing a far more important equator, I thought we should have some kind of ceremony."

The crew squirmed irritably.

I *do* tend to be verbose, Brunei thought.

"Well . . . anyway, I just thought we all oughta take the first pills together," he said, somewhat defensively.

"So come on, Ollie," said a skinny, sour-looking man of about thirty years.

"O.K., Lazar, O.K." Marashovski's gonna be trouble, Brunei thought. Why did they put *him* on the ship?

He handed the pills around. Lazar Marashovski was about to gulp his down.

"Wait a minute!" said Brunei. "Let's all do it together."

"One, two, *three!*"

They swallowed the pills. In about ten minutes, thought Brunei, we should be feeling it.

He looked at the crew. Ten of us, he thought, ten brilliant misfits. Lazar, who has spent half his life high on baronite; Vera Galindez, would-be medium, trying to make herself telepathic with mescalin; Jorge Donner . . . Why is *he* here?

Me, at least with me it's simple—this or jail.

What a crew! Drug addicts, occultists, sensationalists . . . *and what else?* What makes a person do a thing like this?

It'll all come out, thought Brunei. In sixteen years, it'll all come out.

"Feel anything yet, Ollie?" said Marsha Johnson. No doubt why *she* came along. Just an ugly old maid liking the idea of being cooped up with five men.

"Nothing yet," said Brunei.

He looked around the room. Plain steel walls, lined with cabinets full of Omnidrene on two sides, viewscreen on the ceiling, bare floor, the other two walls decked out like an automat. Plain, gray steel walls . . .

Then why were the gray steel walls turning pink?

"Oh, oh . . ." said Joby Krail, rolling her pretty blond head, "oh, oh . . . here it comes. The walls are dancing . . ."

"The ceiling is a spiral," muttered Vera, "a winding red spiral."

"O.K., fellow inmates," said Brunei, "it's hitting." Now the walls were red, bright fire-engine red, and they were melting. No, not melting, but evaporating . . .

"Like crystal it is," said Lin Pey, waving his delicate oriental hands, "like jade as transparent as crystal."

"There is a camel in the circle," said Lazar, "a brown camel."

"Let's all try and see the camel together," said Vera Galindez sharply. "Tell us what it looks like, Lazar."

"It's brown, it's the two-humped kind, it has a two-foot tail."

"And big feet," said Lin Pey.

"A stupid face," said Donner.

"Very stupid."

"Your camel is a great bore," said the stocky, scowling Bram Daker.

"Let's have something else," said Joby.

"Okay," replied Brunei, "now someone else tell what they see."

"A lizard," said Linda Tobias, a strange, somber girl, inclined to the morbid.

"A lizard?" squeaked Ingrid Solin.

"No," said Lin Pey, "a dragon. A green dragon, with a forked red tongue . . ."

"He has little useless wings," said Lazar.

"He is totally oblivious to us," said Vera.

Brunei saw the dragon. It was five feet long, green and scaly. It was a conventional dragon, except for the most bovine expression in its eyes . . .

Yes, he thought, the dragon is *here*. But the greater part of him knew that it was an illusion.

How long would this go on?

"It's *good* that we see the same things," said Marsha. "Let's always see the same things . . ."

"Yes."

"Yes!"

"Now, a mountain, a tall blue mountain."

"With snow on the peak."

"Yes, and clouds . . ."

One week out:

Oliver Brunei stepped into the common room. Lin Pey, Vera, and Lazar were sitting together, on what appeared to be a huge purple toadstool.

But that's *my* hallucination, thought Brunei. *At least, I think it is.*

"Hello Ollie," said Lazar.

"Hi. What're you doing?"

"We're looking at the dragon again," said Vera. "Join us?"

Brunei thought of the dragon for a moment. The toadstool disappeared, and the by-now-familiar bovine dragon took its place. In the last few days, they had discovered that if any two of them concentrated on something long enough to "materialize" it, anyone else who wanted to could see it in a moment.

"What's so interesting about that silly dragon?" said Brunei.

"How about the camel?" said Lazar.

The dragon turned into the two-humped brown camel.

"Phooey!" said Lin Pey.

"O.K.," said Vera, "so what do *you* want?"

Lin Pey thought for a moment.

"How about a meadow?" he said. "A soft lawn of green grass, the sky is blue, and there are a few white clouds . . ."

"Clover is blooming," said Lazar. "Smell it."

Brunei reclined on the soft green grass. The smell of the earth beneath him was warm and moist. "A few apple trees here and there," he said, and there was shade.

"Look over the hill!" said Lazar. "There's the dragon!"

"Will you *please* get rid of that dragon?" snapped Brunei.

"O.K., Ollie, O.K."

One month out:

"Get out of the way!" yelled Brunei. He gave the dragon a kick. It mooed plaintively.

"That wasn't very nice, Ollie," said Lazar.

"That dragon is always underfoot," said Brunei. "Why don't you get rid of it?"

"I've taken a liking to it," said Lazar. "Besides, what about your Saint Bernard?"

"This ship is getting too cluttered up with everyone's hallucinations," said Brunei. "Ever since . . . when was it, a week ago? . . . ever since we've been able to conjure 'em up by ourselves, and make everyone else see 'em."

Daker dematerialized the woman on his lap. "Why don't we get together?" he said.

"Get together?"

"Yes. We could agree on an environment. Look at this common room for example. What a mess! Here, it's a meadow, there it's a beach, a palace, a boudoir."

"You mean we should make it the same for all of us?" asked Lazar.

"Sure. We can have whatever we want in our cabins, but let's make some sense out of the common room."

"Good idea," said Brunei. "I'll call the others."

Three months out:

Brunei stepped through the stuccoed portal, and into the central Spanish garden. He noticed that the sky was blue, with a few fleecy white clouds.

But then, the weather was always good. They had agreed on it.

Lazar, Ingrid, Lin Pey and Vera were sitting on the green lawn surrounding the fountain.

Daker, Joby, Linda and Donner preferred the shade, and lounged against the white arabesqued wall which enclosed the garden on four sides, broken only by four arched entrance portals.

The garden had been a good compromise, thought Brunei. Something for everyone. Fresh air and sunshine, but also the mental security offered by the walls, which also provided shade for those who wanted it. A fountain, a few palm trees, grass, flowers, even the little formal Japanese rock garden that Lin Pey had insisted on.

"Hello, Ollie," said Lazar. "Nice day."

"Isn't it always?" replied Brunei. "How about a little shower?"

"Maybe tomorrow."

"I notice a lot of sleeping people today," said Brunei.

"Yes," said Lin Pey. "By now, the garden seems to be able to maintain itself."

"You think it has a separate existence?" asked Ingrid.

"Of course not," said Vera. "Our subconscious minds are maintaining it. It's probably here when we're all asleep."

"No way of telling *that*," said Brunei. "Besides, how can it exist when we're asleep, when it doesn't really exist to begin with?"

"Semantics, Ollie, semantics."

Brunei took a bottle of Omnidrene out of his pocket. "Time to charge up the old batteries again," he said.

He passed out the pills.

"I notice Marsha is still in her cabin."

"Yeah," said Lazar, "she keeps to herself a lot. No great—"

Just then, Marsha burst into the garden, screaming: "Make it go away! Make it go away!"

Behind her slithered a gigantic black snake, with a head as big as a horse's, and bulging red eyes.

"I thought we agreed to leave our private hallucinations in our cabins," snapped Brunei.

"I tried! I tried! I *don't want* it around, but it won't go away! Do something!"

Ten feet of snake had already entered the garden. The thing seemed endless.

"Take it easy," said Lazar. "Let's all concentrate and think it away."

They tried to erase the snake, but it just rolled its big red eyes.

"That won't work," said Vera. "Her subconscious is still fighting us. Part of her must *want* the snake here. We've *all* got to be together to erase it."

Marsha began to cry. The snake advanced another two feet.

"Oh, quiet!" rasped Lazar. "Ollie, do I have your permission to bring my dragon into the garden? He'll make short work of the snake."

Brunei scowled. "You and your dragon . . . Oh, maybe it'll work."

Instantly, the green dragon was in the garden. But it was no longer five feet long and bovine.

It was a good *twelve* feet long, with cold reptilian eyes and big yellow fangs.

It took one look at the snake, opened its powerful jaws, and belched a huge tongue of orange flame.

The serpent was incinerated. It disappeared.

Brunei was trembling. "What happened, Lazar?" he said. "That's not the same stupid little dragon."

"Hah . . . hah . . ." squeaked Lazar. "He's . . . uh . . . grown . . ."

Brunei suddenly noticed that Lazar was ashen. He also noticed that the dragon was turning in their direction.

"Get it out of here, Lazar! Get it out of here!"

Lazar nodded. The dragon flickered and went pale, but it was over a minute before it disappeared entirely.

Six months out:

Things wandered the passageways and haunted the cabins. Marsha's snake was back. There was Lazar's dragon, which seemed to grow larger every day. There was also a basilisk, a pterodactyl, a vampire bat with a five-foot wingspread, an old-fashioned red spade-tailed demon and other assorted horrors.

Even Oliver Brunei's friendly Saint Bernard had grown to monstrous size, turned pale green, and grown large yellow fangs.

Only the Spanish garden in the common room was free of the monstrosities. Here, the combined conscious minds of the ten crew members were still strong enough to banish the rampaging hallucinations.

The ten of them sat around the fountain, which seemed a shade less sparkling.

There were even rainclouds in the sky.

"I don't like it," said Bram Daker. "It's getting completely out of control."

"So we just have to stay in the garden, that's all," said Brunei. "The food's all here, and so is the Omnidrene. And *they* can't come here."

"Not yet," said Marsha.

They all shuddered.

"What went wrong?" asked Ingrid.

"Nothing," said Donner. "They didn't know what would happen when they sent us out, so we can't say they were *wrong.*"

"Very comforting," croaked Lazar. "But can someone tell me why we can't control *them* any more?"

"Who knows?" said Brunei. "At least we can keep them out of here. That's—"

There was a snuffling at the wall. The head of something like a Tyrannosaurus Rex peered over the wall at them.

"Ugh!" said Lin Pey. "I think that's a new one."

The dragon's head appeared alongside the Tyrannosaur's.

"Well, at least *there's* a familiar face," tittered Linda.

"Very funny."

Marsha screamed. The huge black snake thrust its head through a portal.

And the flap of leathery wings could be heard. And the smell of sulphur.

"Come on! Come on!" shouted Brunei. "Let's get these things out of here!"

After five minutes of intense group concentration, the last of the horrors was banished.

"It was a lot harder this time," said Daker.

"There were more of them," said Donner.

"They're getting stronger and bolder."

"Maybe some day they'll break through, and . . ." Lin Pey let the sentence hang. Everyone supplied his own ending.

"Don't be ridiculous!" snapped Brunei. "They're not real. *They can't kill us!*"

"Maybe we should stop taking the Omnidrene?" suggested Vera, without very much conviction.

"At *this* point?" said Brunei. He shuddered. "If the garden disappeared, and we had nothing but the bare ship for the next fifteen and a half years, and we *knew* it, and at the same time knew that we had the Omnidrene to bring it back . . . How long do you think we'd hold off?"

"You're right," said Vera.

"We just have to stick it out," said Brunei. "Just remember: *They can't kill us. They aren't real.*"

"Yes," the crew whispered in a tiny, frail voice, "they aren't real . . ."

Seven months out:

The garden was covered with a gloomy gray cloud layer. Even the "weather" was getting harder and harder to control.

The crew of starship Number Thirteen huddled around the fountain, staring into the water, trying desperately to ignore the snufflings, flappings, wheezes and growls coming from outside the walls. But occasionally, a scaly head would raise itself above the wall, or a pterodactyl or bat would flap overhead, and there would be violent shudders.

"I still think we should stop taking the Omnidrene," said Vera Galindez.

"If we stopped taking it," asked Brunei, "which would disappear first, *them . . . or the garden?*"

Vera grimaced. "But we've got to do something," she said. "We can't even make them disappear at all, any more. And it's becoming a full time job just to keep them outside the walls."

"And sooner or later," interjected Lazar, "we're *not* going to be strong enough to keep them out . . ."

"Brr!"

"The snake! The snake!" screamed Marsha. "It's coming in again!"

The huge black head was already through a portal.

"Stop the snake, everyone!" yelled Brunei. Eyes were riveted on the ugly serpent, in intense concentration.

After five minutes, it was obviously a stalemate. The snake had not been able to advance, nor could the humans force it to retreat.

Then smoke began to rise behind the far wall.

"The dragon's burning down the wall!" shrieked Lazar. "Stop him!"

They concentrated on the dragon. The smoke disappeared.

But the snake began to advance again.

"They're too strong!" moaned Brunei. "We can't hold them back."

They stopped the snake for a few moments, but the smoke began to billow again.

"They're gonna break through!" screamed Donner. "We can't stop 'em!"

"What are we gonna do?"

"Help!"

Creakings, cracklings, groanings, as the walls began to crack and blister and shake.

Suddenly Bram Daker stood up, his dark eyes aflame.

"Only one thing's strong enough!" he bellowed. "Earth! *Earth!* EARTH! Think of Earth! All of you! We're back on Earth. Visualize it, make it real, and the monsters'll have to disappear."

"But *where* on Earth?" said Vera, bewildered.

"The Spaceport!" shouted Brunei. "The Spaceport! We all remember the Spaceport."

"We're back on Earth! The Spaceport!"

"Earth!"

"Earth!"

"EARTH!   EARTH!"

The garden was beginning to flicker. It became red, orange, yellow, green, blue, violet, invisible; then back again through the spectrum the other way—violet, blue, green, yellow, orange, red, invisible.

Back and forth, like a pendulum through the spectrum . . .

Oliver Brunei's head hurt unbearably, he could see the pain on the other faces, but he allowed only one thought to fill his being—

Earth! The Spaceport! EARTH!

More and more, faster and faster, the garden flickered, and now it was the old common room again, and *that* was flickering.

Light was flickering, mind was flickering, time, too, seemed to flicker . . .

Only Earth! thought Brunei. Earth doesn't flicker, the Spaceport doesn't flicker.

Earth! EARTH!

Now all the flickerings, of color, time, mind and dimensions, were coalescing into one gigantic vortex, that was a thing neither of time, nor space, nor mind, but all three somehow fused into one . . .

They're screaming! Brunei thought. Listen to the horrible screams! Suddenly he noticed that he, too, was screaming.

The vortex was growing, swirling, undulating, and it, too, began to flicker . . .

There was an unbearable, impossible pain, and . . .

The sight of starship Number Thirteen suddenly appearing out of nowhere, and sitting itself calmly down in the middle of the Spaceport was somewhat disconcerting to the Spaceport officials. Especially since at the very moment it appeared, and even afterward, they continued to have visual and laser contact with its image, over three light-months from Earth.

However, the Solar Government itself was much more pragmatic. One instant, starship Thirteen had been light-months from Earth, the next it was sitting in the Spaceport. Therefore, starship Thirteen had exceeded the speed of light somehow. Therefore, it was possible to exceed the speed of light, and a thorough examination of the ship and its contents would show *how*.

Therefore . . . You idiots, throw a security cordon around that ship!

In such matters, the long-conditioned reflexes of the Solar Government worked marvelously. Before the airwaves had cooled, two hundred heavily armed soldiers had surrounded the ship.

Two hours later, the Solar Co-ordinator was on the scene, with ten Orders of Sol to present to the returning heroes, and a large well-armored vehicle to convey them to laboratories, where they would be gone over with the proverbial fine-tooth comb.

An honor guard of two hundred men standing at attention made a pathway from the ship's main hatch to the armored carrier, in front of which stood the Solar Co-ordinator, with his ten medals.

They opened the hatch.

One, two, five, seven, ten dazed and bewildered "heroes" staggered past the honor guard, to face the Co-ordinator.

He opened his mouth to begin his welcoming speech, and start the five years of questioning and experiments which would eventually kill five of the crew and give Man the secret of faster-than-light drive.

But instead of speaking, he screamed.

So did two hundred heavily armed soldiers.

Because, out of starship Thirteen's main hatch sauntered a twelve-foot green dragon, followed by a Tyrannosaurus Rex, a pterodactyl, a vampire bat with a five-foot wingspan, an old-fashioned red, spade-tailed demon, and finally, big as a horse's, the pop-eyed head of an enormous black serpent . . .

The Entropic Gang Bang Caper

PBA THREATENS STRIKE OVER
DEMONSTRATION TACTICS

New York, N.Y. The President of the Patrolmen's Benevolent Association threatened to call a general police strike unless all riot police were immediately disarmed. "Armed police have a tough time getting laid at demonstrations," he explained. "It's bad for morale."

The Arsenal of Entropy

Some common human phobias include fear of close spaces, fear of heights, fear of spiders, fear of suffocation, fear of dogs, fear of injury to the eyes, fear of rats, fear of faeces, fear of insects, fear of slime, fear of injury to the genitals, fear of buggery, fear of impotence, fear of a public display of cowardice.

Scenario One:

War is any means of breaking the will of the enemy. Violence is a means of waging war. A violence-war breaks the will of the enemy through fear. In a violence-war, the enemy is defeated when his fear of further violence is greater than his fear of the consequences of defeat.

VIOLENCE IS THE LAST RESORT OF DESPERATE MEN ARE THE LAST RESORT OF VIOLENCE IS DESPERATE RESORT OF THE LAST MEN

The Arsenal of Entropy

DMSO is a chemical which when combined with a wide spectrum

of liquids will cause the liquid with which it is mixed to be absorbed
into the bloodstream through skin-contact.

Spray-guns may be purchased on the open market.

LSD is a colorless, odorless, tasteless liquid which may be intro-
duced into any fluid medium without fear of detection.

Scenario Two:

*War is any means of breaking the will of the enemy. Revulsion
is a means of waging war. A revulsion-war breaks the will of the
enemy through disgust. In a revulsion-war, the enemy is defeated
when his disgust for further conflict is greater than his fear of the
consequences of defeat.*

WAR NEGOTIATIONS SUSPENDED

Miami Beach, Fla. Negotiations were suspended until next Fri-
day today between the Pentagon and the Military Association of
Soldiers, Sailors and Airmen over the unresolved issue of combat
coffee-breaks. Although MASSA has accepted the Pentagon pro-
posal of a $2.25 an hour wage-increase for enlisted men, to be
spread out over the duration of the next three-year contract,
MASSA spokesmen indicated that the Pentagon refusal to grant
combat coffee-breaks could lead to an indefinite prolongation of
the current strike.

Regular coffee-breaks have been standard procedure in most
other industries for years, MASSA negotiators pointed out, in
refusing the Pentagon's counter-proposal of double-time for night
patrols.

**REVOLUTION IS THE OPIUM OF THE INTELLECTUAL CLASS IS THE
OPIUM REVOLUTION IS INTELLECTUAL OPIUM IS THE CLASS REVO-
LUTION OF THE INTELLECTUAL CLASS OPIUM IS THE REVOLUTION**

Scenario Three:

*War is any means of breaking the will of the enemy. Sour
grapes is a means of waging war. A sour-grapes-war breaks the
will of the enemy through envy. In a sour-grapes-war, the enemy is
defeated when his envy of the pleasures enjoyed by the opponent is
greater than his fear of the consequences of defeat.*

The Arsenal of Entropy

Many men (including police, public officials and military personnel) strongly relish the prospect of sexual intercourse with young, nubile, willing, attractive women. They have been known to abandon more onerous tasks when confronted with the immediate prospect of a good lay. Other men (including police, public officials and military personnel) experience an equivalent reaction at the prospect of sexual congress with young, nubile, willing, attractive men. A small minority of men (including police, public officials, and military personnel) have a similar lust for sexual objects such as dogs, goats, or dirty sweatsocks. Science has discovered few men in whom a sexual desire cannot be provoked.

YOU CAN NEVER FIND A COP WHEN YOU NEED ONE COP A NEED WHEN YOU FIND ONE COP NEVER NEED A COP CAN NEVER FIND YOU WHEN YOU NEED YOU CAN NEVER FIND A NEED WHEN YOU COP ONE

Scenario Four:

War is any means of breaking the will of the enemy. Lust is a means of waging war. A lust-war breaks the will of the enemy through tantalization. In a lust-war, the enemy is defeated when his sexual lust for the enemy is greater than his fear of the consequences of defeat.

SCOTUS RULES ON CONSTITUTIONAL ISSUE

Washington, D.C. The Supreme Court, in a unanimous decision today, declared the Constitution Unconstitutional. "There is no provision whatsoever in the Constitution for the Constitution," the Court decision pointed out.

The Arsenal of Entropy

Many human beings experience a violent disgust-reaction when showered with the entrails of freshly-killed animals.

A violently nauseous man is incapable of violence.

A variety of readily-obtainable substances provoke an irresistible biological urge to vomit.

Scenario Five:

War is any means of breaking the will of the enemy. Love is a

means of waging war. A love-war breaks the will of the enemy through desire. In a love-war, the enemy is defeated when his desire to be loved by the enemy is greater than his fear of the consequences of defeat.

VD EPIDEMIC AMONG POLICE LAID TO HIPPY DEMONSTRATORS VD EPIDEMIC LAID TO POLICE LAID AMONG HIPPY DEMONSTRATORS VD EPIDEMIC AMONG POLICE LAID TO VD EPIDEMIC AMONG HIPPY DEMONSTRATORS LAID TO POLICE VD

LA COPS MOBBED BY GROUPIES

Los Angeles, Calif. Three hundred Los Angeles riot police were brutally sexually assaulted today by a screaming mob of several thousand naked fifteen-to-eighteen-year-old groupies. Five rock stars had to be summoned to restore order using charisma and amplified guitars. The management of the Shrine Auditorium threatened to revoke the LAPD's entertainment licence if this outrage were to be repeated.

"Blue cloth and brass buttons turn me on," explained the seventeen-year-old President of the Cop-You-Laters, the new fan club which is causing serious concern in anti-government circles. "I just can't help it, the sight of a nightstick makes me throb inside."

"Shocking!" declared a rock star who preferred to remain anonymous. "These groupies should be setting an example for our impressionable police. Do they treat their fathers like that?"

Scenario Six:
War is any means of breaking the will of the enemy. Guilt is a means of waging war. A guilt-war breaks the will of the enemy through remorse. In a guilt-war, the enemy is defeated when his remorse for the actions he is committing is greater than his fear of the consequences of defeat.

The Arsenal of Entropy

Shit is a substance easily obtained by anyone. It is neither colorless, odorless, nor tasteless. Its odor, taste, appearance, and concept provoke severe disgust in many people, including police, public officials, and military personnel.

UNIVERSITY DEMANDS DEMONSTRATOR CONTROL OF POLICE

Berkeley, Calif. At a news conference called after the latest Berkeley riot, the Chancellor of the University of California demanded tighter demonstrator control of police. "The situation would never have gotten out of hand if the police had been forced to summon demonstrators earlier," he declared. "It's time the anarchists stopped coddling the police."

Scenario Seven:

War is any means of breaking the will of the enemy. Reality-alteration is a means of waging war. A reality-alteration-war breaks the will of the enemy through alienation. In a reality-alteration-war, the enemy is defeated when his fear of alienation from the current reality is greater than his fear of the consequences of defeat.

IF YOU CAN'T BEAT 'EM EAT 'EM IF YOU BEAT 'EM YOU CAN'T EAT 'EM IF YOU CAN'T BEAT 'EM YOU CAN'T EAT 'EM

MUGGER CLEARED OF POLICE BRUTALITY RAP

New York, N.Y. Superior Court Judge Arthur Cranz today dismissed charges of intent to commit police brutality against Herbert Smith, 29. Smith, a member of the International Brotherhood of Muggers, had been accused of police brutality against Patrolman David MacDougal of the New York City Vice Squad, when the latter's nightstick was buggered during a routine mugging in New York's Central Park. Judge Cranz ruled that since both men were under the influence of capitalist propaganda at the time, intent could not be proven. However, all three paternity suits arising out of the incident are still pending in civil court.

Scenario Eight:

War is any means of breaking the will of the enemy. Identity is a means of waging war. An identity-war breaks the will of the enemy through absorbtion. In an identity-war, the enemy is defeated when his degree of merger with the enemy is greater than his fear of the consequences of defeat.

SECRETARY OF TREASURY ABSCONDS

New York, N.Y. The Secretary of the Treasury today announced his formal abscondence with the National Debt at a press conference held in a Wall Street crash-pad. He told reporters that he planned to sell the Debt to the Mafia as a tax-loss, deposit the proceeds in municipal bonds, and accept a Presidential appointment to the Mothers of Invention.

Scenario Nine:

War is any means of breaking the will of the enemy. Chaos is a means of waging war. A chaos-war breaks the will of the enemy through entropy. In a chaos-war, the enemy is defeated when further action on his part becomes the consequences of defeat.

BECAUSE WE LOVE EACH OTHER, THAT'S WHY!

Reno, Nevada. At a press conference in Reno today, the President and the Vice President announced that they had been married during the night in a private ceremony conducted by the Chief of Naval Operations.

"I just don't see what all the fuss is about," the Vice President said. "We're just two people in love, that's all."

"This time it's for keeps!" the President assured reporters as the newlyweds left for a two-week honeymoon in Niagara Falls.

The Last Hurrah of the Golden Horde

Eastward across the Gobi, three hundred old men ride upon three hundred shaggy, wizened Mongolian ponies. The ponies, like their riders, are the tag-end of a dying breed. The men are dressed in filthy, cracked, badly-tanned leathers. Across their backs are strapped short Mongolian bows; swords dangle from their waists and they carry lances in their horny hands as they ride toward the sunrise.

In the dingy storefront on Sullivan Street identified as the D'Mato Social Club by the peeling green letters on the fly-specked translucent area above the black-painted area of the plate glass window that hid the cave-like interior from the view of casual assassins in the street, Jerry Cornelius, a not-so-casual (or in his own way a *more* casual) assassin, sat on a gray-enameled metal folding chair facing a gnarled old man with a Jimmy Durante nose across the cracked surface of a rickety card-table. Jerry wore a carefully-dated black suit, a black silk shirt, a white tie, and white boots. His black vinyl raincoat was draped across a counter which paralleled one wall of the room and which held a display of candy bars and a cardboard showcase of De Nobili cigars. Behind the counter hung a faded photograph of Franklin D. Roosevelt framed in black. The man with the Jimmy Durante nose was smoking a De Nobili and the semipoisonous smoke that he blew across the table was clearly designed to blow Jerry's cool. Jerry, however, had expected this, and as a counter-measure kept his violin case close at hand. It seemed a draw.

"This is a big one, Cornelius," the old man said.

"Flesh is flesh, Mr. Siciliano," Jerry replied. "Metal is metal."

"Have you ever hit a Cabinet-level official before?"

Jerry pondered. "It's open to doubt," he finally admitted. "I got a head of state once, but it was a benevolent despotism."

The old man chewed his cigar, much to Jerry's disgust. "It'll have to do," he said. "You've got the contract. How soon can you be in Sinkiang?"

"Three days. I'll have to change passports again."

"Make it two."

"I'd have to pull strings. It'll cost you."

The old man shrugged. "Do it," he said.

Jerry grinned. "My motto, Mr. Siciliano. Who's the contract on?"

"Mao Tze Tung's heir-apparent."

"Who's that these days?" Jerry asked. The situation in China had gotten somewhat muddled.

"That's your problem," Durante-nose said.

Jerry shrugged. "And my cover?"

"Arrange it yourself."

Jerry got up clutching his violin case, ran his hand through his great bush of blonde natural, retrieved his raincoat, took a De Nobili from the counter, and said with an evil smirk: "Don't say I didn't warn you."

The railroad train consisted of a locomotive, a sealed boxcar, three flatcars and a caboose. The boxcar contained one ton of (uncut?) heroin. The open flatcars held three hundred members of the People's Army of China armed with machineguns, protected from the elements by the thought of Chairman Mao. The caboose held the negotiating team. The locomotive was a diesel job.

"You'll be working with the Russians on this, Inspector Cornelius," Q said. "Our interests happen to coincide."

Jerry frowned. The last time he had worked with a Russian, he had contracted the clap. "I don't trust those buggers," he told Q.

"Neither do we," Q said crisply, "but it's the only way we can get you into Sinkiang. You leave for Moscow on Aeroflot in the morning."

"Aeroflot?" whined Jerry. Christ, those Russian stewardesses! he thought. "I get airsick on Aeroflot," he complained.

Q glared at Jerry firmly. "We're getting the family plan discount," he explained.

"But I'm flying alone. . . ."

"Precisely."

"Dramamine?"

"If you insist," Q said primly. "But the Bureau frowns on foreign substances."

"My mission?" Jerry asked.

"Catch the Chinks and the Maf in the act. Bust them."

"But we have no jurisdiction."

"Hence the Russians," said Q. "Use your head, Cornelius."

"They have no jurisdiction either."

"You're not that naive, Cornelius."

"I suppose not," Jerry said wistfully.

According to the thought of Chairman Mao, the village was an anachronism: one hundred and fifty-three flea-bitten nomads, along with their animals (mostly diseased horses and threadbare yaks) encamped in a cluster of leather yurts on the margin of the Gobi. From the correct point of view, the village might be said not to exist.

From this same point of view (as well as from several others) the three hundred old men who galloped in from the wastes of the Gobi might also be said to be nonexistent. Nevertheless, the nomad encampment had a certain reality for the old warriors; in fact an archetypal reality stretching back in a line of unbroken tradition from the days of the Great Khan and his Golden Horde still burning clearly in their ancestral memory to the misty and arthritic present.

Village. Burn. Pillage. Rape. Kill.

Outside the umbrella of the thoughts of Chairman Mao, the old barbarians existed in a happier reality of simple, straightforward traditional imperatives.

Therefore, unmindful of the fact that the village was an anachronism, the old warriors, in the time-honored tradition of the Golden Horde, rode into the encampment, slew the men and children, made a pass at raping the women to death, slaughtered the animals, burned the yurts, and continued to ride eastward, secure in the knowledge that they had fulfilled another quantum of their timeless destiny.

A long concrete runway broke the monotony of the Sinkiang wastelands with the more absolute monotony of its geometric perfection. At right angles to the runway, a railroad spur wandered off toward the horizon. From the viewpoint of the pilot of the C-5A approaching this three-dimensional nexus, the runway and the railroad spur formed a T with a finite bar and an infinite upright. If anything, the pilot thought this sloppy. It is likely that he did not fully comprehend the thought of Chairman Mao; a more erudite man might have appreciated the symbolism.

"It is a clear demonstration of the cynical perfidy of the Chinese gangster element enshrined behind the facade of the Maoist clique, Comrade Cornelius," Commissar Krapotkin observed genially, drawing a glass of tea from the silver samovar and handing it across the table to Jerry. Krapotkin was a short barrel of a man who wore his double-breasted Mod suit like a uniform. Perhaps it is a uniform, Jerry thought, as he took a spiked sugar-cube out of his mother-of-pearl pillbox and inserted it between his teeth. The Russians were doing their best to be hip these days and it was hard to keep up.

As Jerry sipped tea through the sugar-cube between his teeth, Krapotkin lit up an Acapulco Gold and continued to make small-talk: "While they gibber and squeak their anti-Soviet obscenities in Peking, they deal with the worst gangster element of the decadent capitalist society by their back door in Sinkiang, which, by the way, is of course rightfully Soviet territory."

"I wouldn't call the Maf the *worst* gangster element of decadent capitalist society," Jerry observed mildly.

Krapotkin produced a metallic sound which Jerry tentatively identified as a laugh. "Ah, very good, Comrade Cornelius. Indeed, one might argue that the distribution of heroin, contributing as it does to the further corruption of the already decadent West, is an act which contributes to the long range progress of the working-class."

"But providing the reactionary adventurist regime in Peking with hard American currency does not," Jerry rejoined.

"Exactly, Comrade! Which is why my government has decided to cooperate with the American narcs. Once the Maoist clique has been exposed in the act of selling heroin to the Maf, we should have no trouble totally discrediting them with progressive elements throughout the world."

"And of course the Mafia will be discredited as well."

"?"

"The Maf is essentially a patriotic organization like the K.K.K. or the Loyal Order of Moose."

Krapotkin roached his joint. "Enough of the pleasantries, Comrade," he said. "Are you prepared for the drop?"

Jerry fingered his violin case. "My cover?" he inquired.

"You will be a Mafia hit man assigned a contract on the heir-apparent to Mao Tze Tung," Krapotkin said. "Our agents in Palermo have uncovered just such a plot."

"The real hit man?"

Krapotkin smiled. "He has been disposed of, I assure you."

From a certain viewpoint, Jerry reflected, Krapotkin was right.

Not 90 seconds after the C-5A had taxied to a halt with its tail facing the juncture of the rail-spur-runway T as if preparing to fart along the track, the great doors in the nose opened like the petals of an aluminium flower, a ramp was lowered, and a black Cadillac disgorged, pulling a house trailer of grandiose proportions and Miami-Beach-Gothic design. The C-5A continued to disgorge Cadillacs like a pregnant guppy, each one pulling a trailer larger and more rococo than the last.

Something less than three hundred old men galloped haltingly across the wastes of Sinkiang on faltering ponies. A dozen or more of the Mongol warriors had burst blood vessels in their tired old brains from the excitement of the last massacre. The blood was running thin. Where once the steppes had echoed to the pounding hooves of the Golden Horde as the whole world trembled before a tide of barbarians that filled the field of vision from horizon to horizon, now there was naught but an expiring handful of decrepit savages. *Sic transit gloria mundi*. The spirit was willing, but the flesh was practically moribund. The survivors envied those few of their comrades lucky enough to have died a warrior's death sacking the last village in an endless chain reaching back to the glory days when the villages had names like Peking and Samarkand and Damascus.

But something—call it pride or manly virtue—kept the pitiful remnant of the Horde going, riding ever eastward into the sunrise. Perhaps it was the hope that somewhere on the endless steppe there still remained a village large enough (but not *too* large) to bring them all the glory of death in one last gory, triumphant, final massacre. Flailing like tattered battle flags in their befuddled old brains the simple imperatives which shaped their lives and hopes and destinies: Village. Burn. Pillage. Rape. Kill.

Jerry Cornelius, still clutching the violin case, stood alone in the gray wasteland, and watched the Russian helicopter disappear into the slate-colored sky with a certain sense of foreboding. You just can't trust those Russians, he thought. Now where was the car?

To the east was a large boulder. Behind it, and not without a certain sense of relief, Jerry found a late model black Cadillac sedan, well-waxed and shiny. So far, so good.

Inside the car, Jerry found his new persona. Doffing his clothes, he assumed the persona: a black pin-striped suit with pegged pants and thin lapels, a white button-down shirt, a white tie, a diamond stickpin, pointed black Italian loafers, argyl socks, a box of De Nobilis, and jars of black shoe polish and vaseline, with which he gave himself a Rudolph Valentino job, atop which he affixed a green porkpie hat with a leopard skin band. Thus accoutered, and with a round toothpick in his mouth at a jaunty angle, he sealed the car, turned on the air-conditioning, and set out across the wasteland.

Only when he discovered that the radio would bring in nothing but Radio Moscow and that the tape library contained naught but Tschaikowsky did the full extent of Krapotkin's treachery become apparent.

As the train hove into sight of the rail-spur-runway junction, the soldiers of the People's Army were able to contain cries of awe, amazement and dismay only by diligent application of the thought of Chairman Mao.

For there in the depths of Sinkiang was, considering the circumstances, quite a decent facsimile of Las Vegas. A semicircle of trailers rimmed a large kidney-shaped swimming pool. Done up in pastels, sporting picture windows, and sprouting numerous extensions, wings, and breezeways, the trailers resembled the lower or casino floors of Las Vegas hotels. Complex mazes of cabanas, beach chairs, bocci courts, pavillions, greenhouses, handball courts and pidgeon coups which filled the interstices between the trailers completed the illusion. Behind the semicircular Las Vegas facade towered the tail of the C-5A, reminiscent, somehow, of Howard Hughes and all that his shadowy persona implied. Parked among the spectral casino hotels were an indeterminate number of black Cadillacs.

Around the pool, waiters in red tuxedoes served tepid Collinses to fat men in sunglasses stretched out in beach chairs, warming themselves with complex arrays of sunlamps. Starlets in bikinis paraded their pinchable asses by the poolside.

The officials in the caboose immediately called for the reserve train which had been parked fifty miles down the track in anticipation of such a necessity.

Approaching his destination from the south, Jerry Cornelius spotted a cluster of pagodas, huts and barracks, among which huge billboards had been erected bearing immense portraits of Mao, Lenin, Stalin, Enver Hoxha, and other popular personalities of the People's Republic of China. Everything was festooned with calligraphy like a wedding cake. Intermittent strings of firecrackers exploded. Hatchet men chased each other through the winding streets. Soldiers of the People's Army performed calisthenics. The sharp syllables of Chinese dialects filled the air like razorblades. Gongs sounded. Paper dragons danced in the streets. Perpetual twilight hovered over the scene, which, upon closer inspection, proved to be constructed of balsa wood, rice paper and papier-mâché.

Warily, Jerry swung the Cadillac wide of this Chinese version of Disneyland and circled toward the tail of a C-5A which dominated the landscape. Soon reality (such as it was) changed and he found himself on the outskirts of what appeared to be a suburb of Las Vegas: the lower stories of casino hotels mounted on wheels and parked in a semicircle around a huge kidney-shaped pool, facing the Chinese apparition across the chlorinated waters.

Having spied a heavily-guarded boxcar behind the facade of the Chinese reality, Jerry was not surprised to see a dozen thugs with machineguns guarding the C-5A. The $50,000,000 must be on the plane.

For a moment, Jerry parked the Cad along the Orient-Vegas interface, playing at pondering his next move.

Shortly, he drove on into the Mafia camp, parked the Cadillac next to a fire hydrant outside a barbershop, and melted into the scene with barely a ripple. Yes indeed, this was his kind of town!

Eastward across the wastelands, here and there a rider dead on his horse, a scungy pony faltering under its rider, the spirit burning brighter as the blood thinned as if their ancient flesh were ectoplasmating into naught but the weathered parchment-dry quintessence of tradition-cum-desire, the desperate determination not to die a peasant's death, the image of the Final Massacre burning its forlorn hope into the backs of what was left of their arteriosclerotic brains, the husks of the Golden Horde doddered onward, ever onward.

"Ya get da Big Picture, Cornelius?" The Rock said, sipping at his Collins as he and Jerry lay side by side in beach chairs, sunning themselves at poolside. Jerry, dressed in neon-blue bathing suit, contrasting yellow terrycloth robe, Japanese rubber sandals and silvered Air Force shades, had resisted the dangerous urge to order Pernod, and as a consequence was nursing a foul rum concoction. Only the presence of his violin case close at hand soothed his jangled nerves. And the sunlamps threatened to melt the shoe-polish in his hair.

"I'm not paid to get the Big Picture, Rock," Jerry said, keeping in character, though from a certain viewpoint what he was saying was true.

The Rock scratched his hairy paunch with one hand and with the other, clawlike, pinched the ass of a passing starlet, who giggled appropriately.

"I like yer style, kid," The Rock said. "But doncha have any curiosity?"

"Curiosity killed a cat."

"I'm a dog man myself, Cornelius, so who gives a shit? What I say is dese Chinks have been asking for it. Just because da punks got a few H-bombs and ICBMs is no reason for them to get the idea they can burn the Maf and live ta talk about it. Yeah, after ya hit their number two *padron,* that smart-ass punk in Peking will have ta look over his shoulder a few times before he tries putting milk-sugar in our heroin again."

"Just who is their number two?"

Rock pointed his De Nobili at the empty raft anchored out in the center of the kidney-shaped pool. "Da Big Boy will make this year's deal out on da raft—neutral turf. Whatever Chink is out there with him—zap!"

"Won't the Reds . . . ?" Jerry inquired.

"Da Cads are full of heavies with choppers," The Rock grinned. "When you hit da number two, dey hit da People's Army." The Rock chucked himself under the chin with his right forefinger as if flicking a bead of sweat at the giant posters of Mao, Stalin, Hoxha and Lenin glowering like spectral Internal Revenue agents across the moat-waters of the pool.

Jerry decided to develop a sudden hankering for Egg Foo Yung.

Major Sung passed the opium pipe across the black-lacquered table to Jerry, who inhaled the sweet smoke and fingered his violin case voluptuously as Major Sung caressed his copy of the Little Red Book obscenely and said: "Of course I am familiar with your work in England, Colonel Kor Ne Loos."

"Your English is excellent, Major," Jerry lied. "Harvard?"

"Berlitz."

"I should be reporting to the honorable Heir-Apparent to godlike Mao," Jerry chided.

Major Sung frowned and kicked the brass gong which sat upon the table. Kung-fu, Jerry noted warily. He revised his estimate of Major Sung laterally. "As you of course know," Sung said with an oriental leer, "the peacock often hides his egg behind an embroidered fan."

Jerry started—he certainly hadn't expected anything like this! "The dragon has been known to preen his scales before he pounces," he rejoined.

Outside the pagoda, a chorus of two hundred kindergarten students were chanting the latest Number One on the Chinese Top 40, "Death To The Violaters Of The Spirit Of Mao's Urine." Jerry tapped his fingers on the table in time to the catchy rhythm, which he recognized as a variation on "Rock Around The Clock."

"May I take that to imply that the pasta contains an asp?" Major
Sung said. It was clearly not a question.

Jerry smiled. "As Confucius says, a fox with a dagger may be-
head a drunken lion."

Major Sung laughed. "As Chairman Mao has observed, the
enemies of the Revolution will devour their own entrails if they
can make a fast buck in the process."

Bowing and scraping, a Sergeant in a kimono entered the
chamber with tea and fortune cookies.

Major Sung cracked open his pastry and read aloud: "Death to
the revisionist running dogs of the Wall Street imperialists and
their would-be lackies in Prague."

Jerry's fortune cookie said: "Tension, apprehension and dis-
sension have begun."

As Jerry, in his pin-stripe suit, porkpie hat, and Italian loafers,
lounged against the right front fender of the Cadillac, which he had
parked inconspicuously at poolside, a fat man in a flowered
Hawaiian shirt and black Bermuda shorts boarded a speedboat at
the Vegas end of the pool. Stuffed between his thick lips was an
El Ropo Supremo Perfecto Grande. Set jauntily on his bald head
was a red sailor cap on the brim of which "The Big Boy" had been
embroidered in Atlantic City in bold blue thread.

As a Meyer Davis orchestra in one of the poolside cabanas
struck up "Amore" and a stripper began to peel on the diving
board, the white speedboat set out across the pool toward the raft.

Meanwhile across the pool, fifty soldiers of the People's Army
marched back and forth bearing placards serializing the menu of
Hong Fat's restaurant in severe calligraphy and psychedelic posters
of Mao, Stalin, Lenin and Jim Morrison while the People's Army
Brass Band played "Chinatown, My Chinatown" to which a chorus
of Red Guards waving the Little Red Book sung the "Internatio-
nale" in Sinosized Albanian. To this heady send-off, an old
bearded Chinese in a military tunic (with a curious if superficial
resemblance to Ho Chi Minh) rowed a punt toward the raft in
neutral waters.

At poolside, Jerry's trained eye picked out heavies in blue serge
suits moving unobtrusively toward their Cadillacs. They all carried
violin cases. Jerry placed a bet with a convenient bookie that the

cases did not contain violins. The best he could get was the wrong end of 9-4 odds.

Alone on the raft at last, The Big Boy and the Heir-Apparent swapped bon mots as the strains of "High Hopes" mingled with the thin voices of schoolchildren chanting "My Mao Can Lick Your Mao" in a corrupt Canton dialect.

"Ya dirty mother, last year's dope was cut with milk-sugar."

"As Chairman Mao has observed, when dealing with corrupt mercenaries of the exploitative class, the doctrine of 'no tickee, no washee' is fully justified."

"Remember what happened to Bugsy Siegal!"

"Confucius once said that a toothless dragon does not fear the orthodontist."

Behind the Chinese Disneyland, the People's Army had placed six machinegun nests in a circle around the boxcar of heroin.

Twenty heavies with choppers ringed the C-5A. Inside, five more heavies guarded $50,000,000 in unmarked small bills.

"Fifty million! That's robbery. You Chinks are crooks."

The Meyer Davis orchestra played "It Takes Two To Tango." The People's Army Brass Band countered with a Chinese version of "Die Fahne Hoch."

"As Chairman Mao has said," the Heir-Apparent threatened, "I may not be the best man in town, but I'll be the best till the best comes round."

Hidden behind a facade of placards, posters, pagodas, dancing paper dragons, hatchet men, schoolchildren performing calisthenics, rioting Red Guards, captured American airmen in chains, opium dens and filthy peasant huts, three hundred soldiers of the People's Army of the People's Republic of China girded themselves for a human wave attack.

"We only deal with you Commie pinko Chink bastards because you're the only mass suppliers of heroin aside from the Federal narcs that we can find."

"As Chairman Mao has said, tough shit."

Ominously, the Meyer Davis orchestra began playing "Hawaiian War Chant."

Jerry Cornelius stubbed out his roach and reached for his violin case. "The time has come, the Walrus said, to speak of many things," he observed as, out on the raft, The Big Boy gave the finger to the Heir-Apparent.

"Fifty million for the boxcar, take it or leave it," the Heir-Apparent said.

The People's Army Brass Band broke into "Light My Fire" as seven hundred Red Guards doused themselves with gasoline and immolated themselves while singing "Chairman Mao ist unser Fuehrer" contrapuntally, but since they were all off-key, the ploy was a failure.

"As Al Capone once observed, play ball, or we lean on you."

Jerry Cornelius opened his violin case and withdrew a violin. To the untrained observer, it appeared to be merely an ordinary electric violin with self-contained power supply, built-in amp and speaker rated at 100 watts. However, an Underground electronics expert on 150 mg of methedrene had made a significant modification: the high notes registered well into the ultrasonic and the lows were deep down in the subsonic, while all audible frequencies were eliminated.

When Jerry tucked the violin under his chin and began to play "Wipeout," the brains of everyone within a five mile radius began to vibrate to the beat of a drummer who was ultra-and-supersonic as well as different and nonexistent. To the naked human ear, Jerry appeared to be playing "The Sounds of Silence."

Out on the raft, The Big Boy was growing quite cross as the subliminal strains of "Wipeout" inflamed cells deep within his paretic brain. "Mao Tze Tung eats shit!" he informed the Heir-Apparent.

"Al Capone was a faggot, according to the infallible thought of Mao Tze Tung!"

The Meyer Davis orchestra began to play "The Battle Hymn of the Republic."

The People's Army Brass Band immolated their tuba-player.

As Jerry segued into a subliminal rendition of "Heartbreak Hotel," fifty slot machines produced spontaneous jackpots, Cadillacs gunned their engines, whores' poodles howled, thirteen plate glass windows shattered, and every starlet at poolside achieved climax. (Some of them had not come since their first screentests.)

Hatchet men began chopping at papier-mâché pagodas. A paper dragon set itself on fire. Three hundred soldiers preparing themselves for a human wave attack began to drool and got erections. Seven hundred chanting kindergarten children achieved satori and began to devour an American flag drenched with soy sauce. A giant poster of Stalin broke into a grin and thumbed its nose at a poster of Mao.

"Mao Tze Tung eats the hairy canary!"
"The Maf sucks!"
"Faggot!"
"Creep!"
"Chink!"
"Wop!"
"ARGH!"

Salivating, The Big Boy leapt at the Heir-Apparent, chomping his El Ropo Supremo Perfecto Grande to bits, and buried teeth and cigar in the old Chinaman's beard, setting it aflame. The two men wrestled on the raft, biting, spitting and cursing for a few moments, then toppled each other into the pool, which proved to be filled with crocodiles.

Pleased with his work, Jerry Cornelius began to play "Fire."

A phalanx of Cadillacs screamed around the pool and barreled into the People's Army Brass Band spewing machinegun bullets which ripped into a poster of Mao Tze Tung, enraging a rioting mob of Red Guards who set themselves on fire and threw themselves under the wheels of the cars, causing them to skid into a balsa wood pagoda which toppled into the pool in splinters which

L

were devoured by the blood-crazed crocodiles who expired in agony from the splinters in their stomachs some time later.

Three hundred soldiers of the People's Army launched a human wave attack, firing their machineguns at random.

Jerry continued to play "Fire," seeing no particular reason to change the tune.

Major Sung shrieked: "Capitalistic running dogs of the demographic People's revisionist lackies of Elvis Presley have over-run the ideological manifestations of decadent elements within the amplifier of the pagoda!" and committed hara-kiri.

The Rock began smashing slot machines with a baseball bat.

Starlets tore off their bikinis and chased terrified hatchet men around the poolside.

The human wave reached the pool, dove in, and proceeded to beat moribund crocodiles to death with their gunbutts.

A suicide squad hurled itself through the plate glass window of a trailer and devoured the rug.

Cadillacs circled the boxcar of heroin like hostile Indians, filling the air with hot lead.

The sopping remnants of the human wave reached the trailer camp and began beating thugs to death with dead crocodiles.

Red Guards showered the C-5A with ink bottles.

Tongues of flame were everywhere.

Explosions, contusions, fire, gore, curses, looting, rape.

Jerry Cornelius began playing "All You Need Is Love," knowing that no one was listening.

Riding eastward across the wastelands on their diseased ponies, something under two hundred decrepit remnants of what once had been the glorious Golden Horde, most of them incoherent with exhaustion, spied a great conflagration on the horizon.

Flaccid adrenals urged near-moribund hearts to beat faster. They flayed their ponies with the shafts of their spears. Drool flecked the lips of doddards and ponies alike. Their backbrains smelled blood and fire in the air.

The smells of gunpowder, gasoline, burning balsa wood and paper mache, sizzling flesh, gave Jerry Cornelius a slight buzz as he began to play "Deck the Halls With Boughs of Holly." The swimming pool was colored a bright carnelian, which did little to mask the chlorine odor. Bits of anodized aluminum struggled to keep afloat amid scraps of charred balsa wood and shards of placards.

A dented Cadillac careened through a barricade of beach chairs and into a squad of Chinese soldiers beating a starlet to death with copies of the Little Red Book before sliding over the rim of the pool to sink bubbling into the churning depths.

The pillar of fire consuming the Chinese Disneyland reminded Jerry of the Dresden firestorm. Sentimentally, he began to play "Bongo, Bongo, Bongo, I Don't Want To Leave The Congo."

In a strange display of gallantry, Red Guards, hit men, capa mafiosas and Chinese soldiers joined hands in a ring around the ruined trailer camp, screaming *"Burn,* baby, burn!" in English, Mandarin, Cantonese, Italian, Pidgin, and Yiddish. At each *"burn"* a canister of napalm dropped from somewhere onto the conflagration.

Reduced to sentimentality despite himself, Jerry played "God Save The Queen."

Two hundred or so pairs of rheumy eyes lit up with feral joy at the sight of a great city (by current Horde standards anyway) going up in flames, at the sight of smashed cars, broken bodies, naked starlets shrieking, and a great pool of what appeared to be blood.

Weeping great nostalgic tears, the last generation of the Golden Horde shouldered their spears, whipped their ponies into a stumbling gallop and charged in a body into the fray, the image of the Final Massacre burning like a city in the fevered brains of the aged savages:

Village! Burn! Pillage! Rape! Kill!

Mongolian ponies wheezing and gasping under them, the crazed doddards reached the conflagration and found to their chagrin that there was precious little unburnt, unpillaged, unraped, unkilled.

They found a boxcar guarded by machinegunners and charged it en masse, sacrificing half their number to impale the befuddled Chinese troops on their spears and set the boxcar aflame. As a strangely-intoxicating aromatic smoke billowed from the burning boxcar, the remnant of the remnant scattered, looking for more things or people to burn, rape, and kill.

A dozen of the doddards expired attempting to rape an aged whore to death, and another dozen were compelled to shame-facedly trample her to death under the hooves of their ponies, eight of which expired from the effort.

Fifteen of the Horde had heart attacks trying to beat Cadillacs to death.

A half-dozen doddards died of broken hearts when the slot machines they were torturing failed to cry out in pain.

Several of the Horde fell to devouring the corpses of crocodiles and choked to death on the splinters.

As the last Khan of the Golden Horde watched in senile befuddlement, the great silver bird issued a terrible battlecry and began to move. The doddard's bleary eyes bugged as the C-5A picked up speed, shot by him, and actually left the ground!

A feeble nervous impulse traveled spastically from his optic nerve into his brain, and thence to his arm and throat.

"Kill!" he wheezed asthmatically, and hurled his spear at the unnatural thing.

The spear was sucked into the intake of the left inboard jet engine, lodged in the turbine, and shattered it. The jet engine exploded, shearing off the wing. The C-5A nearly completed a loop before it crashed upside-down to the runway and exploded into flames.

From an aerial viewpoint, the runway and the railroad spur formed a T with a finite bar and an infinite upright, but the only living being in the area did not notice the symbolism. Riding into the sunset on his pony, his back to what in the distance seemed naught but a smoldering refuse-heap, the last Khan of the Golden Horde, sole survivor of the Final Massacre, filled his dying brain with one thought, like a dwindling chord: fulfillment; Golden Horde died in glory; village; burned; pillaged; raped; killed; ancestors proud.

This thought flared brightly in his brain like a dying ember and then he went to that Great Carnage Heap in the Sky. The wheezing pony tripped over a rock, dislodging the body, which fell to the ground in a twisted heap. A vulture descended, pecked at the body, sniffed, and departed.

The pony staggered on for a few steps, then halted, its dim brain perhaps mesmerized by the glare of the setting sun.

The Mongolian pony was still standing there an hour later when Jerry Cornelius, in his pin-stripe suit, porkpie hat, and Italian loafers, wandered dazedly up to it out of the wasteland.

"Here's a bit of luck," Jerry muttered, perking up a bit. (The short-circuiting of his electric violin had seriously vexed him.)

Jerry mounted the pony, kneed its flanks and shouted: "Git 'em up, Scout!"

The pony waddled forward a few steps, puked, and died.

Jerry extricated himself from the corpse, brushed himself off, and consulted a fortune cookie he had secreted in a pocket.

"It's a long way to Tipperary," the fortune cookie informed him.

Munching the soggy rice pastry, Jerry trudged off into the setting sun whistling "Dem bones, dem bones, dem dry bones, now hear de word of de Lord. . . ."